KINGDOM
KEEPERS II
DISNEY AT DAWN

ALSO BY RIDLEY PEARSON

The Kingdom Keepers—Disney After Dark
Steel Trapp—The Challenge

❀

WRITING WITH DAVE BARRY

Peter and the Starcatchers
Peter and the Shadow Thieves
Peter and the Secret of Rundoon
Escape from the Carnivale
Cave of the Dark Wind
Blood Tide

❀

RIDLEY PEARSON

KINGDOM KEEPERS II

DISNEY AT DAWN

EDITIONS

New York

An Imprint of Disney Book Group

Copyright © 2008 Page One, Inc.
All rights reserved. Published by Disney Editions, an imprint of Disney Book Group. No part of this book may be reproduced or transmitted in any form or by any means, electronic or mechanical, including photocopying, recording, or by any information storage and retrieval system, without written permission from the publisher. For information address Disney Editions, 114 Fifth Avenue, New York, New York 10011-5690.
Printed in the United States of America
First Edition
10 9 8 7 6 5 4 3 2 1
Reinforced binding
Library of Congress Cataloging-in-Publication Data on file.
ISBN 978-1-4231-0365-3

This book is dedicated to all those readers who,
by e-mail, demanded it be written.
You see?
Someone's listening. . . .

1

LIGHTNING FLASHED ON THE HORIZON. A breeze swirled around the Cast Members. The air tasted dusty, almost bitter, with electrical charge.

Finn Whitman, one of five kids on top of the final parade float, pointed to the far gate where the Magic Kingdom's DHI-Day parade was to pass through, where five *identical* kids, wearing *identical* clothing to theirs, stood waiting.

DHI stood for Disney Host Interactive or Daylight Hologram Imaging—depending on whom you asked—a recent addition to the Magic Kingdom that offered the holograms of five teenage kids as Park hosts. The five kids who had auditioned for those roles were typically forbidden to enter the Magic Kingdom. But tonight was special: it was a DHI celebration.

Finn sensed trouble coming, wondering if it had to do with the electronic illusions waiting by the gate.

"How weird is that?" he said, seeing himself as a hologram not thirty yards away. The Finn Whitman standing by the gate looked no different from himself, except for a slight sparkle, a glow, when viewed from a certain angle.

"It gives me the weebies," said Charlene, regarding her identical, though electronically projected, twin. She too wore a cheerleader's outfit; she too had her blond hair pulled back severely into a ponytail, not a hair out of place; she too looked slightly embarrassed to have the body of a young woman, instead of a girl. Charlene was an athlete and champion gymnast and had clearly been recruited as a Disney Host for her clean, cheerleader looks and her uncanny physical ability. She was good with people and could make friends with anyone. Most kids at school were jealous of her—but the other DHIs appreciated the skills and abilities she brought to the team.

The hologram of Charlene stood next to the hologram of Finn, but the software had all five holograms in PAUSE, making them look more like glowing mannequins than kids. They awaited the start of the parade with the patience of the robots they were.

"We've been here before *as* them," said Willa, "but never *with* them."

"I was, once," corrected Finn. "Only the one time, and I was being chased by Security. I have to admit, it was plenty strange to see myself guiding some guests while I was also running for my life."

"What's that?" asked Philby, pointing up at the rise behind the tall boundary fence inside the Magic Kingdom.

"Cinderella Castle," answered Charlene.

"No, the gray balloon," Philby said. "It's massive."

"Looks like a weather balloon," said Terry Maybeck, who seemed to stand more than a head taller than all of them. An African American, Maybeck currently wore his hair in dreads, making him look older than the others.

The swarming clouds suddenly swallowed the large balloon.

"It doesn't make sense," said Philby. "You don't release a weather balloon in an electrical storm unless you're Ben Franklin."

"Not our problem," said Maybeck. "All we've got to do is ride the float and wave to the guests. Let's stick with the program."

At that moment, music started and the first float moved toward the open gate. The five holograms came to life, as if a switch had been thrown. They formed a line at the front of the parade, waving to the bushes, as if guests were waving back.

"Sometimes our DHIs look *so stupid*," Willa said.

"Sometimes?" Philby said sarcastically.

"They paid us well," Maybeck reminded them, "and we got Gold Fastpasses for our families. We've got nothing to complain about."

"And they're having a parade to celebrate our DHIs

returning to the Kingdom," Finn said, "and we get to be part of it. Things could be worse."

"Who here doesn't miss the way it used to be? *Before* they patched the source code?" Maybeck met eyes with each of them.

Finn had been the first to "cross over" during his sleep: to wake up as his own hologram in the Magic Kingdom. Initially it had seemed impossible, but encounters with pirates and witches had made him reconsider what was real and what was make-believe. Soon, all five kids had come to the same realization: when they went to sleep at night they awoke *inside* the Magic Kingdom as their DHI holograms. In reality, it had not been a corruption in the software's source code but the ingenious work of a veteran Disney Imagineer named Wayne, who had needed their help. But no one at Disney knew this other than them, so recently programmers had inserted a software patch to correct "the problem."

None of them knew if Wayne could, or would, undo it, allowing them to return to the Magic Kingdom as nighttime holograms. But all of them secretly hoped he would.

"Here we go!" said Finn. "Hang on!"

Their float jerked and climbed up the sloping asphalt just behind another float carrying Aladdin and

Jasmine. With all the floats strung out in a line, the kids had lost sight of their matching holograms out in front, leading the way.

The music swelled, and a man's voice dramatically announced, "Welcome to DHI-Day at Magic Kingdom!" The sound of applause rose above the lush jungle landscaping.

"Keep your smiles on," said Maybeck, "and hang on tight."

But at that moment, all five kids lost their balance and stumbled into each other. Jasmine and Aladdin also slipped off their pillows as their float accelerated to close a sudden gap that had appeared in the parade line.

It took Finn a moment to spot the problem: one of the floats—the villains float—had been pulled out of the line and off to the side. The Aladdin float, and the one carrying the DHIs, had sped up to close the gap.

"What's with that?" said Maybeck. "Broken down?"

"No," said Philby. "It's empty."

He was right: the float's platform lacked a character or Cast Member. It was just an empty wooden rectangle. Below it, the Cast Members responsible for preparing the floats scurried around frantically, hurrying to get the empty float out of the way and to fill the void created by its absence.

"What happened?" Finn called down to one of the

Cast Members just before reaching the gate and the adoring guests.

The man didn't answer immediately. But his face gave away his concern. "He was right there a minute ago," he mumbled, nearly drowned out by the music. "I swear he was!"

"Who?" called Finn. "Which character?"

He and the others had long since learned to take nothing for granted. Not when there were Overtakers in the Park, who wanted to gain control of the Magic Kingdom. There were no accidents here: everything happened for a reason, even if the other Cast Members didn't recognize it.

"That float should have Chernabog on it!" said Philby, shouting to be heard above the music. "Only he's not there." He turned and looked back at the empty float as they passed fully through the gate and into the Park. Finn had turned around as well. So had Maybeck.

"Who's Chernabog?" grumbled Maybeck.

Philby answered, "Only the most powerful villain Walt Disney ever created."

Finn's voice was overpowered by the joyous music and the crush of applause. "And he's gone missing? That can't be good."

2

FINN FELT THE QUICKENING BREEZE of the lightning storm bearing down on the Park. He hoped the weather would hold off at least until the parade finished. It was an evening parade with fireworks to follow. He didn't want it canceled. It wasn't every day he was asked to ride a float in Disney World.

He kept checking the sky as the line of floats reached a view of Tom Sawyer Island. He noted that the water looked oddly green and mysterious. His four friends waved and smiled at the crowds—big crowds. All but Maybeck, who nodded with his whole body but never actually waved, his head bopping and moving to the parade music.

As their float moved through Frontierland, Finn caught sight of a girl among the crowd. She was like a beam of light or a bright star in the night sky, the way she stood out. Amid the hundreds of guests—thousands?—she had appeared almost magically. Nut-colored skin, thanks to an Asian mother and African American father; a tangle of dark hair bouncing as, running now, she kept up with the steady movement of the parade. She seemed almost to float above the ground. Immediately behind her followed Jezebel. And though they claimed to be sisters, it had to be by adoption. Amanda's skin was a rich caramel, her hair so dark brown it was mistaken for black. Jez had once had jet black hair as well, though it was no longer so. But her pale, translucent skin set her apart, not just from Amanda, but from every girl Finn had ever met; it had depth, as if you could see into and through the first layer to some part of her that lay beyond.

"Amanda!" Finn shouted, breaking a strict rule that required silence of any Cast Members on a float.

The other kids hurried over and waved enthusiastically at both girls.

Amanda and Jez waved back, glad to have been spotted. Amanda gave Finn an enthusiastic thumbs-up—or at least he thought she'd intended it for him. He hadn't seen or heard from her in weeks. She hadn't been in school. She'd disappeared the same day her sister had somehow been transformed by Finn—an event he still didn't fully understand. Jez had gone from evil twin to a sweet, even angelic, girl, all in less than a minute. Only then had Amanda dropped the bomb that Jezebel was her sister, an explanation that had never been fully clarified.

"Where did they come from?" Charlene asked. Even now Finn heard a tinge of jealousy in her voice.

Or was that suspicion? There was a lot unanswered about Jez and Amanda. "And check out that hair color. Since when is she a strawberry blonde? Last time we saw her she had hair like my granny's."

"What the heck are they doing here?" Philby called out. He didn't mean the sisters.

Two big monkeys were moving in the bushes, swinging and keeping perfect pace with . . . *was it possible?* . . . the float. *Their* float.

"Since when are there monkeys in the Magic Kingdom?" Maybeck said.

"Are they wild?" Charlene asked, having noticed them as well.

Finn saw something his friends apparently didn't: the monkeys weren't following the float; they were following Jez and Amanda, keeping perfect pace with *their* movements.

"There aren't any primates in the wild in northern Florida," Philby said, ever the expert. Philby was a walking encyclopedia—he knew everything, and what he didn't know he knew how to research. His red hair and rock-climbing, thrill-seeking mind-set played against the geek he really was. A favorite of the girls at school, he wanted nothing to do with them. He spent his weekends with a climbing wall and a laptop.

The parade turned just then, making a graceful arc

past the Hall of Presidents. The crowds thickened. Amanda's efforts to keep up with the DHI float failed. She and Jez stopped, caught in a bottleneck of Park guests. Finn waved, and Amanda waved back, but it wasn't a pleasant or friendly wave; it was more like panic.

Growing smaller now and being absorbed by the crowd, Amanda pointed to Cinderella Castle. Then sharply up. Finn nodded, hoping to communicate that he too was aware of the oversize gray balloon. But Amanda shook her head violently, as if he didn't understand. He nodded, again trying to say that he did understand. He felt constrained by not being able to shout down at her. Amanda frantically pointed toward the sky. Then she tore a leaf off a plant and pushed it against her face. Again she pointed toward the castle. Then the float rounded the corner, and Amanda was gone.

Finn looked up at the swirling, dark clouds. *They'll cancel the parade*, he wanted to shout. Maybe she was concerned that he and the others were so high above ground when lightning threatened. But surely the Park authorities had it under control. He wasn't worried about their safety—he just didn't want the parade canceled.

Maybeck edged closer to Finn, pushing past Charlene, who was waving two pom-poms. "What do you suppose they're doing here?" Maybeck asked, while bobbing his head and trying to keep a smile on his face.

"No clue."

"AWOL all this time, and they suddenly reappear for our reopening celebration. Doesn't that strike you as just a little bit odd?"

"Everything about them is odd, if you ask me," said Charlene, overhearing.

"What was with the leaf?" Finn mumbled. No one heard him.

"I like them both," said Willa, joining in. Willa looked constantly on edge. She had chocolate-colored, captivating eyes and a somewhat grating voice.

"You like everybody," Charlene said.

"So what?" Willa complained.

"It just doesn't work. You can't like everybody," Charlene said.

"Why not? Of course you can!" Willa said.

"Oh, forget it," Charlene said, shaking her pompoms. She looked more eighteen than fourteen.

"Amanda knows where I live," Finn said. "Otherwise I might have said that they came here to catch up with us after reading about the grand opening."

"If she'd wanted to catch up with *you*, she'd have come by your place," Maybeck said.

"So it's you, I suppose," Finn said. Maybeck

believed every girl was in love with him. "She knows where you and Jelly live, too, don't forget."

"I'm just saying the timing's kind of interesting," Maybeck said. "We know there's something strange about those two, and there just happens to be a pair of monkeys following them."

Both Jez and Amanda reappeared, staying with the parade float once again.

With Amanda stabbing the sky and looking worried, Finn pointed back, behind her, trying to show her the monkeys. But before he could tell if she saw them, he lost sight of Amanda.

"She could have been pointing to the balloon," Finn said. "Even though it disappeared, maybe they saw it too. Whatever she saw, she was . . . I don't know . . . agitated. I don't think they came here to celebrate. I think they came to warn us."

"Warn us?" Charlene said.

"About the weather?" Maybeck said skeptically. "I doubt it."

"Could have been about the primates," Philby said.

"Yeah. A couple of monkeys," snapped Maybeck sarcastically. "Now, there's something to set your legs trembling."

"Maybe they were running from the monkeys," Willa said.

"I'm not even sure they *saw* the monkeys," said Finn.

The parade kept moving, and their float along with it. They crossed the lagoon, heading for the Hub, the density of the crowds increasing. Cheers arose. Kids screamed out their names.

"We're rock stars," said Maybeck.

"Our DHIs are the rock stars," clarified Finn. "Let's not confuse the two."

Finn caught a lightning flash out of the corner of his eye. The storm was moving closer. He looked up at the sky to see that it was far darker than even a few minutes ago. Was this what Amanda had wanted him to see? His mind reeled with possibilities. Why had she seemed so agitated? The low clouds and swirling fog obscured any sight of the gray weather balloon. Would anyone believe him now?

Suddenly the music was interrupted. "Ladies and gentlemen!" the booming voice announced. "Welcome to the Magic Kingdom's DHI-Day celebration! Please direct your attention to Cinderella Castle, where the fireworks will begin shortly."

"Look!" Philby said. "They're cutting the parade short!"

Sure enough, the parade now hooked around the Hub, and instead of heading down Main Street, USA, for its final segment, it went fully around the Hub and back the way it had come. Finn briefly saw the five DHIs far ahead, leading the way.

Whoever was in charge didn't want the parade caught in the storm.

"Don't you think we should tell someone about that balloon?" Willa asked. "That's got to be dangerous in an electrical storm."

"They must already know, don't you think?" said Finn.

Philby said, "The string or wire holding it is tied to that window. Maybe it's some kind of experiment."

"Isn't that the window to the apartment?" Finn asked. As DHIs, the kids had previously used the castle's penthouse apartment as a hiding place.

"What if that's what Amanda was pointing to?" Finn continued. "What if she was trying to show us the balloon?"

"But why?" Willa asked.

"What's so important about a balloon?"

"Nothing the Overtakers would like more than to ruin the DHI celebration," said Philby. "What if they're trying to use lightning to set Cinderella Castle on fire or something?"

"I wouldn't put it past them," said Finn.

"We don't know if the Overtakers exist anymore," said Maybeck. "If they do, don't you think Wayne would contact

14

us? Has anyone heard from the old dude, by the way?"

The Overtakers were a group of Magic Kingdom characters, rebels led by Maleficent, the evil sorceress from *Sleeping Beauty*. Their goal was to overthrow the good and take control of the Park for themselves. Wayne and others believed the Overtakers intended to imprison any characters and Cast Members not part of their group. They had been caught preparing vast dungeons beneath Pirates of the Caribbean, which were said to be for this purpose.

The DHIs were now also known as the Kingdom Keepers—one of the most popular attractions in the Park. The last thing the Kingdom Keepers could afford was for Maleficent to gain power again. They had barely stopped her the first time, and she now considered them among her greatest enemies—a distinction they could have done without.

"We should probably tell someone about the balloon," Finn said, moving to the back of the float and the small ladder there. "At the very least, it shouldn't be up in the storm."

The peculiar phenomenon that had been discovered shortly after the Disney Host Interactives had been installed in the Magic Kingdom had carried all five kids into a struggle with the Overtakers and the evil fairy Maleficent.

Wayne had showed them an astonishing three-story maze called Escher's Keep in Cinderella Castle, which led to the little-known penthouse apartment, now a secret hideaway used by Wayne.

Finn wondered aloud if the balloon might be something Wayne was responsible for.

"If Wayne's up there," Philby said, "we should go see him."

"You can't leave now," complained Charlene, waving her pom-poms eagerly for the cheering crowd.

"Cover for me," said Finn. "No one's going to notice if one of us isn't here."

"They'll notice if *you* aren't," Willa said. "They won't notice if I'm not."

"That's not true. Besides, I'm the one going, so I don't think it really matters."

"We never go solo. Remember what happened to Maybeck?"

Finn stopped, one foot over the rail and on the small ladder leading down. Maybeck's DHI had once fallen into a trap that had prevented the real Terry Maybeck from waking up. The so-called "Sleeping Beauty Syndrome" might have killed him.

"It was *your* rule," Willa reminded him. "And it was a good one. We've had no trouble since we started pairing up."

"Okay," Finn said. "So?"

"Someone's going to notice if you leave," Maybeck warned.

"Just keep moving," said Finn. "The more the three of you move around up here, the less likely I'll be missed."

"You don't actually think we're going to let you do this alone, do you?" Maybeck said.

"We're all coming," Philby said. "Here's the plan. . . ." He pulled them all into a huddle at the center of the float. "The fewest number of guests will be on the bridge to Liberty Square. We get off and start shaking hands and signing autographs like it's all part of the parade. That's also the closest we're going to get to the castle. When we make our break, we all go at once—again, like it's scripted. If we get separated, we meet inside the castle in Escher's Keep."

Lightning flashed again. A few seconds passed before the first rumble of thunder rippled through the air.

"That lightning is still some distance away from here, right?" Charlene asked anxiously.

"Closer than it was. You couldn't hear thunder a few minutes ago," Philby said. "I'll bet they're closing the rides—the mountain attractions and roller coasters. That's going to mean a whole bunch of the guests in and around the Hub for the fireworks."

"If we really saw a balloon, whether they believe us or not, we've got to convince them to check it out before that lightning gets here." Finn couldn't stop thinking about Amanda holding up that leaf to her face. *Green skin?* Was that the message? More than anything, he hoped they might find the two sisters. He sensed they had some of the answers.

"And if they don't care about the balloon?" Willa said.

"We're approaching the bridge, people," Philby announced. "If we're going to do this, now's our chance."

"Okay," Finn said, working his way down the ladder. The others followed.

He happened to look up at Charlene just as she blinked furiously to protest leaving the float. "We can't do this!" she said.

Her blinking revealed a subtle green shadow on her lids, which enhanced the color of her eyes.

Finn spoke what he'd been thinking—what Amanda had been trying to tell him by putting the green leaf to her cheek.

He called out to the others, "Maleficent is inside the castle. That's what Amanda was trying to tell us."

3

THE KINGDOM KEEPERS MET UP AGAIN at the base of Escher's Keep, a confusing maze of interlocking staircases, mirrors, and doors that crawled up the inside of Cinderella Castle. It had been built years ago as an attraction but had never opened to the public, as it had proved too dangerous. One misstep, and you were dumped into chutes or slides, some of which landed you in the castle moat.

"I tried to tell a Cast Member about the balloon," Finn said. "But he thought I was my DHI playing some kind of trick on him. I shook him, and he said, 'Amazing technology! That feels so real!' What a jerk! I tried to point out the balloon, but with the clouds, you can't even see the string or wire or whatever."

"We've got to get up there," Philby said, "Maleficent or not."

"But what if Amanda was trying to *warn* us?" Charlene asked nervously. "Wouldn't that mean we might be walking into a trap?"

"She's got a point," Maybeck said.

Finn quickly reorganized them: he and Philby

would ascend Escher's Keep to the apartment; Maybeck and Willa would try to find Amanda and Jez while Charlene stood sentry on the path to Fantasyland, giving Philby and Finn eyes on the castle from the outside.

They said their good-byes, Maybeck uncharacteristically wishing them luck, his dark, troubled eyes expressing concern. They agreed to meet after the fireworks in front of Cinderella's Golden Carrousel, immediately behind the castle.

"And if you guys don't show up?" Willa asked Finn.

Thankfully, Maybeck dragged her out the door and into the castle gift shop's storage room before Finn had to think of something plucky to say.

"You okay with this?" Philby asked nervously, his foot on the first step of Escher's Keep. It was a route that had to be memorized, and neither boy had attempted to climb it in several months.

"Let's do it," said Finn.

Philby stepped aside, allowing Finn to lead the way. It was no picnic. Sometimes stairs led nowhere. A single misstep would mean falling down a slide to the ground floor or into the moat. The route up to an elevator that accessed the penthouse apartment included invisible bridges, upside-down staircases, and trapdoors. The illusions were the result of mirrors, projections, and trick lighting, their combined effect overpowering.

"Do you remember the way?" Finn asked. He faced four doors, all in different colors. They formed a semicircle on a small platform of polished floor tiles. He and Philby were fifteen feet above the ground floor, having ascended the first staircase correctly—skipping every other tread.

"I want to say second from the right: blue. But it's your call," Philby said.

Turning the wrong door handle caused a trapdoor to open.

Philby stayed off the platform in case Finn chose incorrectly. The plan was to take turns until they got it right.

Finn tried the blue door, and the floor fell out from under him. Down, down, he raced, the slick slide spinning him in tight coils before throwing him out onto the floor. He headed to the slanted stairs and began climbing again.

Philby tried the yellow door. The trapdoor opened beneath him.

Green—for "go"—seemed too simple a choice, so on Finn's next attempt he tried the purple door, and it opened.

"Purple," Finn called down to Philby, who was gingerly skipping steps as he made his way up the slanted staircase.

Once through the purple door, Finn started across an invisible bridge—an effect so convincing he would have sworn there was nothing beneath his feet. He moved across it in tiny steps, just barely sliding each running shoe forward, making sure something solid was beneath it. Philby, behind him, took the novel approach of getting down on hands and knees and breathing low onto what turned out to be glass, and then following the orbs of fog.

"It's a mirror," said Philby, sneaking up behind the slower Finn. The trick was compounded by the fact that a false destination—a second purple door—was projected at the other end of the invisible bridge, making Finn want to head in that direction. In fact, at its midpoint, the bridge veered right, arriving at what looked like a solid wall, which wasn't solid at all. The two boys ended up on a second small platform.

"I remember this part," Philby said. "This is where we go *down* the stairs in order to go back up."

"Are you sure?" Finn tested the "up" staircase: it was real. He thought Philby had it wrong.

But Philby waved his hand across the step four steps above this first step, and then punched his hand right *through* the illusion—the stairs stopped midflight, nothing but a projected image. He led the way down a staircase and then back up a longer staircase, which would make it appear to anyone standing below as though the boys were walking upside down.

"You two!" a low voice called out loudly. "Come down from there!"

Finn caught sight of an upside-down Cast Member. He was dressed as a barbershop singer, in white pants, a red-and-white-striped shirt, and a straw hat: a Dapper Dan Cast Member.

"Security," Finn whispered to Philby. "I faced Dapper Dans just like him that time Amanda and I were here taking pictures of everyone's DHIs. They were trying to catch me."

"You are not permitted in this area!" the man hollered. "Come down at once."

"I don't think we should trust him."

They reached a third platform and ducked behind a false wall with two windows. "You think he'll come after us?" Philby asked.

Thunder cracked high above them.

"I think there's something going on here," Finn answered. "The weather balloon, the monkeys, Amanda and Jez showing up for the first time in forever. And personally, I don't trust *anyone* dressed up like he's selling fried chicken. He could be anybody. That's an easy costume to fake."

"So we ignore him?"

Another crack of thunder. It was getting close.

"*Outrun* him," Finn said, "is probably more like it."

"And if we're caught?" Philby said. "You ever read those contracts we signed? They'll remove our DHIs from the server. They'll replace us with other kids. We'll no longer be Disney Hosts, no longer have the Gold Fastpasses. We'll lose it all." He hesitated. "All that for some weird balloon? You sure it's worth it?"

"You're the one who saw it, not me. Listen, I'm not sure of anything," Finn said. "You want to head down, I'm not going to stop you or anything." He added, "But I'm going after that balloon, Security or no Security. Amanda was pointing at the castle, and that's good enough for me."

"How could she possibly know anything about it?" Philby asked.

"How can we possibly go to sleep at night and wake up as DHIs inside the Park? When was the last time *any of this* made sense?"

Philby pursed his lips. He nodded. "Yeah, okay. You're right. If they toss us, so what? We go down fighting."

"Exactly." Finn peered around the edge of the wall.

"What do you see?"

The man in the straw hat was gone.

"I think he's coming after us."

4

MAYBECK DUCKED INSTINCTIVELY as the sky flashed, and, only moments later, thunder boomed and rolled in a long series of endless echoes. A few early raindrops splattered in huge globs onto the footpath, and the air smelled dusty and sweet—ozone— foretelling the electrical charge it carried.

Charlene stiffened with the crack of thunder. "I . . . do . . . not . . . do . . . lightning," she said.

The Park guests scattered for cover, quickly emptying the paths.

"Then forget what Finn said and come with me!" Willa said, taking Charlene by the hand. "The parade blocked Jez and Amanda from coming over the bridge. They'll probably head past the Haunted Mansion and through Fantasyland to reach the castle. We're going this way," she said, pointing in the direction of Cinderella's Golden Carrousel, "to cut them off. Maybeck, you go around past the Mansion. Hopefully, one of us finds them before we meet up somewhere near Peter Pan."

"See you in a minute," Maybeck said.

"It's hard to see much, so pay attention," she said.

The swirling clouds had brought an early darkness.

"Never fret. Eyes like a hawk," said Maybeck.

"What about the monkeys?" Charlene mumbled. "What if that was some kind of omen?"

"I'll keep that in mind," said Maybeck.

They split up, Willa dragging Charlene by the arm. Maybeck jogged off.

Park guests waved at Willa and Charlene. Some braved the increasingly steady rain to chase after them, calling for autographs. Willa pressed on.

Charlene said, "We're getting wet."

"That's what usually happens with rain," Willa said.

"We can't get wet!" she complained. "DHIs don't get wet. The rain runs right through them. We can't disappoint the kids like that!"

"Are you worried about the kids, or your hair?"

"Both, I guess."

"Okay. So let's run faster."

5

AMANDA AND JEZ RAN THROUGH the light rain, dodging clusters of guests who were determined to stick it out and wait for the fireworks.

"It's not far now," Amanda said, spotting the spires of Cinderella Castle.

Jez didn't answer.

Amanda glanced back. It wasn't like her sister to avoid a chance to make a snide comment. "Keep up! You're falling behind," she called out. Jez was a fast runner; it made no sense that she should lag. She seemed to be running at a steady pace, no faster, no slower, no matter what Amanda said or how fast she ran.

The rain made the walkway more slippery. Amanda slowed and shortened her strides to avoid falling. When she looked back, Jez was still running at the same pace, the same stride. She apparently had magical footing—she didn't slip.

Amanda stopped and turned fully around and stared at her sister. *How could she not slip even a little bit?*

Despite the falling rain, Jez's shirt was . . . dry, her hair perfectly in place.

What a princess, Amanda thought.

But then she tensed.

Jez's feet landed on the wet walkway. No splash.

"Jez? Stop! Answer me, Jez!" Amanda cried out.

But Jez just kept on running toward her. The same perfect form and posture. The same perfect Jez.

Jez finally did stop, though she remained several yards off, like a fearful animal.

There was a reason her shirt and hair were both dry: the rain fell *through* her, hitting the walkway below.

Amanda stepped forward, now only inches from her sister. The rain fell harder, soaking her own hair and shoulders. Jez remained dry.

"Say something," Amanda whispered.

She reached out her arm and swung it from right to left, cutting her sister in half, her hand passing right through.

A hologram. A DHI.

"Where's my sister?" Amanda managed to choke out, the drops of water now flowing down her cheeks having nothing to do with the rain. "What have you done to her?"

6

"**H**E CAN'T POSSIBLY KNOW the way up here," Finn whispered. "Only Wayne understands Escher's Keep. He said so." But he could hear the swishing of the man's clothing as he climbed the upside-down staircase. He not only knew the way, he seemed to be quickly closing in on them.

"I don't think that actually matters right now," Philby said. "We are going to be in some serious—" He gasped. "What are you doing, Finn?"

Before him, Finn Whitman, the fourteen-year-old boy, transformed into a glowing version of himself with a slightly shorter haircut. He was now his DHI hologram.

"Willa said she s-saw you do this." Philby stuttered when nervous. "But I d-didn't believe her."

"It's not very stable. I can't hold it for very long," Finn said. "Go. Black tiles. Never two in a row. It's the left staircase when you reach the other side. There's the final invisible bridge and then the black hole. I'll meet you there. Wait for me."

Philby waved his arm through Finn just to confirm what he'd seen him do. "But if you're here as your DHI, then where's the real you? Not back asleep in bed? And why can't any of the rest of us do this when we're awake?"

"Philby, I don't know. Maybeck said he's had the same thing happen. Willa, once or twice. We can discuss this later, okay? For some reason, I'm able to will myself to cross over. I don't understand it, but I don't try to understand it. It just *happens* if I let it. Wrap your mind around *that*. It doesn't last long, and it's exhausting. So I'll meet you in the black hole, and I'm going to need your help from there on."

"And you're going to stay and . . . what? . . . *fight* this guy?"

"Yeah, right," Finn said sarcastically, his voice sounding a little bit different, like the buzzing of something electronic. "I'm going to make him wonder what he's chasing. I'm going to freak him out of his shorts. If I'm lucky . . . well . . . let's hope I'm lucky." He waited only seconds. "GO!"

Philby took off across the checkerboard floor, making sure the toes of his shoes landed only on the black squares, and never two black squares in the same horizontal row. It required a kind of dancing across and down the floor that made him look like a kid in *Riverdance*.

Finn's ability to cross over while awake had to do with achieving a kind of meditative state. If he focused on having no fear, no worries, he temporarily crossed over. He didn't know the rules or how it worked, only that he could make it happen—though only inside the Magic Kingdom, where hologram projectors existed throughout the Park. He took a moment to test his ability, aware of its unpredictability and his lack of control over it. He grabbed for the nearby doorknob. His hand landed on it, and he was able to *turn* the doorknob. Then he pulled his hand away, closed his eyes briefly, and concentrated on just a single idea: light. He opened his eyes and reached for the doorknob once again. This time the doorknob passed *through* his hand. It sparkled and glowed as he swept his hand on through the doorjamb and back out.

So far, he seemed to be in control of his hologram, but he knew from previous attempts that his hologram quickly deteriorated. A few minutes was all he had, until Finn, the fourteen-year-old boy, came back to replace the DHI.

He stepped out of the way as he heard footsteps approaching. The man arrived at the platform. Finn hid behind him. The man was big, with thick, heavy legs and broad shoulders. He looked a little foolish in his red-and-white-striped jacket and straw hat. He studied the checkerboard floor like a person trying to remember the code, bringing his thick hand to his scrabbly chin in contemplation.

"White or black? Odds or evens?" Finn said, startling the man.

The man spun around, his face a knot of anger. "You're not allowed here," he said in a deep, dry voice. Incredibly quickly for his size, he jumped toward Finn and swiped at him, his hands passing *right through* the DHI, at which point he stood up in astonishment, looking at his own hands as if they'd betrayed him.

"One wrong step, and you fall," Finn said, darting past the man and out onto the checkerboard floor. He concentrated on the idea of light—*pure light*. A DHI weighed nothing, and only weight triggered the tiles in the floor. But he knew he couldn't maintain this pure state for very long. He had to lure the man out onto the floor quickly. There wasn't much time.

He tried another tack. "I'm a Cast Member," Finn said, "like you."

"I don't care. You're not allowed up there," he said. By saying this he confirmed he knew about the penthouse—Walt Disney's former apartment—the secret room Wayne had offered the DHIs as a place to hide.

An Overtaker? Finn wondered. The group loyal to Maleficent, dedicated to changing the balance of power in the Parks.

"I said you're not allowed up there," the man said.

"White or black?" Finn said, his DHI standing on one of each.

The pleasant warmth of the DHI gave way to a slight chill, and Finn knew the internal light was giving way to flesh and blood. He wished he understood how to control this transformation better, but that was for another time. He took advantage of his brief weightlessness and crossed the checkerboard floor to a platform that presented another three ascending staircases. He had one last trick left.

The man stepped out onto the checkerboard, keeping his eyes on the squares. It was a long fall below—thirty feet or more, though the floor had been painted in perspective, which made it appear more like three hundred: a bottomless, rocky cavern. He took that in, and then, as he looked across at Finn, his face turned scarlet with anger.

"You won't talk your way out of this, son." He stepped onto a black tile. Then another. *He knew the pattern!* Making sure he avoided any two black squares in the same horizontal line, he progressed cautiously but quickly across the floor.

Finn felt the DHI fading. He'd managed to maintain it for a minute or more, but he suspected he weighed something now. Would he trip the sensors that opened the floor, or could he make it across?

His plan was to run *right through* the man. He believed if he concentrated, he could summon his pure

DHI for the fraction of a second it would take to pass through him. In doing so, he was certain to cause the intruder to misstep, which would send him plummeting. But Finn would have to move quickly to avoid being on the floor when it fell out and gave way.

He stepped out onto two black squares. He could *feel* his weight on his feet. He was about equal parts boy and DHI. *How much longer?*

The Dapper Dan stopped halfway, his face a scowl. Then something occurred to him, and he belched out a laugh. "Going to wrestle me, are you?" He grinned mischievously. "I'll save you the trouble." His right foot reached out for a white square.

Finn had not considered that the fastest way for the man to catch Finn was to make Finn fall *with* him.

Finn ran forward on the black tiles, simultaneously letting go of all fear. He felt the warmth return like a blast from a furnace. But well before he reached the other side—in fact, before he even reached his adversary—the floor went out from under him.

The man fell, letting out a short scream as he was funneled into a red plastic chute.

Finn was floating. The trapdoor had opened beneath him, but his DHI simply hovered. He was suspended ten feet above the evacuation chute, with only air beneath him.

He felt the chill returning. He managed three steps toward the edge of the open pit and then fell. His fingers caught the lip of the hinged flooring, and his body smacked into the hanging trapdoor. Normally not good at pull-ups, he must have been partially DHI, because he managed to lift himself, hook a leg, and pull himself up. Seconds later, the trapdoor snapped back into position. He stayed on the black squares and recrossed.

Middle staircase. Red door. He remembered this section well.

He heard the Dapper Dan hit bottom and, seconds later, the sound of him climbing stairs again. Faster now. Ever more determined to apprehend Finn.

Finn stepped forward into total darkness, a matter of extreme trust. The first time he'd followed Wayne in here, he'd nearly puked from fear. The black hole.

He ran smack into Philby.

"There's no elevator," Philby said.

"What?"

"No elevator. It's not here."

"It has to be here," Finn said.

"No such luck, Sherlock."

"But that means—"

"Somebody's up there," Philby said. "Already in the apartment. And what do you want to bet it's not Wayne?"

"There's got to be another way up," Finn said. "Fire stairs. Something for an emergency."

"In case you hadn't noticed, it's pitch black. You don't happen to have a flashlight on you, I suppose?"

"Turn your back to me," Finn said. He mustered his strength. Transforming into his DHI sapped his energy. He felt exhausted from having challenged the man just now, but knew he had to do this. He closed his eyes. He felt the warmth return. He couldn't hold it for more than a few seconds. He came out of it, his legs weak, his head swooning.

"Oh, man! How cool is that?" Philby said excitedly. "Hold on to my shirt, lightning bug. I saw some stairs over here."

Finn reached out and held on, as much to keep his balance as to stay with Philby. They reached a set of metal stairs, the handrail cool to the touch.

"Going up," said Philby.

They started climbing the spiral stairs. Higher and higher.

From below them came the heavy breathing of the man pursuing them.

He'd already caught back up. He sounded incredibly close.

7

MAYBECK PROVED HIMSELF the faster runner, arriving next to Amanda at nearly the same instant as Charlene and Willa despite having come the long way around. The rain was falling in punishing waves, and thunder was cracking menacingly overhead.

Amanda, soaking wet, was on her knees, crying. Jez just stood there, the rain passing through her. It took Maybeck and the girls a few seconds to realize what Amanda already knew.

"Oh, man," said Maybeck. "How long ago did this happen?"

Willa and Charlene helped Amanda to her feet. Everyone but Jez was now drenched. Charlene held her hands over her hair, as if that would do any good.

"She didn't keep up," Amanda said. "I thought she was probably fiddling with her iPod—trying to protect it from the rain. She won't stop messing with that thing. So I looked back, and . . . *she* was there." She pointed to the DHI of her sister.

"But how is that possible?" Willa asked. "Jez isn't a DHI."

37

"She is now," said Maybeck, contradicting. He ran his hand right through Jez's body and out the other side.

Some kids cheered and called out from the crowded area in front of Peter Pan's Flight, where they stood protected from the rain.

"Somebody did this," Amanda said. "They programmed a DHI for her. But it's not much of a program. She's just . . . standing there."

"But why?" Maybeck said.

"Who?" Willa said. "The Imagineers wouldn't do this without Wayne telling us."

More kids called out from the line, this time wanting autographs.

"We can't stay here," said Maybeck.

"I have to find her," Amanda said. "The *real* her."

"We need Finn and Philby," Willa said.

Hunched over and miserable in the rain, Charlene added, "Could we maybe move this meeting somewhere dry?"

Maybeck said, "We saw you two not five minutes ago. If they grabbed her . . . if they made a switch . . . it had to have happened between then and now. Somewhere really close to here."

"Are you saying she was . . . kidnapped?" Charlene said, a little too concerned with her hair to have stayed with the discussion.

"If humans take you, you're kidnapped," Maybeck answered. "I doubt there's a name for it when it's a band of Disney villains. But yeah. She's missing."

"But why?" Charlene asked Maybeck. "Why kidnap Jez?"

The three kids stared at Amanda, waiting for an answer. She pursed her lips as if she'd swallowed something bitter. "If I told you—which I can't—you wouldn't believe me."

"Try us," Maybeck said.

"You'd be surprised at what we can handle," said Willa.

"The Overtakers?" Maybeck asked, winning Amanda's attention.

"You don't know the half of it," Amanda said.

"Try us," Maybeck repeated.

"Please tell us," Willa pleaded. She wiped the rain from her eyes. "We want to help, but we need to know what's going on, what we're involved in."

Charlene proved she'd been paying attention after all. "This has to do with Finn, doesn't it? When Finn got tangled up with Jez, and you said some kind of spell had been removed. Maleficent's spell."

That incident had happened months ago, though the kids remembered it as if it were yesterday. Maleficent had kept Jez under her control to prevent Jez's own powers from interfering with Maleficent's plan. The DHIs had managed to trap Maleficent, and Finn had helped free Jez from the spell—though her powers had yet to be explained to any of them. Maybe this was why the sisters had vanished recently: to keep from having to explain themselves.

"We have to hurry," Willa said. "For one thing, those kids are blowing our cover. For another, every second counts. She can't be far."

"Since when are you a detective? You've been reading too many American Girl books," snapped Charlene.

"No, she's right," Maybeck said. "Time is in our favor, but not for long. Amanda and I will retrace her route, looking for her. Willa, you and Charlene get Finn and Philby out of the castle and meet up with us."

Amanda jerked her head toward Cinderella Castle. "He's *in* there?" she gasped, and then mumbled, "I'd nearly forgotten."

"Forgotten what?" Maybeck asked.

Amanda looked back and forth from the sputtering and sparking DHI of her sister to the colorful lights illuminating the castle.

"Something horrible's going to happen," Amanda whispered. "Jezebel dreamed about it. We came here to warn all of you." She met eyes with Maybeck and then Willa. "He's actually *in* there?"

"She dreamed about it?" Charlene said, distrustful and sarcastic. "Your sister can dream the future, I suppose? Is that what you're trying to tell us?"

"Fairlies have abilities you wouldn't believe."

"What's a Fairlie?" Willa blurted out.

"I told you you wouldn't believe me."

8

FINN FOLLOWED PHILBY up the tightly wound spiral staircase in complete darkness, his lungs and legs burning, his head pounding. Transforming himself into a DHI—twice in a matter of minutes—had taxed him. He climbed, half in, half out of consciousness, sliding his hand along the cool steel handrail, faint of head but not of heart. Someone was trying to attract lightning to Cinderella Castle. He envisioned the penthouse apartment converted into a Frankenstein laboratory, some Disney monster strapped to a stainless-steel table with wires attached to his head and heart. He didn't know what to think—except that the Overtakers had sent the Dapper Dan to stop them. That had to mean something big was going down.

Thunder cracked outside, sending a rumble up his legs. Climbing higher in a lightning storm was not the smartest move. He felt another tremor in his chest.

Speaking in a breathless whisper as they climbed, Finn said, "What if it's all a trap? An elaborate trap? What if this guy is supposed to drive us to the top of the castle? What if the weather balloon and lightning are intended for us? To *kill* us?"

Philby stopped, and Finn bumped into him. He had trouble catching his breath. His heart was about to explode.

The staircase vibrated: the man was climbing toward them.

"But if that's the case, then this guy's suicidal," Philby said, "because he's right behind us."

"But if he's an Overtaker, how do we even know he's real?"

"How do we know if any of this is real?" Philby quipped. "Not one of us has ever told our parents about what happens to us at night. Why do you think that is?" He answered his own question. "Because they wouldn't believe it."

Shadows flickered on the wall. A flashlight. *The guy!*

"Climb!" Finn hissed.

They started climbing higher, running up the stairs as fast as they could. Their pursuer wasn't nearly as light on his feet as they were. The beam from his flashlight and the strange, shifting shadows it cast propelled them hurriedly up, up, up. At last, they faced a door.

It was bolted shut; there was no doorknob or handle.

In the dim light, Finn caught sight of a handwritten sign taped to the wall:

OPEN <u>ONLY</u> IN EMERGENCY

"Do we dare?" Finn asked.

"It has to lead into the apartment," said Philby.

"Agreed."

The light from the flashlight rose more quickly now. "And we're trying to get into the apartment."

Finn moved the bolt, and the door popped open.

Together they entered into another dark space. Finn reached out. It was narrow and tight. The sound of bells . . . no . . . Finn knew that sound. It wasn't bells. It was . . . *hangers*.

"We're in a closet," Finn said softly. "A closet inside the apartment, I'll bet."

"The stairs are the apartment's fire escape," said Philby. "Makes sense." But why lock a fire escape from the *outside*? Finn wondered silently.

He groped in the dark and touched another door in front of them and opened it a crack. The closet led into the apartment's small bedroom, the shiny bedspread a hideous shade of grass green. The air smelled stale and dusty. The boys slipped into the bedroom. It felt unbearably warm.

Heavy footsteps clomped up the stairs.

"Hurry!" Finn hissed. He and Philby rushed out of the closet, shut its door and, working together, slid the bed to block it. At the very least they had bought themselves a few seconds.

They hurried to the bedroom door, and Finn put his ear to it.

"Anything?" Philby asked, one eye nervously on the blocked closet behind them.

"It sounds like someone mumbling." Finn opened the door carefully and then quietly stepped through. Philby followed. They were in a small hallway with a view into a larger living room. The décor might have once been called modern. Now it looked slightly cheesy.

Finn angled his head around the corner to get a better view into the living room. Then he jerked back.

Maleficent—the most powerful of the Disney fairies and Finn's greatest enemy—stood by the apartment window. Amanda had somehow known! Maleficent had enormous evil powers, including the ability to conjure spells with nothing more than incantations. Finn had once seen her transfigure a trash bag into a rat. She had demonstrated powers of fire and electricity, conjuring a cage of glowing "wires" around him. Her one weakness was temperature—she could only conjure when cold, which helped explain her being jailed in an apartment kept so warm. He doubted she was at her full powers, given the warmth of the apartment, but that could change in an instant. She had her back to them, and her dark robe hung to the floor. Now Finn understood what he'd heard: Maleficent was chanting while facing the open window. It was blocked on the outside by a heavy iron grate—like a jail cell.

Casting a spell? Finn wondered.

His legs shook with fear. The last he'd known, she'd been locked in a jail cell in the catacombs beneath Pirates of the Caribbean. What was she doing here?

She stepped away from the window but continued chanting. Through the window, the sky darkened. The storm roared as lightning flashed and thunder cracked. Finn tensed with the next lightning strike: a tremendous flash was followed instantly by a crack and boom. Was she summoning the lightning? Another loud crack. A bolt of electricity struck the iron grate. It glowed red hot, and then sparks flew. The iron grate melted and fell open, the window no longer blocked. The evening's cool breeze blew through.

Maleficent climbed up onto the sill. The crowd cheered from below.

Color filled the sky—the fireworks display had begun.

"Stop!" he shouted.

She turned. "YOU!"

It was no trap. Their being here clearly surprised her.

Her red eyes locked on to his. Her green, hideous

skin scrunched tightly around her eyes. *If looks could kill . . .* he thought.

Finn stepped back, afraid. *The cool air . . .* Three loud bangs of thunder mixed with the fireworks, making a war zone out of the sky. A fiery backdrop played out behind the green creature standing in the window.

She glanced back at him one more time and then climbed outside.

Finn and Philby hurried to the smoldering window opening and looked out.

Maleficent was climbing the castle wall, her cape swirling in the wind. She moved like an insect.

He looked down and gasped. They had to be a hundred feet up.

"I'm not going out there!" Finn said.

"The stairs!" Philby said.

With every second she would be cooling off, regaining her powers. The boys hurried back to the bedroom, determined to follow her. The Dapper Dan was pounding on the closet door from the other side.

"Ready?" Finn said, his hands against the bed frame.

Philby, selected as a DHI in large part for his brainpower, did not need to hear what Finn had in mind. He knew intuitively.

"One . . . two . . ."

On *three* the boys shoved the bed out of the way. The door flew open.

The Dapper Dan, who'd been pushing hard on the closet door, fell through and tumbled down onto the carpet. Finn and Philby ducked into the closet, hurried out the emergency door, and threw the bolt before the Dapper Dan had climbed to his feet. They had trapped him inside.

They hesitated on the landing.

"Up or down?" Finn asked Philby, the challenge obvious to both boys.

Philby looked down the stairs, knowing this meant safety. Then he looked at Finn. "If she gets free, we'll never be safe again," he said.

"Up!" the two boys said in unison.

The boys climbed the dark staircase, slowly at first, but then, holding the rail, Finn picked up the pace.

As they neared the top, the sound of the crowd grew louder. The stairs ended in a small stone chamber with an open window.

It took only seconds for Finn's eyes to adjust. There was a young woman tied up in the corner. She had wings, and for a moment he thought she, too, was an Overtaker. Then he recognized her as Tinker Bell. She was a Cast Member, in costume.

Maleficent stood in the open window, her robe

fluttering, the fireworks flashing colors in the sky beyond her. Now Finn saw the metal wire secured to the wall.

"Silly boys!" Maleficent said in a raspy voice. "The end is near."

She jumped.

Finn ran to the window.

But she hadn't fallen. Instead, she flew off, away from them.

She could fly!

But then Finn understood: near the conclusion of the fireworks show, Tinker Bell flew from the castle. Tinker Bell was actually a Cast Member riding a zip line from the castle onto a roof in Tomorrowland. But on this night, it wasn't Tinker Bell riding the zip line.

Maleficent let out a bloodcurdling screech—to the delight of the crowd—as she rode the wire high in the sky. She grew smaller and smaller.

The crowd went crazy with cheers and screams.

Her hideous screech rang in the air until swallowed by the next thumping blast of fireworks—the grand finale—that joined the rippling of thunder echoing off the Florida landscape like the aftereffect of a bomb exploding.

9

THE LIGHTNING STRIKE that hit Cinderella Castle charged the night sky with intense light as fire rained down. The bolt of lightning had grounded out on the thin wire holding the weather balloon. Next, the lights went out in a large area encircling the castle, including the street lamps surrounding the Hub, most of Liberty Square, and as far away as Tomorrowland. Spotlights that normally lit the sky went black, leaving the colorful glow of the fireworks' grand finale.

Then something—or someone—flew out toward Tomorrowland, and it was quite obviously *not* Tinker Bell. The caped figure was chased by a ball of swirling orange flame. A chorus of cheers arose. No one was exactly sure what they'd just witnessed, but whatever it was, it was amazing.

Willa and the others heard the cheer. Only moments later a swirl of rumor reached them: a witch had flown from the castle. Maybeck said a few words that would have gotten him detention in school.

"Which witch?" Charlene wondered aloud.

"Three guesses," said Amanda.

The three others looked at her sharply.

"Finn!" Charlene muttered, her worry hanging in the air.

"What do we do now?" Willa gasped.

"You've got to tell us what you know," Maybeck demanded of Amanda.

"It's Jez that saw this coming, not me," Amanda said.

"Saw *what* coming?" he asked.

"Trouble."

"You already said that. You gotta give us more."

"I told you: Jez is different."

"She's your sister!" he complained.

"Yeah," she said, sounding apologetic. "Kind of. I guess you could say I'm a little different as well."

"Different how?"

"Just . . . different."

"She's not on trial," Willa complained to Maybeck. "She and Jez came to *warn* us!" She addressed Amanda. "What did Jez think was going to happen?"

"She *saw* things. She wrote them down—drew things—in her journal. Kept track of them—dreams mostly. And daydreams. But . . ." She cut herself off and looked at each of the others searchingly. "The really creepy part is she showed me a sketch she made of lightning striking the castle. She knew it was going to happen, and I think she knew that Finn was going to be inside."

"You owe us an explanation," Maybeck said impatiently.

"And you'll have it," Amanda agreed. She glanced around—a number of guests were braving the rain to get a better look at the castle. "But not here. Not now. You have to help Finn. He's in danger. More danger than from just the lightning. It's the Overtakers. They did this. They're responsible. Jez . . . I have to find Jez. They're afraid of her . . . powers. She can stop this by warning you and others, but not if they control her."

"Stop what?" Maybeck asked.

"I wish I knew."

"The lightning?" Willa asked. "We're a little late, if that's the case."

"It was more than that," Amanda said. "Listen, I've got to find Jez. You all need to help Finn and Philby. They're in danger. Jez saw that coming. *That* was what she was trying to prevent."

"Okay," Maybeck said, "enough chit-chat. Let's get going. Amanda and I are going to head back to look for Jez while you two check out the castle and find Finn and Philby."

"With the power out, they'll close the Park," Willa warned. "They're not going to let us run around for long. And if they recognize us, they're not going to want us in the Park at all."

"Well, then, pull up your hood. Mess up your hair. We gotta do this," Maybeck said. "If they close the Park, we'll IM and figure this out." He grabbed Amanda's arm and tugged. She hesitated, then moved with him.

They took off at a run.

"Everyone IM at midnight," he yelled over his shoulder.

Charlene and Willa headed for the castle, which was shrouded in darkness and a veil of smoke left over from both the fireworks and the lightning strike.

Behind them, they left the sputtering hologram of Jez, who, as another series of street lamps flickered and failed in the spreading blackout, sputtered and went dark.

Gone, just like the real Jez.

Some kids cheered from under awnings. Rain continued to fall.

One of them shouted, "The Kingdom Keepers *rule!*"

Willa winced at hearing the nickname that a local newspaper had adopted for the kids and their DHIs. She felt a chill down her spine and a pain in her stomach. They weren't superheroes; they were teen models mixed up in some confused technology that no one fully understood—not even the people who'd invented it.

She'd gotten a good look at the thing flying. She hadn't mentioned what she'd seen to the others, because who would have believed it?

But she knew what she'd seen—*whom* she'd seen—and the chill was replaced with a spasm of terror.

Maleficent had escaped. Jez had been turned into a DHI.

To think that those two events were some kind of freak coincidence and unrelated was just plain wrong.

10

IT SOUNDED LIKE DOZENS of footsteps were hurrying up the spiral staircase as Finn and Philby rushed to untie the woman dressed up as Tinker Bell. Finn got the tape off her mouth.

"Are you all right?"

She looked terrified. "Who . . . *what* . . . was that?"

Philby said, "Finn, we're cooked."

The approaching footsteps were noticeably closer. They were either security guards or Overtakers. Either way spelled disaster for the boys.

"Who's coming?" the Tinker Bell woman asked.

"We don't know."

"I'm not sticking around to find out," she said.

The boys looked paralyzed.

She said, "Harnesses," pointing to the wall. "They're rescue harnesses, in case I get stuck out there." She hesitated only a second before grabbing one. "Put them on!"

She helped both boys into the harnesses and double-checked them for safety. "Have you ever ridden a zip line?"

Finn shook his head.

Philby said, "In camp once."

"Same thing," she said. "I'm going to go first." She clipped a pulley to the guy wire. "That way I can catch you two as you arrive on the other end. Ready?"

Whoever was coming up the spiral stairs was moving fast.

"See you down there," she said. With that, she jumped.

Finn watched as she zoomed away, into the dark of the night. She disappeared.

"I am *not* going out that window," Finn declared.

"Listen," Philby said, "we have two choices: we can get busted and blamed for everything that just happened, or we can go out that window."

"You're insane."

The sounds coming up the stairs grew even louder.

Philby grunted and pushed Finn toward the window. "You're first," he said.

"I don't think so."

"Those guys are going to be here in about two seconds."

"What if it doesn't support us?

"This is Disney. The thing will probably support a tank."

"What if Tinker Bell doesn't catch us?"

"My advice? Don't look down."

Philby tested the pulley and pushed Finn.

Finn felt a blistering wind on his face.

He was . . . *flying*. It was, for an instant, the coolest thing he'd ever done. He was zooming down the wire, high above the grass and the water, headed for the lights of Tomorrowland.

The whine of the pulley rose to a high-pitched whir. Philby was behind him now. Down, down, down they raced. Then the wire leveled off, and their speed decreased. They were headed above a set of rooftops. Finn caught sight of the MONSTERS, INC. COMEDY CLUB sign to his left. With the wire more level, they continued to slow.

Tinker Bell caught them at the far end, in front of a set of pads. She unhooked the pulleys and helped them both out of the harnesses.

Finn looked back to see several men huddled in the tower they'd just left.

"Nice timing," Finn said. Seeing how far they had traveled, his knees went weak. "That was not a smart thing to do."

"It was *incredibly* stupid!" Philby agreed. He looked at Finn sheepishly. "But man, was that fun!"

Tinker Bell led them down a very steep metal

staircase and into an alley. A moment later, she'd showed them how to reenter the Park. They hurried toward the Hub.

"FINN!" He heard his name shouted from far away. It took him a moment to see in the glow of a few emergency lights what Philby saw first: two figures up near the castle. Girls.

"It's Willa and Charlene," Finn said.

"How can you be sure?" Philby said, squinting.

"Trust me. It's them."

The boys ran toward the girls, circled carefully, and hid on the other side of a stone wall, waiting. They squatted down and caught their breath.

Finn dared to raise an eye above the wall: he saw a pair of Cast Members that he took to be security guards, searching the crowd.

"They're looking for us," he told Philby. "Might be Overtakers. Might just be Disney Security."

"We'll get across the Hub and catch up to the girls. We're just two kids now among all the others."

It was true: the rain had stopped and the crowds had returned. An announcement was repeated several times, apologizing for the fact that the Park would close early due to the weather. Cinderella Castle had been roped off.

Finn nodded his agreement.

The two boys crossed the busy Hub outside of the castle. As they reached its center a number of lights came back on, and the look and feel of the castle was restored. Some firemen were packing up.

And there, looking down on them from the castle plaza, were Charlene and Willa.

The girls looked terrified.

11

AT TWO MINUTES BEFORE MIDNIGHT, as Finn was preparing to IM with Philby, Maybeck, and the others, his messaging window showed an unexpected visitor. The Instant Messaging program was only connected to people on his buddy list, so the appearance of this uninvited visitor was somewhat surprising, unsettling, and even alarming. His parents made a big deal out of how unsafe the Internet could be, how stalkers often trolled for kids by pretending to be kids themselves. And while he thought his parents overdid their warnings, he knew that stuff happened. The appearance of the uninvited guest made him wonder if it was happening to him.

I'm from the firehouse.

Finn's breath caught. Wayne lived above the firehouse in the Magic Kingdom. Could this possibly be Wayne? His Wayne? He'd been missing for a long time now.

WAYNE? Finn typed. But nothing appeared in the IM window. It was as if the program was blocking that name from being written, the way some Web sites prevented the use of certain words. He considered how to work around the problem. Then he typed again.

W . . . A . . . Y . . . N . . . E . . . ?

you always were the clever one. my name was supposed to be blocked, but separating the letters! brilliant!

Finn wasn't convinced it was Wayne on the other end of this written conversation. He could be an imposter.

Finn typed: **you have something I found, but you kept. it's magical. what is it?**

He anxiously awaited the answer. This question, he felt, would determine if it was in fact Wayne.

uncle walt's pen

Finn cursed at the screen, not meaning to. It really was Wayne. No one but he and the other DHIs knew that answer.

An unusual feeling overcame Finn. For months he'd wondered if Wayne had died or been captured by the Overtakers. Thrilled to now reconnect with him, he let his fingers hover over the keyboard.

Where to start?

A Disney old-timer and former Imagineer, Wayne knew more about Disney World than any living person. He had once counted Walt Disney himself as a personal friend. A legend in Disney circles, his name often appeared on blogs.

He was responsible for Finn and his friends' becoming DHIs in the first place. He had created the concept and had overseen the development of the software. More important, as far as Finn could tell, he controlled a secret group of Cast Members that opposed the Overtakers' attempt to gain control of the Magic Kingdom.

we're not safe here. do you have video abilities?

yes.

then go onto the web site: www.dgamer.com/vmk. it's a secure link. but before you do that, you'll need to write something something down.

Finn wondered if Wayne had been in a coma or something. He typed: **vmk was shut down months ago.**

to the public, yes. the site had to be closed for security reasons. write this down. at the sign-on, use the username: imagineer1. your password is our uncle's full name spelled backward with no dashes or spaces.

Finn quickly scribbled down *yensidtlaw*. waltdisney spelled backward.

okay. got it.

you will see a video link button on the landing page. right click on that button: it will open up a video chat with me. see you in a minute.

The sudden closing of VMK had come as a shock to Finn and his friends. News that the Web site remained accessible surprised him. But he didn't doubt Wayne for a moment. Wayne lived and worked in a secret world. He was full of surprises.

*　*　*

"It's really you," Finn gasped, seeing the man's weathered face on his computer screen. There was no telling how old Wayne was, but he wasn't young.

The video signal wasn't perfect: static overlaid Wayne's face, and the sound of his voice was crackling and uneven. He looked and sounded older than Finn remembered him.

"You don't have much time," he said, causing gooseflesh to ripple up Finn's arms.

"Excuse me?" Finn replied.

Wayne was continually checking over his shoulder, as if afraid of being found out, which Finn found disturbing.

"You were lucky at the Park tonight," Wayne said.

"You were there?"

"Never mind about me. You were there. That's all that matters."

"It was Maleficent."

"Tell me exactly what happened."

Finn kept his summary of the evening's events as short and succinct as possible. He described spotting Amanda and Jez during the start of the parade; of later seeing a pair of monkeys in the bushes near the crowd. Wayne quizzed him about the monkeys. Then Finn described his being chased up Escher's Keep, and finished with Maleficent's daring escape out the window and down Tinker Bell's zip line.

"We'd moved her there," Wayne said. "Third move in as many weeks. We had intelligence that the Overtakers were planning for her escape. We thought by moving her around frequently . . . But it obviously wasn't enough."

"What about the weather balloon? The lightning strike?"

"The apartment was locked down like a jail cell. Sealed tight. We had to provide a way out in case of fire, but the closest exit was locked from the inside. Our security guard would have had to open that door for her to escape."

"The Dapper Dan chasing us . . . was he one of your guys?"

"You had no way of knowing that."

But I should have, Finn thought. The Dapper Dan had known the way up the Keep. Only Wayne could have taught him the route.

"We put on an ankle bracelet that would send an alarm if she moved more than fifty feet from the transmitter," Wayne explained. "It housed a GPS transmitter, so we could track her down. They used the power of the lightning strike to break open the bars. Nothing short of a small bomb would have accomplished that. The lightning also temporarily knocked out the power, which was crucial for her to escape. They bought her enough time to cut the ankle bracelet off. We found it up there in the Tinker Bell tower."

That didn't sound good. "So she's just . . . gone?"

"I doubt very far. A green face tends to stick out. It's control of the Park that she's after. She'll stay in the Park, we think. But to accomplish her goal of domination, she'll have to rebuild, and reorganize the Overtakers. And she'll need the five of you out of the way. You defeated her last time. She won't risk that happening again."

Finn didn't like the way Wayne said that so calmly. Out of the way? He tried to wrap his mind around the fact that they were talking about a Disney character—villain or not—as if she were human. And after all that he and the other DHIs had been through, it wasn't so hard. Something weird was going on, and somehow they were now a big part of it. Whatever kind of being Maleficent was, however it was that she existed, her presence was very real, as was the threat to the DHIs.

"She needs cold, don't forget, or at least the illusion of cold. She loses her powers in the heat. For this and other reasons, we think she's likely gone to the Animal Kingdom."

"Because?"

"There are several attractions there that are kept quite chilly. And of course there's Everest."

"Is that where Jez is?"

Wayne's face tightened. "You want to explain that, please?"

Finn told him the rest of what had happened. He related what Willa had told him briefly upon their meeting by the castle: that Jez had been replaced by a DHI and the real Jez had vanished.

"That's why I was IMing the others," he explained. "At midnight we were going to meet and try to figure out how to get Jez back." He listened to himself say that, and wondered what chance they had against Maleficent. Then he checked the computer clock and, seeing it was well past midnight, wondered why no one else had joined the chat.

"Amanda," Finn continued, "supposedly said something about Jez being . . . different. Like she's a Cast Member or something."

"She's not a Cast Member," Wayne said knowingly. If he knew something about Jez, he hid it well, for although the reception was poor—sparking and sputtering—his expression didn't change.

"What I'm going to tell you now," Wayne said, "is done so in the strictest confidence. Do you understand me, Finn? You can share what you must with your friends, but only if absolutely necessary, and only if they promise to protect the information. It's critical to the safety of all of us."

"I promise." A second chill raced through Finn.

Wayne glanced suspiciously over his shoulder for the umpteenth time. "I'm in hiding, as you must be aware by now. The Overtakers are said to have obtained the DHI technology. They are working on projecting me—turning me into a DHI so that they could mislead our efforts to defeat them. And if they managed to contain my DHI when I was sleeping . . . well . . . you saw what happened to your friend Maybeck."

Months earlier, Maybeck's DHI had been prevented from crossing back over—a process that was triggered by a small black remote control device that Wayne possessed. As a result, the human Maybeck had remained asleep in bed in a kind of induced coma while his DHI had been trapped in a maintenance cage in Space Mountain. Finn had freed Maybeck's DHI, and Wayne had then crossed them over, allowing the human Maybeck to awaken from his comatose state. But the idea of that happening to Wayne or any of the other DHIs ever again was terrifying. Unthinkable.

"What you've just told me about Jezebel's disappearance," Wayne said, "figures into this theory, I'm afraid. It suggests the Overtakers do, in fact, have the DHI technology at their disposal, and that presents us with some difficult choices."

"Our DHIs went back on line tonight," Finn muttered.

"Precisely! You're aware of the DHI expansion plan?"

Finn had heard rumors that the Animal Kingdom was planning Disney Host Interactive characters—using DHIs of Animal Kingdom animals to guide guests through the Park the same way holograms of Finn and his friends guided guests around the Magic Kingdom.

"Animal Kingdom this year," Wayne said. "Then they'll put your DHIs at Disneyland and the cruise ships within two years. You and the other DHIs have become so popular that the Imagineers are ramping up expansion into all the Parks around the world: Paris, Hong Kong, Japan. You have developed an enormous fan base."

The video briefly sputtered and went dark, but a moment later Wayne's face grew larger as he leaned toward the camera.

Wayne spoke softly. "Imagineering won't confirm or deny my team's accusations that the Animal Kingdom's DHI server was cloned, but now with what you've told me, I'm sure of it. The Overtakers have a second DHI server, Finn. No one around here is ever going to admit it, but that doesn't mean it's not true. They have stolen the software responsible for projecting you five kids as holograms. If they've created DHI data for me, as I believe—and for Jezebel, as you've just told me—then it's in an effort to trick us or spy on us or manipulate us. What if my DHI is used so that I give my people orders that they, the Overtakers, want given?"

"That would give them control of the Park." Finn paused, deep in thought. "But wait a second. If they have the same server, the same software, does that give them control over our DHIs too?"

"You see? You understand things so quickly. There's a reason you're the leader," Wayne said, his eyes briefly looking brighter.

"I'm not the leader."

"Of course you are."

"We've never voted on a leader."

"Not all leaders are elected, Finn. Some just rise to the occasion."

Finn ignored that. He and his friends worked as a group. Wayne wouldn't understand that.

"So what you're saying," Finn said, "is that the Overtakers may be able to use our DHIs like they used Jez to trick Amanda? They could have us doing stuff we wouldn't want."

"It's not only that, I'm afraid. If they have a second server up and running—and by everything you've told me about Jez's disappearance, they must—then the greater concern is their generating DHIs for each of you inside the Animal Kingdom. If they trap those DHIs and prevent them from crossing back over when you're asleep . . ."

"We'd end up like Maybeck was."

"Sleeping Beauty Syndrome," Wayne said.

"Yeah: SBS," Finn whispered so softly to himself that Wayne didn't hear. It was the nickname Wayne had given to the comatose state. "But why would they want to do that to us?"

"Because Maleficent wants you out of the way. For good. They can only accomplish that if you go to sleep," Wayne reminded Finn. "That's the key, you see? If none of you goes to sleep, there's no way you'll cross over in the first place, no way you could be trapped in the Syndrome. They cannot gain that control over you as long as you remain awake."

"I thought the software was rewritten so that SBS couldn't happen again. Wasn't that the point of the DHI server being down for the past couple months? The Grand Opening was to celebrate everything working again."

"Yes, yes, yes. And I'd like to think the same rewritten software had been installed at the Animal Kingdom, but that installation has been going on while the original software was being debugged. I know a software update was made available to the Animal Kingdom, but I can't get anyone over there to confirm it ever took place."

Finn stared at Wayne's flickering face, his thoughts whirring. Wayne was warning him that the Overtakers had a DHI server with the original flawed software that allowed Sleeping Beauty Syndrome. "You're freaking me out," Finn said.

"Yes. I can understand that."

"How do you know any of this is for real?"

"I don't. All I can tell you is, as a precaution, I've been taking twenty-minute naps—never a minute longer, hoping to keep them from crossing me over. So far it has worked. But for how long? The crossing over has to do with the dream state. We designed it that way. It occurs in the first few moments of REM sleep, which is about twenty minutes into a decent night's sleep. The crossing over feels to you like it happens immediately—instantly—but that's not the case. And another thing: I designed the crossing over to synchronize—that is, if you all go to sleep at about the same time, all five of you would then cross over at roughly the same moment. It saves the code from having to reload for each of you."

"But what about the remote control? If we got in trouble, couldn't you use that to cross us back over?"

"If your DHIs were all in the same place at the same time. Yes, that's more than likely possible. But they could prevent that easily enough."

"By keeping our DHIs apart." Finn didn't like what he was hearing. "So, what am I supposed to do?" he asked. Wayne was making it sound as if there was no hope: they were doomed.

"You need to stay awake. You need to find where the real Jezebel is being kept," Wayne explained. "And you need to find that second server and take it back. At the very least, you need to crash it. But only once Jezebel is safe and you see that she's fully awake. I wouldn't mind if you contacted me then as well. If you crash that server before saving Jezebel . . . well . . . I'm not sure you or anyone else will ever see her again."

"And if they catch you sleeping, then the same applies to you."

"Never mind about me. It's Jezebel we must concentrate on."

"Why? Who is she?" Finn asked, hearing something different, something urgent, in Wayne's voice. He knew something he wasn't sharing.

Wayne grimaced. He looked sternly into the camera. "It's not for me to say."

"But you know?"

"I suspect. Knowing and suspecting are two different things."

"Then tell me."

"I can't. That wouldn't be fair to her or you. For one thing, I could be wrong. Listen, Finn, there are powers at work far greater than my own. It's not for me to guess. If you're to learn about Jezebel, it will have to come from another source."

"Amanda."

"Perhaps."

"They're sisters."

"That's a loosely thrown around term, now isn't it,

Finn? We're all sisters and brothers, depending how far back you go."

"They aren't sisters," Finn said, seeking an answer.

"It isn't for me to say. That's the best I can do."

"Find Jez," Finn said, repeating his instructions. "Find and crash the second server. Recover it if we can."

"It's challenge enough, I know," Wayne said. "But the bigger challenge will be how quickly you can accomplish any of this. You absolutely must have Jezebel safe and the server crashed before any of you fall asleep. If you sleep, you very well may be crossed over into that second server, the Overtakers' server, and that would leave you—the real Finn—"

"SBS," Finn said, cutting him off. "The Sleeping Beauty Syndrome."

"Yes, I'm afraid so."

"*You're* afraid?" said Finn sarcastically. "How do you think I feel?"

"There's one last thing I need to explain."

Wayne was constantly doing this: holding stuff back, and Finn found it frustrating and annoying. It was as if . . . as if he were testing him.

"You're surprised your friends haven't IMed you," Wayne said.

"Yes." But how do you know that?

"And you're probably wondering how I know that."

"Okay. You win."

"You'll find them in your private room inside VMK. Maybe I'll have time to explain about VMK at some point. For now, all you need to know is that I sent your friends the same link and password I just gave you. When we end this chat, all you have to do is click on the VMK logo on the landing page. It'll link you directly to VMK."

"No way!" Excitement filled Finn. He had loved the virtual community. The idea of returning . . .

"I promise you it's true. Remember the link: dgamer-dot-com, forward slash VMK. You'll use the same user ID and password I've just given you. And by the way, something you may need . . . There's a new Web terminal in Camp Minnie-Mickey. It's supposed to be used for making Disney vacations reservations, but if you click on Dream Vacations and type the password I gave you, it will grant you Web access and through it, a way into VMK."

"But Camp Minnie-Mickey is in the Animal Kingdom," Finn said.

"Once you're inside VMK, if you need me type my name. It won't show in the text box, but I'll see it and I'll come find you. Trust no one, not even the avatars in VMK. The Overtakers are everywhere. Take every precaution you can."

"But I'm going to Animal Kingdom?" Finn said, repeating himself. After all he'd been told, he wasn't sure he wanted to get anywhere near the park.

"You must find Maleficent and destroy the second server. So, yes. You and the others are going to Animal Kingdom."

Wayne turned to look over his shoulder again. "Oh, no . . ." he said, his voice panicked. The screen erupted into static, and Wayne was gone.

* * *

Finn found his way to to the DHIs' private room inside the Virtual Magic Kingdom. He was disappointed he didn't have time to enjoy being back in VMK. The game was nearly empty of players, and the effect was chilling. As he reached and entered the room, he found Maybeck sitting on a virtual couch; Willa and Charlene were over in a corner, their text boxes filled with dialogue about what had happened during the lightning storm.

Philby stood near to the room's only door, guarding the entrance. Text bubbles appeared above each of the avatars as the Kingdom Keepers began "talking."

philitup: he's here

mybest: about time

Maybeck's avatar stood up and crossed to the door, meeting up with Finn. Quickly the other avatars swarmed around Finn as well.

willatree: we got the message to wait, but we worried what it meant.

Finn: it was _ _ _ _ _ . He'd forgotten that the VMK server wouldn't allow him to type Wayne's name.

philitup: who?

Finn: the old guy with the white hair. five letters.

mybest: you mean _ _ _ _ _? But the system again refused the name. **where's he been?**

Finn: he appeared on my IM buddy list and we had a video chat. he's in trouble. we're all in trouble.

philitup: and?

Finn: serious problems. philby, stay by the door. we don't want anyone entering unannounced and reading us.

Philby's and Maybeck's avatars pushed the couch to block the room's entrance. Philby stood there, just behind the couch, while the others moved to the far side of the room. Charlene brushed her hair in the mirror. Maybeck's avatar shot free throws at a basketball hoop on the wall.

Finn described the meeting with Wayne as simply as possible.

Finn: the Animal Kingdom is installing a DHI server—animal hosts as guides. our old friend thinks the original server may have been cloned, possibly when Maleficent was hiding out in the server room. remember that? if that's right, the Overtakers may have their own DHI server, or they may have control of the new one at AK. that means if we go to sleep they may be able to cross us over—to control us and prevent our return. we'd be in perma-sleep the same way Maybeck was at Space Mountain. Sleeping Beauty Syndrome.

willatree: Jez's DHI

Finn: exactly. that was them. it confirms some kind of second server is up and working.

philitup: are you saying we can't go to sleep?

Finn: he's warning us not to.

philitup: exactly how long does he think we can stay awake?

Finn: depends on how much Coke we can drink.

angelface13: i'm tired right now. Charlene's avatar finally turned away from the mirror.

mybest: this is crazy.

Finn: we can do whatever we want. he's just warning us.

mybest: not to sleep.

Finn: yes.

mybest: and I'm saying that's crazy.

philitup: so what's the drill?

Finn: we find jez and get her to safety. then we find or destroy this cloned DHI server and put it out of commission.

mybest: all before we go to sleep.

Finn: that's the safest for all of us

It was a long time before any dialogue lines appeared above any of the avatars. Finally, Willa's avatar stepped away from the others.

willatree: if it was my sister, i'd be freaking out.

angelface13: same here.

mybest: do we know they've got her in AK?

Finn: remember the monkeys we saw tonight?
they've got to be from the Animal Kingdom! and it
fits with what the old guy said about the server—
that's AK as well.

philitup: AK's a big park

angelface13: i love Animal Kingdom

mybest: we can't get in there at night without being
busted. i don't need any trouble. my aunt is using
my DHI money for my college.

Finn: the guy who chased philby and me . . . turns
out he's with the old guy . . . he can get us in
around 5 AM, when the park is waking up. there's
work to do before then. we need to know everything
there is to know about the park

mybest: such as?

Finn: layout and cast members—that'll be willa.
electronics and security—philby, of course,
including the coldest buildings. maybeck will find
out everything about the animals—their feeding,
where they're kept, how dangerous they are.
charlene, we may need costumes, ways to blend in.

i'll IM with amanda. she mentioned her sister's diary. amanda will be part of this. Anyone have any trouble with that?

No one typed a thing.

Finn: okay. good luck getting out of your houses. i'm going on bike. we should all bring our DSs so we can communicate. everyone has one, right?

He waited. No one came on to say they didn't own a DS.

Finn: meet up with a food truck at 4:45 AM outside the entrance to the Animal Kingdom Lodge. the dapper dan guy will be driving. if anyone can't make it early, we'll all meet after the main gates open on the path leading in to the Rainforest Café. agreed?

mybest: i'm in

philitup: me too.

willatree: likewise

angelface13: what if we can't find jez?

Finn had half expected a question like that from Charlene. But he wasn't prepared for the sinking feeling in his gut as he read it. His fingers hesitated briefly above the keyboard. And then he typed.

Finn: that's not an option.

12

FINN DIDN'T GET ANY great joy from sneaking out of his house at 1 AM. His parents were pretty good about giving him his privacy and space. The two things they asked in return were honesty and trust. He broke their trust by opening his second-story window and shinnying down the fire rope installed for emergencies. The only justification for his actions was that this qualified as an emergency—though he'd never be able to explain it to them. If caught, he'd be grounded for all eternity.

He quietly walked the Hawk Tracer BMX out to the sidewalk. Then he climbed onto the bike and took off down the sidewalk. It was the most beautiful bike he'd ever owned—silver-and-black frame, monkey bars, alloy levers—and it ripped along, teasing him into trying a few tricks, such as jumping curbs and popping wheelies, which he resisted because of the dark.

He kept to the residential streets as much as possible, avoiding the busier avenues, afraid that a policeman would stop and question a kid on a bike. It was a long ride, and he settled into a rhythm of slowing at stop signs, looking in all directions for headlights, and then crossing—but never fully stopping. The residential streets were totally quiet and empty of cars. Soon he had two miles behind him. Then three. He crossed two major avenues, finding his way into Orlando's older neighborhoods, one connecting to another. Finally, the residential gave way to the commercial. He flew past shuttered buildings, businesses of every kind: psychic readings, dry cleaning, a yarn store, a bakery, dozens of restaurants and coffee shops, dog grooming, curtains and drapes, lamps, a half dozen banks, and a copy shop. He spotted the red tile roof and stucco walls of a building he'd been to once before. Amanda's house.

It had a tall, stained-glass window in the front, just below a squared-off steeple that showed a white angel against a blue background. Maybe it had once been a church.

He pulled the bike around back to an apron of cracked blacktop that had once been a parking lot. He locked the BMX to a metal railing and then circled the building, wondering, *What now?* He'd never been inside Amanda's house before, though he assumed, from what she'd said, that she and Jez had separate bedrooms. Each ground-level window had a grid of heavy wrought-iron bars on the outside to protect against burglars; it gave Finn a ladder to climb. He went from the railing to the bars on a window, grabbed hold of an iron pipe running from the gutters, threw a knee up over the edge, and pulled himself onto the Spanish-tile roof. He walked gingerly, for the first tile he stepped on cracked.

A shade was pulled down blocking the first window he reached. Finn edged around the corner to another window with its shade up. There was a small solar panel propped up on the window ledge. It was dark behind the glass. Finn cupped his face to the glass and was able to make out an empty bed. There were no posters on the wall—no artwork at all. The place looked dumpy and unlived-in. He took this to be Jez's room. There were no bars across the second-story windows, so he tried to open one, but it didn't budge. He moved along slowly; the roof was steeply pitched. The Spanish tile felt smooth and slippery beneath his sneakers.

The last window on this side had its shade up, but gauzy curtains were pulled across it. It also had the same kind of solar panel outside—this one taped to the jamb. He tried cupping his eyes with his hands to the glass but could barely see anything in the dark room. What he did see was a pair of sneakers on the floor: Amanda's black high-tops. Convinced he had the right room, he tapped lightly on the pane. Waited. Tapped again.

All at once, black objects fled from the overhead eves. Bats! Finn instinctively jumped back, slipped, and fell face-first to the curved tile roof. He reached out and clawed his fingertips into the windowsill. Just then, the curtains sprang back, and there was Amanda looking out the rain-stained window at him, her face a sleepy, twisted knot of curiosity. She wore a spaghetti-strap top and plaid pajama bottoms.

Finn's fingers slipped an inch, leaving scratch marks on the sill. Another half inch, and he was gone.

Amanda threw open the window and grabbed both his wrists. They locked grips. She put her foot to the wall and heaved and pulled. Finn grabbed the inside of the sill, got his knees under him, and, with her help, climbed inside.

"Sorry," he whispered.

"The front door is easier," Amanda said in a normal voice. "Or you could have called."

"Shhh!" he said, ducking low, as if that would help.

"Why?" she said, again in her normal voice. "I'm the only one here."

"What?"

"I . . . ah . . ." Amanda switched on the light. It was a dim compact fluorescent bulb hanging from a wire that led to a car battery. A second wire led from the battery to the window and the solar panel beyond. As Finn took all this in, Amanda spoke, but unlike the Amanda he knew, she wasn't telling the truth. "Our mother . . . my mother

". . . she . . . she . . . her sister down in Boca needed her. She had to leave suddenly. Left me by myself."

"All alone?"

"I'm a big girl."

"You're fourteen. My parents *never* leave me alone overnight." He paused as their situation sank in. "You're alone? We're alone?" He spoke in his normal voice.

He took in the light, the battery, and the solar panel outside the window. He saw no light in the hallway. He'd seen no other lights from the street.

"We are. Stay there." She went to a closet and put on a robe. She sat down on the edge of her bed and pointed to a rickety chair at the desk.

Finn moved the chair closer.

"It's two in the morning," she said. "Just for the record."

The air from the open window was cool. The curtains danced at the sides. Amanda stood and closed the window. "Whoa!" she said. "Check it out!"

It took Finn a moment to spot the bat hanging upside down from the eaves above the window. It was *big*, though Finn didn't want to appear scared by a bat. It had a blue iridescence to its black wings, tucked at its sides. It looked dangerous.

"Creepy," he said.

"There are a lot of bats here," she said. "I think they

live in the attic. Though that's the biggest one I've seen, by far."

She pulled the curtains, shuddered, and sat back down on the bed. "They make the weirdest sounds at night. Sometimes I have trouble sleeping."

"Flying rodents. Never been a big fan. I'm not one of those guys with rats for pets. No thanks."

"I've never had a pet."

"Seriously?"

"We moved around a lot." She blushed and looked away; he wondered what that was about.

"You remember Wayne?" he asked.

Her eyes went wide. "I thought he'd disappeared."

"Yeah, So did I." Finn went on to explain his encounter with Wayne, and then the meeting that had followed. Amanda interrupted several times, clarifying the connection between Jez's disappearance, her DHI being seen at the Magic Kingdom, and the possibility that the DHI server had been cloned.

She sat for several long minutes with her head in her hands, her hair cascading over her forearms and forming a veil she hid behind.

"I'm going to trust you," she said.

Finn felt a shiver. He looked up at the bat, a long, dark silhouette seen through the translucent curtains. "Okay," he said.

"I can trust you, right?"

"Right."

"Because I'm not supposed to tell anyone."

He didn't say anything, but she had every cell in his body focused on her.

"Most people, they would never believe it. And that's a *good thing*. It's better if people don't believe it. It's safer for everyone. There's some saying about hiding behind ignorance, isn't there? There should be, if there isn't. Am I rambling?"

"Sort of."

"Nervous."

"It's just me."

She came up from under the veil of hair and met Finn's eyes. Hers were close to tears, shining like marbles. "You, of all people, might understand. You and the others. I can't think of anyone else. Maybe you won't believe—and that's okay," she said, reaching out and touching his knee. "I won't be mad or anything."

"I can't believe it if I never hear what it is," he said, a little impatiently.

She nodded, her eyes apologetic. "Jez and I are different," she said.

"I know that," he said quickly. "You're very different."

"No . . . I don't mean from each other. I think it might be better if you just listen. No offense or anything, but this is kind of hard to explain."

He nodded, thinking he shouldn't speak.

She saw this and giggled. Covered her mouth. Looked as if she might cry. When she spoke, it was very softly.

"I guess the only way to explain this is just to say it."

Works for me, he thought, but didn't say so.

"We're Fairlies."

"You mean: fairies?"

"No. Fairlies. As in, fairly human. It was supposedly a joke a long, long time ago, but it stuck. Fairlies. Go figure. We're not witches or fairies, or anything like that. We're just kids with . . . unusual abilities."

"Such as?"

"I'm not allowed to say. Sorry. Rules, you know?"

"You and Jez are sisters?"

"Sort of, I guess. Not exactly. We're both orphans. All Fairlies are orphans. My parents drowned. Jez's went on this trip to South America and never came back. They think pirates—*real pirates*—got them. She and I were raised in the same foster home. That's why I call her my sister. Fairlies display certain qualities at a very young age: spoon-benders, mind readers, clairvoyants. There was a boy who could set fire to things by just *looking* at them. Very strange. But real. Jez dreamed the trouble here in the Parks. This was way before you guys were hired to be the models for the DHIs. She and I . . . we kind of ran away. Not recommended, I might add."

Finn understood the solar panels then: there were no parents. Jez and Amanda lived by themselves.

"The day we got here, Maleficent put a spell on Jez or bewitched her or something. Jez didn't even recognize me. Then you and the DHIs came along. Somehow, you released her right before Maleficent was captured. I wanted to go back after that, to the foster home, but Jez had more dreams. She keeps them in a diary, a journal," she explained.

"So, she can dream the future?" Finn asked skeptically.

"Believe whatever you want to," Amanda said, "or not. *I believe* the Overtakers have taken Jez prisoner to prevent her from interfering with whatever they have planned."

Finn's skin crawled. He felt slightly sick to his stomach.

She stared at Finn long and hard, her eyes fiery pinpricks. "I can't expect you to believe any of this. Asking that is probably too much. I hope you do someday. I hope this makes us better friends, not worse. I'm trusting you in ways I've never trusted anyone." She paused. Her breathing was labored, her skin flushed. Finn felt as if he might explode with anticipation.

"And your powers?" he asked.

"Sorry," she said squinting. "Can't say. Not now. Not yet, anyway."

"You and Jez are squatting. Here, in this house, this church. Whatever it once was. The solar power." He pointed.

Amanda eyed Finn cautiously. "You're not going to tell."

"I've got bigger secrets than this, believe me."

"It was closed up. Abandoned. We always enter by the back. We're very careful. Only once have I used the front door, and that's when you and your mother dropped me off here. I wasn't even sure it could open."

"And the neighbors?"

"What neighbors? It's stores and stuff. No one's ever said anything. It's only been a couple of months. The water's on. It's cold; no hot water, but it works. We shower at school. The toilets work."

"This is way cool."

"It's not great, but it's what was available. We had to think fast."

"Don't Fairlies have money?" he asked.

"If you're going to tease me, we're done here."

"Can't take a joke?"

"Not about that. And yes, I have an after-school job. But right now, I think we both could use some sleep." She yawned.

"No! We can't sleep," he said. "Wayne says if any of us—the DHIs—go to sleep, we might get trapped the way Maybeck did last time. He said the only way to protect ourselves is to find Jez, get her to safety, and then find and crash the second server." He let this sink in. "We need your help. That is, only if you want to."

"Of course I want to."

He liked the idea of her being involved. She was the most unusual girl he'd ever met. He wondered what powers she might have and why she wouldn't tell him about them. "You were going to join us on IM," he reminded her.

"Yeah, well . . . my computer access is through our local library. A little late for that."

"So what about her journal? Can I see it? Maybe she left clues or something. We don't know what we're looking for, and it's a huge park. We're all real tired, and we haven't started. We don't know for sure she's in the Animal Kingdom. Wayne thinks so, but no one knows for sure. I don't know if you can help, but—"

"Absolutely. I absolutely want to help if I can."

She took off, out the bedroom and down the dark hall. A light popped on in the next room, casting a trapezoid of light against the far wall, where a mural of a woman's stern face had been painted. She seemed to be looking at Finn. He ducked back into Amanda's room.

She returned, clutching a leather journal. Reluctantly, she passed it to Finn. "This is private stuff, remember?"

Finn nodded and flipped through the pages. The diary was filled with writing, drawings, sketches. Clippings and photographs had been pasted, paperclipped, and stapled to the pages. Fortunes from fortune cookies. Ticket stubs.

In the upper-right-hand corner of a page crowded with sketches was a drawing of a castle being struck by lightning. Finn pointed to it. "Okay," he said. "Now I believe."

13

FINN CLIMBED BACK UP the fire rope to his bedroom window, while below him, barely seen, Amanda waited for him, straddling his mother's mountain bike, which he'd loaned her.

His mission was to get hold of his father's BlackBerry; to make sure his parents didn't worry about him or question where he'd gone; and to borrow his little sister's DS for Amanda, who didn't own one.

He reached his parents' bedroom on tiptoe and quietly opened the door. His mother was snoring; his father lay on his side facing the window. The clock on his mother's end table read 4:08 AM.

He found his father's dresser in the dark and patted around, searching for his BlackBerry. On Saturdays, his father only took his phone if he went on an extended errand. Finn could only hope that his father had no such errands planned. If he did, and he looked for his phone, he wasn't going to find it.

He returned to his mother's side of the bed and quietly turned the clock so that it faced away from the bed, where it couldn't be read by his mother. Then he gently shook her awake. She was a heavy sleeper, and he was counting on her not coming fully awake.

"Mom . . ."

Her eyes squinted open, saw him, and then shut again.

"Finn," she complained.

"It's just after six," he lied, wishing he didn't have to. "I'm going on my bike over to the skate park. Might go to Blizzard Beach later. I'll call."

"Don't forget sunscreen." She opened her eyes a little more and looked for the clock, but she made no effort to turn it around. This he'd been counting on.

"I'll call," he repeated.

There was precedent here: early Saturday morning rides at the skate park were part of his routine. Bikes weren't allowed in the half pipe after 9 AM on weekends. He often got up early and returned for a late breakfast. By adding the bit about Blizzard Beach—a favorite among his friends—he'd bought himself the rest of the day.

"Take your father's phone," she said, rolling over.

"Ah . . . okay," he said, his hand tapping his pocket.

He put away the fire-escape rope and left the house by the back door, joining Amanda and climbing onto his bike.

"How'd it go?" she asked.

"Worked out great. I'm good to go for the rest of the day."

"Your parents let you leave the house at four in the morning?"

"Not exactly. But we're cool."

Had he looked overhead he might have felt otherwise: hanging upside down from the gutter of his house, the large bat with the blue tint on its wings dropped free and flew away. Flapping frantically, it circled just above the two bikes as they sped off down the empty street, red safety lights flashing in the dark.

14

THE FOOD-SERVICE STEP VAN had double tires in the back and mud flaps that carried silhouettes of silver mouse ears on their black rubber.

The man behind the wheel had florid cheeks, blue eyes, and bushy eyebrows. He spoke in a deep voice to Finn, who pulled the passenger door open.

"Everyone in back. Find places to hide in case they check back there." He popped open his door. "It'll be pitch black in there once I pull that door down, so hurry!"

Finn rushed the others into the back. They climbed up into a refrigerated area of cardboard boxes filled with fresh fruits and vegetables stacked onto wooden pallets and strapped to the walls. Each stack offered a place to hide behind. The kids doubled up. Charlene and Willa hid behind a tower of raspberry and strawberry flats. Maybeck and Philby ducked behind the lettuce, leaving Finn and Amanda to press into a small space behind six stacked boxes of carrots.

"Okay," the driver said. "That's good. Stay like that. All set?"

The door came down hard, with a bang of finality. It was dark as a cave inside. The refrigerator unit up near the cab wheezed loudly as it blew an icy wind, freezing them.

"Dang . . ." Maybeck said. "This is how I always imagined prison."

"What if one of us is afraid of the dark?" Charlene asked timidly.

"Then she should hold on to Willa, Charlene," said Maybeck.

"I didn't say it was me!" Charlene said.

"Right," said Maybeck.

The truck grumbled and groaned as it lurched around a series of corners toward the back side of the Animal Kingdom. Pretty soon its brakes squealed to a stop. Finn and the others had been in the same situation before—at the reinforced, militarylike security gates at the back of the Magic Kingdom. He could picture the guards outside. Supplies and merchandise and employees came through these entrances. The driver's credentials were checked, manifests and work schedules cross-referenced. The kids heard some talking through the shell, though the words were indiscernible. Then a single *thump*. The Dapper Dan had elbowed the back wall of the cab, trying to warn his passengers.

"I dropped my purse," Charlene announced in a

harsh whisper. "I can't find it! I can't find my purse."

Finn knew that if Security saw a purse, they would probably climb up into the back of the truck to retrieve it. And if so, then they'd spot the kids.

"I can't see!" she hissed again.

Sounds of the door hardware rattled at the back of the truck. The back door was definitely about to be lifted.

"My purse . . ." Charlene moaned.

Finn stepped out from behind the stack of carrots. Amanda reached out to stop him, but she was too late.

He felt around the floor. *Nothing.* Then he remembered his father's BlackBerry. He pulled it out of his pocket and hit a button on the keypad, and the screen came to life like a flashlight.

Charlene's arm shot out from behind a stack of boxes, and she grabbed hold of her purse. It vanished.

The door rolled open a crack. Finn shoved the BlackBerry into his pocket, snuffing its light. His knees didn't flex. He didn't move. He just stood there. Light flooded into the back of the truck. He turned, but it was too late. The door continued up.

In an instant everything changed: he was suddenly pasted to the ceiling—floating—hidden by the rolling door, which was carried on tracks like a garage door.

"Clear," one of the Security guys announced.

Finn sank toward the truck bed. From the light of the BlackBerry he saw Amanda facing him, her arm extended. As her arm fell, so did Finn.

The back door clattered shut and the *clunk* of hardware confirmed they were locked inside again.

"You did that!" he said, accusing Amanda.

"No idea what you're talking about," she whispered.

"You saved us," he said.

"That was way cool, Finn," said Maybeck. "You mind telling me how you did that?"

Amanda whispered warmly into Finn's ear. "No . . . not yet."

Finn said into the dark: "Ah . . . I could show you, but I'd have to kill you."

Maybeck chuckled.

"I want some, too," added Philby.

"Later, dudes," said Finn.

Again, he felt Amanda's breath warm against his neck as she whispered softly, "Thank you."

He wanted to say something, but his voice had gone dry, and he couldn't get a word out.

15

A MOMENT AFTER the truck finally pulled to a stop, the Dapper Dan climbed up inside and then lowered the garagelike door behind himself, leaving it open just enough to admit some light from the nearby light poles.

"This is as far as I go with the truck. Finn gave each of you an assignment, as I understand it."

"I've got a pretty good handle on the tech side of the Park," Philby said. "There are cameras all over the place, some for Security, some for the Park visitors. Basically, we won't be alone wherever we go. But there's a very cool element to this I think we should consider." He glanced around at the group. Charlene was trying to wipe a smudge off her clothes, but everyone else was paying strict attention to him. "Out at Conservation Station— which everyone in the Park calls 'CS,' by the way—is a bank of camera monitors that are interactive. Visitors can actually move and zoom the cameras, searching for animals and that kind of thing. But I think they give us a real good opportunity to monitor what's going on."

"That could be my job," Amanda said, volunteering. "If no one else wants it," she added carefully.

Everyone nodded.

"Other than that," Philby said, swinging his backpack around and reaching inside, "I got nothin'."

"Is anyone going to explain to me why I brought along my DS?" Charlene asked.

"The Parks all have free Wi-Fi," Philby said, as if this answered her.

"Yeah? So?" she said.

"So I've set-up a DGamer chat room so we can IM each other," he explained. "It's totally secure. No one can eavesdrop."

"A D what?" she asked.

"DGamer," he said. "Let me show you." Philby took her DS from her and changed her settings to allow Wi-Fi access. Then he showed her how to enter DGamer mode. Turning on his own DS, he typed a message to her. An alert appeared on her screen and she answered it. Then he switched devices with her and sent one from her device to his.

"How totally awsome," she said, marveling. Taking back her own DS, she sent Philby a text message:

angelface13: i never knew it could do that.

philitup: it's a new feature, added last spring.

Finn set up his sister's DS for Amanda. Philby had invited them all to join the private chat, and soon they were all texting back and forth.

The Dapper Dan cleared his throat to stop them, and they put their Nintendos away. He asked if they knew their way around the Park. "I'm acquainted with the layout," Willa said, piping up. She handed out maps for each of them. "Basically there are five areas—Asia, Africa, Camp Minnie-Mickey, and DinoLand USA. These four surround a lake that holds the fifth, Discovery Island, in the middle—the Tree of Life, some food stalls, and shopping. I don't know our plan, if we have one, but there are five of us, not counting Amanda, and five areas. Seems pretty obvious."

"And I'll be watching you from the Conservation Station," said Amanda, reminding everyone.

"In terms of costumes," Charlene said, "the best thing we could do is just dress as rangers or animal care. Either light green or dark green short-sleeve shirts and shorts. It would be best if we could get the real thing, but I don't see how that'll happen."

"That will happen because I'm going to help you," the driver said. "Cast Members are now responsible for their own uniforms. But there's a costuming shed that used to be for outfitting everyone. Now it's more of a storage facility and costume-repair facility, but I can get you in there."

Finn said, "Here's what I suggest: Willa will be a conservation ranger; Maybeck an animal-care worker; Amanda, Philby, and I stay dressed as we are. Charlene . . . you get the tricky one."

"Which is?" she asked, finally looking up from the smudge.

"DeVine."

"Thank you," she said.

"The character," Willa corrected. "He wasn't giving you a compliment!"

"Who knew?" Charlene asked.

"I thought your cheerleading experience might make you a better gymnast than the rest of us. DeVine walks on huge stilts and dresses in total camouflage so that it's almost impossible to see her. Can you use stilts?"

"I've used stilts before, though not real high ones."

"These are real high," said Willa.

"There are four complete DeVine outfits," the driver explained. "But I've got to warn you: DeVine enters the Park at ten, twelve, two, and four. If two DeVines are seen in the Park at the same time, that will alert Security. So if you do this, you'll need to hide deep within the jungle when the real DeVine is in the Park."

They were all staring at Charlene.

"Will you do it?" Finn asked.

"What's the costume like?" she asked the driver.

But it was Willa who answered. "It's amazing. With the makeup, she blends into the jungle so well you can't even see her when you're only a few feet away."

"There's makeup involved?" Charlene asked. "This is so totally my thing, I can't believe it. Of course I'll do it."

"Wayne wanted me to tell you," the driver said, "that Maleficent can transform herself from human to animal. It doesn't last long, and it exhausts her, but any animal you see in the Park could be her. He said it's incredibly important to keep that in mind: *any animal.*"

"And remember about the security cameras," Philby reminded. "The whole Park is watched. Only the washrooms are absolutely safe. No cameras."

He yawned a massive yawn. It was contagious: each of them yawned in succession.

"The hardest part of all of this," Maybeck said, "at least for all of you, is looking older than you really are. Thankfully that's not such an issue for me."

Philby cringed. "Give me a break," he muttered.

"It's true," the driver said. "We can use some makeup to try to help, but those of you in costume must remember that Cast Members are eighteen and up. So act it where possible, and avoid encounters with Park visitors as much as you can. Whatever you do, don't talk to other Cast Members. It's a family here—even as big as it is. Cast Members know the other Cast Members. You will be found out."

"That's encouraging," Maybeck said sarcastically.

"That's reality," the driver said.

"Yeah?" Maybeck snapped a little testily. "Well, that would be the first time we've dealt with reality in a long, long time. So pardon me if I don't recognize it."

"Any questions?" the driver asked.

He hoisted the truck's rear door. And while the sun had not yet risen, they found themselves in a vast, empty parking lot, alongside several steel-sided, mostly windowless buildings that looked like warehouses. The sky was fully aglow with the push of dawn as the kids climbed out of the truck and hurried to follow the Dapper Dan.

16

THE DRIVER SHOWED THEM into the Cast Services building. Even if the lights had been on, it still would have been gloomy and creepy inside, with its rows of hundreds of abandoned lockers. But under the hazy glow of the dim, off-hours lighting, the place looked positively haunted. Not one locker had a person's name on it, nor did any of them look used—no scratches, decals, graffiti, or dents. Nothing like the lockers at school.

"This was originally going to be where Cast Members changed for work," the Dapper Dan said, "but it became impractical because of the distance to the Park. But if anything goes wrong—a missing button, a broken zipper—it comes here. The building's only open a few hours a day."

The six kids stood just inside the building. The driver walked past and unlocked an interior door to the left of a narrow counter, behind which was a retractable metal barrier, padlocked shut.

"Make sure this is locked behind you. When you're ready, you cross the roads out here. Stay to the far left of the parking lots. There's a pedestrian entrance on West Savannah Circle. Philby, if you find you need anything mechanical, any tool of any sort, the adjacent structure is the maintenance facility. The animation training lab is in that building as well. Parts for anything you can dream of to do with the Animal Kingdom can be found over there. You can use these IDs to access it and any other facility," he said, handing each of the kids a plastic ID card. Finn's card had his picture on it and a fake name, Finnian Thomas, with a fake address. "Each of you is in the system as an employee of the company—and you're all in there as being eighteen. So if anyone should ask . . . the department you work for is on there as well. Memorize it. These will get you into and out of the Park via the pedestrian entrances, allow you to charge food, buy merchandise. But don't abuse them. In most cases, you don't need them to go backstage. But in certain buildings, certain facilities, you may, so keep them handy. They get you past the electronic security. Whatever you do, don't lose them. I'll need them back, and I'll need to destroy them."

There was a noise then, like the wind: a swishing, whooshing sound, as if someone had left a window open. But no one felt a breeze, and not a hair moved on anyone's head. However, quite a few hairs raised on the back of Finn's neck.

"What was that?" he asked.

The driver turned to the door they had come through. "I've got to go," he said. "You're on your own from here on out." He was gone in an instant. His hurrying off so quickly added to the sense of impending danger.

He closed the door a little loudly on his way out. The boom echoed around the building.

"Check it out," Maybeck called to the others. He was holding open the door that the driver had unlocked. The others stepped forward and peered inside. The ceiling was thirty feet overhead, steel beams with cross supports—all unfinished and basic. Displayed before them were fifty or sixty rows of clothes hanging from steel pipes. The rows stretched from where they stood to the far side of the building, fifty yards or more.

"Oh . . . my . . . gosh," gushed Charlene.

There had to be thousands, perhaps hundreds of thousands, of garments—every kind of Animal Kingdom costume and Cast Member outfit, in every size. And accessories: hats, boots, belts, buckles, backpacks, clipboards, pointers, pens, notepads—in containers on shelves just above the clothing that matched their theme.

"Wow . . ." Willa said.

"You all know how you're dressing," Finn said. He spotted the signs across the room. "Women's locker rooms to the right, men's to the left. The sooner we're out of here the better. Philby, Amanda, and I will stand guard."

"Against what?" Willa asked.

"Use your imagination," Maybeck said.

"If I whistle like this," Finn said, emitting a whistle that sounded a little bit like a sick bird, a little bit like a leaking balloon, "then hide until you hear it again."

"If you whistle like that," Maybeck said condescendingly, "you're going to get me laughing so hard I'll never be able to hide."

"Your problem, not mine," Finn said.

That silenced Maybeck for the moment, just long enough for Philby to say he'd look for a door at the back where he could stand guard. Amanda would stay basically where they were. Finn would patrol the general locker area where they'd entered.

No one had a good feeling about this. No one but Charlene, who was acting like she'd just unlocked her grandmother's attic.

* * *

Suspended above the impossibly long rows of clothing and costumes were large hand-painted signs done in the Animal Kingdom's African-style lettering. They divided the space into sections, a system used to organize a hundred thousand Cast Member costume pieces into something manageable.

While Maybeck cruised ANIMAL CARE and Willa PARK RANGERS, Charlene browsed the area marked PERFORMERS, searching for DeVine costumes.

The first suggestion that they might not be alone came in the form of noise: the familiar sound of hangers tinkling like dull bells. Charlene noticed it first, or was at least the first to voice her concern. She hurried to find Willa and whispered hotly, "Did you hear that? The hangers? Coming from over there?" She pointed.

"What?" Willa was busy trying to find a shirt that would fit her.

"Hangers. Like someone else is in here," Charlene explained in a conspiratorial hush. "Don't forget Small World."

As DHIs, the kids had once ridden through It's a Small World late at night only to have all the dolls come alive and attack them. It was a memory—more like a nightmare—none of them cherished. Other parts of various attractions in the Magic Kingdom had come alive as well, often threatening them, or outright causing them harm. It had instilled a reluctance in them all, a distrust of what might happen next, that had stayed with them long since, and whether they spoke of it or not, haunted them.

"You're just buggy because it's dark in here."

"I'm not buggy! I heard hangers banging around over there. What's with that? You think I should tell Finn?"

"Boys? We don't need boys."

Some hangers rang out quite near them. Charlene jumped back. Willa stood her ground but peered inquisitively into the room's twilight. "It's got to be Finn or Philby playing a joke," she told Charlene.

"Ha-ha."

Willa stood taller and spoke with authority. "Okay, you guys! You got us. Ally-ally-in-free."

The *ting-ting* of hangers faded, like a clock running down. The girls waited for someone to jump out and surprise them, but it didn't happen.

"Are you going to check it out?" Charlene asked, partly hiding behind Willa.

Together the girls explored the rack in front of them, pushing clothes aside. They did so cautiously, a few garments at a time. Willa grabbed a bunch of shirts and slid them to her right.

A large bat dropped from the rack, unfolded its wings, and flapped violently to gain altitude. Willa ducked. Charlene screamed and went over backward, falling to the floor.

The bat spiraled into the upper reaches of the

warehouse and, because of Charlene's scream, got the attention of everyone on the floor.

It was a big bat, an ugly bat, with a wingspan of at least two feet, but it moved through the air as fast as a cat after a toy, fluttering and flying, weaving and diving, one moment up high near the ceiling, the next dive-bombing down one of the endless aisles.

The commotion drew Finn and Amanda, running. Philby hurried from the back. But it was Maybeck who proved to be the shrewd thinker. He grabbed a butter-fly net from the props section and came after the bat like a lacrosse player, swinging the billowing net with remarkable agility.

"Find the lights!" he shouted, following the bat down a row of grass skirts. "Bats don't like light!"

Where the others might have been satisfied with scaring the bat out of the building, Amanda and Finn understood the tension in Maybeck's voice. Finn had seen a huge bat at Amanda's. The same bat? Not a great believer in coincidence, he, too, wanted to catch it. Clearly Maybeck also believed it was no ordinary bat.

"Philby," Finn shouted, "the lights!" He had no idea how to turn on the lights in a building this size, but if there was a switch, Philby would find it before anyone else.

True to form, the overhead lights came on only

seconds later, and the warehouse lit up like the school gymnasium. As the lights flashed on, the bat dove as if it had been shot, and there was Maybeck, lunging through the air. He swung the net. The bat swooped. The two met in a tangle of nylon mesh, high-pitched squeals. Maybeck skidded down the smooth concrete floor like a base runner diving for home plate. He twisted the net, throwing it over itself and trapping the prize inside.

The kids let out an unplanned cheer.

They had taken a prisoner.

17

MAYBECK APPROACHED the employee pedestrian entrance to the Animal Kingdom holding a pillowcase that wouldn't stay still. The Cast Member entrance—employees only—was a revolving door of steel tines that moved only clockwise and required the employee card to open. The unattended entrance—he was grateful for that—required him to swipe the ID card the driver had provided. A red light turned green, and Maybeck pushed through the turnstile. Use of the pillowcase prevented the contents from being seen: the bat. Still, it was too close for comfort, and he was only too happy to dangle it away from his side as he cleared the entrance.

The pillowcase danced again.

"Settle down!" he said harshly, aware that he was speaking to a white pillowcase. Or more precisely, its contents: a Rousette fruit bat.

To his surprise, it quieted.

Willa, an animal lover, had identified the bat the moment Maybeck had caught it. This led to a group discussion of what to do with the thing. Charlene wanted it released and out of the building as quickly as possible. Philby suggested doing something to it that wouldn't have been approved by the SPCA, and while Willa thought it was "cute" and that it might make an interesting pet, Maybeck and Finn came up with a solution that seemed to please everyone—except Philby, of course, since it meant keeping it alive.

"We can't let it go," Finn had said. "I know it's completely ridiculous to think it might be Maleficent . . ." Willa groaned at the mention of this. "But what if it is? Or what if we've captured Maleficent's spy? Amanda and I saw a bat at her house. What if that was this same one?"

"If it is Maleficent, don't you think she'd turn back into herself and do something bad to us?" Willa suggested sarcastically. "I'd say this would be a good time for that."

"Good point," Charlene said.

"Wayne told me the heat slows the powers she uses to transform herself. It's like her kryptonite. We don't know what she's capable of," Finn said. "I just don't see how it's worth taking any risks."

"It's not," said Maybeck. "We've got to lock it up . . . do something with it, so it can't follow us."

"You all know what I think we should do," said Philby. Everyone ignored him.

"It'll be light out soon. Bats don't fly around in the daylight. The main thing is: we don't want it to find us or Maleficent."

"Why can't we just hide it among the other bats?" Maybeck said. "Have you even seen the bat enclosure? This thing won't be going anywhere. And it's not like Maleficent can walk in there and take it out."

Finn said, "That's brilliant!"

"Earth to Maybeck. It's just a bat. It is *not* Maleficent, or she'd be in our face right now," said Willa emphatically.

"So you'd just let it go?" Finn asked.

"Not me," Maybeck said, speaking directly to Finn. "At the least it deserves a bat jail. I can bluff my way into the bat enclosure."

Maybeck rarely lacked self-confidence.

"And if you're stopped?" asked Charlene, always the cautious one.

"I'll tell whoever stops me I'm returning a bat that was sick. You think anyone's going to want to get up close and personal with this *thing*?" He jiggled the pillowcase. The bat turned and flapped its enormous wings and tried to nip at Maybeck through the fabric.

"Okay. That's settled," said Charlene. "Let's just get it out of here."

And now Maybeck, inside the Park, was telling

the contents of his pillowcase to settle down, and much to his astonishment—it obeyed. He told himself that his tone of voice was responsible, that the bat had responded to his anger. But what if it had actually understood him?

At a few minutes past 6 AM there were more Cast Members in the Park than he would have expected. He realized that employees must arrive between six and seven because they were suddenly everywhere: sweeping, opening up attractions, zipping around in golf carts. It was a frenzy of activity. He followed a road to his left, a road he'd seen a number of Cast Members take, not entirely certain where he was. He'd entered to the left of the main entrance—that much he knew. He sneaked Philby's map out of his back pocket. Philby had done his homework, supplying both a Disney illustrated map with a key and a Google Earth satellite view of the area. On the satellite map he'd drawn and labeled some red circles, including DeVine's entrance gate, the two monkey temples, the Conservation Station, the Park's main entrance, and the group rendezvous spot.

Once on Discovery Island, Maybeck headed for Asia and the Maharajah Jungle Trek.

Some birds called out from the top of a tree. He moved a little faster.

He crossed Discovery Island, to the right of the

Tree of Life, aiming for a bridge to Asia. He texted into the DS.

mybest: i'm inside, on the island.

Finn: okay.

With each of the kids checked in to the chat room, they could all follow the conversation.

Maybeck then wrote to warn them about how many Cast Members were already in the Park.

mybest: until park opens u will stick out unless dressed as a cast member.

Had Maybeck looked back and slightly to his left, he would have seen that what had started as six or seven birds was now many times that number. They flew to the next tree and settled there. Then more joined them, and they flew to the next tree.

Finn: will wait 4 park opening. discovered something useful. meet us @ home base?

mybest: need to play bat boy first. will meet u after park opens.

philitup: agreed. will meet @ home base after park opens.

willatree: how's the bat?

mybest: quiet for now.

He was glad the bat had stopped moving so much. He didn't dare inform the others that he thought the thing understood what he said.

He crossed the bridge—the entrance to the Maharajah Jungle Trek just ahead. A cacophony surrounded him; he could barely hear himself think. He looked up to see two trees full of birds. For a moment, it seemed as if they were following him.

Na . . . he thought. *Couldn't be* . . .

Finn had heightened Maybeck's curiosity. What had they discovered in the short time it had taken him to enter the Park?

More obnoxious bird noises overhead.

He looked up.

Four trees. Hundreds of birds.

What the . . . ?

18

PHILBY SWIPED THE ID through the card reader at the door to the AK Maintenance facility. A small red light turned green, and Philby pulled on the door. It opened, and no alarms sounded.

Finn held out his hand to Amanda, who looked down at her sister's diary and then reluctantly gave the book to him.

"I'm not sure she'd want me doing this," Amanda said, still keeping one hand on the diary, unwilling to fully let it go.

"I promise, only the pages we talked about," Finn said.

"We don't know that they have anything to do with this," Amanda protested.

"You're the one who said she could dream the future."

"Sometimes, sure. But this is personal stuff."

"You said she wrote in it each morning after waking up."

"It's true. She did," Amanda confirmed.

"Then maybe, without knowing, she left us

clues how to find her. She drew lightning striking a castle. There are drawings of monkeys in there." He tugged gently on the journal, but Amanda would not let it go.

"Please," Finn said to her.

For a moment the journal connected them. Then Amanda let go.

"You're standing guard for us," Finn reminded her.

He held up his DS. "Send us a text if you see anyone coming."

"Okay," she said, her eyes filled with concern.

"All we're going to do is make copies," Finn reminded her. "There's got to be a copy machine or a scanner inside."

"And what about bats?" she asked.

"We'll be careful. I promise," Finn said.

He followed Philby inside to a reception area, where a well-organized desk held a telephone and computer. Some Disney cartoons were taped to the computer monitor, and there were framed pictures of three kids. The few lights that had been left on cast murky shadows and offered a dimly lit corridor running in both directions off this front room. There were two signs, each with an arrow: one read MAINTENANCE and pointed left; the other read ANIMATION TRAINING LAB and pointed right.

"Cool," Philby said, turning right. "I've got to see this."

The animation training lab was a garagelike workshop that reminded Finn of the workshop in his grandfather's basement. The L-shaped room had countertops that ran along every wall, behind which were pegboards holding every conceivable kind of tool. Computers and hand tools littered the counters. But what made it much different from Grandpop's basement was its purpose. The room was designed for the repair of the Audio-Animatronics—the talking robots—that were used extensively throughout the Park. The result was the disturbing presence of human torsos, heads, hands, and legs in every stage of creation, from pieces that looked like robots to painted faces dressed in costumes that seemed so real Philby kept spinning in circles, afraid one or more of them might suddenly move or attack. Of equal concern were the dozens of animals under construction, including pieces of tigers, lions, Stitch, Donald Duck, and a fantastic hand—possibly from a gorilla—that was nearly three feet across and supported by a metal superstructure that held it four feet off the floor.

"Whoa . . ." Philby said, taking a look around. Both boys spoke in whispers, as if the "body" parts might overhear them.

"Somehow I don't think we'll find a copier in

here," Finn said, holding Jez's journal.

"Oh, I bet you're wrong. Give me a minute." Philby walked the lines of workbenches. He muttered words like "impressive" and "interesting" and "incredible." Then he addressed Finn. "Articulated, motor-controlled limb movement—very cutting edge." He stopped in front of a six-foot tyrannosaur head with wires sticking out of a missing eye.

"What about a copier?" Finn reminded him, not so impressed.

"Yeah, okay," Philby said. "But I could stay here for hours."

"Let's save the extra-credit work for another time."

Philby's curiosity carried him to the far end of the room, where the lab opened out into a large space that appeared to be used for assembly. Most of the robotic dummies stood on their own here—cables and wires running from them—and many were at least partially clothed and had faces. Most of the Audio-Animatronics were of animals in various poses, all of which looked incredibly lifelike. But it was the far end of the room that intrigued Philby.

"Check it out," he said, approaching the area some-what cautiously and with great respect. "Remember this?" he asked.

The three walls at the end of the room were covered

in jungle-green paper, as was the floor. There were stage lights and tripods and cameras and a dozen computers on rolling stands.

"I do," said Finn. He and the other DHI kids, upon acceptance by Disney, had been computer-modeled by Disney Imagineers. Their movements were recorded to create the DHIs. The empty cages off to their left suggested the obvious.

"Animals," Philby said, immediately understanding the setup. "They motion-modeled animals here to create DHIs."

"Wayne told me they were doing that," Finn said. "Animal hosts." The cameras were all set low to the ground. Then there were the cages and—he realized as he stepped closer—paw marks seen faintly on the green-paper floor covering.

"Check it out," Philby said again, this time directing Finn's attention to five photographs thumbtacked to the wall nearby. There were several monkeys, a baby elephant, a pair of tigers, and a gorilla.

"Got it!" Finn said, pointing to a flatbed scanner hooked up to a computer. He touched the computer's space bar and the machine woke up.

Philby laid Jez's diary on the scanner bed and began scanning the pages. As he printed them out, Finn received a text message.

panda: 2 guys out front!!!

"Visitors!" Finn whispered to Philby.

Finn: got it! thanx

The lab's only door was a long way away. There was one EMERGENCY ONLY door to the right of the green-screen area, but it had an alarm, and Finn had no desire to draw the wrath of Security upon him and Philby before they managed to even get into the Park.

"We can hide!" Philby said in a harsh whisper. He pointed to an area where dozens of parts and partial bodies of the Audio-Animatronics figures had been heaped into a kind of junk pile. Many of the human robots had faces that looked phenomenally real.

Finn grabbed the printouts, and the boys jumped into the junk pile, worming their way down into the parts so that only their shoulders and faces showed. They blended in with the robotic human parts.

Two men entered the room, both wearing dark blue coveralls. Neither seemed surprised to find the lights turned on—something Philby had done upon entering.

"It's always something," the thinner of the two said. "I could have told you the sound system was going to go out at some point. They should have rewired the Asia system when they installed Expedition Everest. Not my fault."

The men scrounged around on the workbenches, apparently looking for parts.

"Finding the break in the wire, if there is one, is going to be a bear," said the heavier man.

"Don't mention bears," said the other one. He pointed to an Audio-Animatronics figure of a standing bear cub designed for the Country Bear Jamboree. "This one will get jealous."

Both men laughed—harder than the joke deserved.

The thin one suddenly turned and headed directly for the junk pile where the boys were hidden. "Didn't we loan these guys our acoustic coupler?"

"It's the tester we're looking for. Forget the coupler."

The thin man picked up a piece of one of the robots. He was about two feet away from Finn, who held his breath in an attempt not to be noticed.

"You know what?" the thin man said, looking right at Finn, then at Philby, then at the stack of robots. "This place gives me the creeps sometimes. Some of these things look so real . . . I gotta tell you."

"Found it!" the bigger man said. He held up a box with a lot of wires running out of it. "I knew the guys had borrowed it."

He tucked the box under his arm. The two men reached the door. The thin man stopped at the light switch.

"Hey," he said, "did you turn on the lights when we came in? Because I didn't."

"I don't think I did."

Finn felt sweat trickling down his rib cage. He calculated the distance to the emergency door, ready to run for it.

"Well," said the big man. He switched off the lights.

19

FINN'S FIRST DECENT look at the contents of Jez's diary came as he, Amanda, and Philby awaited the Park's opening. The main parking lot was a steady stream of arriving vehicles. Awning-covered shuttles were used to transport visitors to the Park entrance. The shuttles were stacked up at the back of the lot awaiting use. The three kids sat on a shuttle bench together and reviewed their personal photocopies of Jez's journal in detail.

Finn had always pictured a girl's diary to be line after line of neatly written cursive on well-organized pages, the contents of which held secrets about her love interests. What he saw here surprised him. Jez's was a stream-of-consciousness collage, a collection of images, sketches of animals, and musings. There were clothing receipts pasted into the pages; pieces of postcards, stapled; a fortune cookie fortune taped to a page; there were recipes, movie ticket stubs, pieces of torn photographs; ribbons and candy wrappers. There was an arch that looked like the letter *M*, with a blob of ink on the right side. Surrounding and interweaving it all were lines from poems, song lyrics, comments, and what looked like quotes from conversations she'd had. It was all mixed up into a mess of heavily scribbled pen and pencil.

"Are these supposed to mean something?" Finn asked, fingering the three photocopied pages.

"They must have meant something to her," Amanda said. "Jez took her journaling very seriously."

"And at what point did she cut off her ear?" asked Philby. "Go van Gogh." He won a few smiles.

"Look," Finn said, indicating the upper right-hand corner of the photocopy. "That's a castle and a lightning bolt."

"That's what I told you about," Amanda said. "And look down here." She pointed to what was obviously a monkey.

"Yeah, but this could be coincidence, right?" Philby said, sounding somewhat apprehensive. "Are we actually going to believe a person can see into the future?"

Finn looked over at him with a dumbfounded expression.

"Okay, okay. But it doesn't mean everything on this page is significant," Philby protested.

"How do we know it isn't?" Finn asked.

"This is several nights' worth of dreams," Amanda said. "You can tell because some are pencil, some pen. The movie tickets and postcards—that stuff is memories, reminders."

"But what about this decal, or whatever it is?" Finn asked.

"No idea. A stamp, maybe," Amanda said.

The letters were reversed, the image backward.

"There's a tiger, a gorilla, and . . . what's this, a bowling pin?" Finn turned the page upside down, but couldn't quite tell what he was looking at.

"I think they're all clues," Amanda said.

Philby exhaled loudly, so as to be noticed. "We *all* want to find her, Amanda. But if we go chasing down sketches from her diary, then that's a lot of valuable time that could have been spent looking for her."

"I think we can trust this," she said.

"We need more proof," Philby complained.

"We have a castle and a lightning bolt!" Finn pointed out.

"On opposite corners of the page. There's also an aqueduct, some balloons, and a railroad track."

"These are dreams, not instant replays," Amanda told Philby. "She had visions. Glimpses. How much of your dreams, your nightmares, do you remember? Bits and pieces are what I get. Sometimes more than that, a piece of a story, but not that often. Maybe we all dream pieces of the future but just don't happen to know it. How often do we write them down or make sketches and keep track? She left us clues, Philby." She waved the photocopy in the air. "This is the map of her dreams. Maybe she didn't know she was leaving it for us, but there's no ignoring the castle and the lightning, is there? So maybe not everything on here is helpful. It probably isn't. But we won't know that until we check it out. Right? We've got to check out each thing on here, because if even *one* other thing on this page can help us find her—" She covered her mouth with her fist, on the verge of crying.

"I'm just saying we don't have much time. I'm nodding out like every other minute. We fall asleep and we may stay asleep forever. That's what Wayne said. I just want us to use our time efficiently, that's all." He studied the sheet. "For instance, who's Rob?" In several places on the cluttered page Jez had written, *Change Rob.*

"Rob Bernowski," Amanda said. "From school."

"A friend? Boyfriend? Or what?" Philby asked.

"A little of both, I think."

"And she wants to change him? And this is relevant to us, how?"

"I don't know. Sure, I guess. She put that into the journal in a bunch of places." Amanda opened up the journal and flipped through several pages around the ones they had copied. "The way she writes it, it's like she's really set on it."

"So are we supposed to talk to Rob about this?" Philby asked sarcastically. "You think Rob has her?"

Amanda glared at him.

Finn asked, "What can it hurt to call him? I don't see why we don't follow up on everything we can. Am I missing something? What if this *is* important, and we ignore it?"

"That's why you called the meeting, isn't it?" Philby asked. "I say we put it to a vote. We could spend all day chasing a bunch of meaningless ramblings, and we haven't got all day. How much longer can we stay awake?" He yawned, and then Finn and Amanda yawned right along with him.

"Stop it," Finn said.

"We're out of time here," Philby complained, "and we haven't even started. I'm going to have to call my mom at some point, or she'll have the cops out looking for me."

"We'll put it to a vote," Finn agreed. "But in the meantime, we're going to make a list of everything on this page and what it might mean, no matter how far out." He addressed Philby. "We'll do it scientifically." He said this knowing it would appeal to him.

"I can get behind that," Philby said.

Amanda looked over at Finn, her eyes red and shining behind tears she struggled to hold back. But her eyes also had a twinkle in them. She seemed to be thanking him. Finn reached out and took her clenched fist in his hand.

"We're going to find her," he said.

20

MAYBECK APPROACHED the bat enclosure from the Maharajah Jungle Trek path. The enclosure was quite large, with colorful prayer flags strung between the facade of a fake building, rock walls, and the large boxlike frame that supported a wall and roof of mesh netting. A three-stage viewing room had been built along the path. A ranger would be on duty once the Park opened at 9 AM, but for now it stood empty. Maybeck avoided the viewing room, just in case, staying outside, moving along the perimeter wall of the netting. He left the path and entered the jungle, keeping close to the enclosure's netted wall.

It was only then he saw the birds. His first reaction was one of astonishment. He thought it beautiful in a way—a thousand or more dark birds so crowded into the treetops that large branches bent under their weight. He thought how fortunate he was to see such a phenomenon—that it probably only happened in the early hours before guests arrived and scared away all but the most brazen of the wild creatures that had adopted the Animal Kingdom as their home.

Then he noticed something strange about the birds: they all seemed to be looking right at him. He knew this was impossible, and yet . . . The thrill of astonishment gave way to the electric jangle of raw nerves. They *were* looking right at him.

Two things happened then: he spotted a door into the enclosure about ten yards farther into the jungle, and the first of the birds left their perches and flew toward him.

He knew he shouldn't panic. It was only birds, after all. But the way they surrounded him . . . the way the jungle went suddenly silent . . . the way the bats in the enclosure awakened with a start—*nocturnal* animals—a restless jittering as they hung from their perches sent a spike of terror through him. Birds flew in flocks, certainly. But they didn't *attack* as a group. Did they?

The birds attacked.

It was as if someone had blotted out the sun. They came at him as a dark cloud of beating wings and unflinching black eyes. Their small bird legs were aimed right at Maybeck. The birds came at him in such numbers that at first it was just plain scary—they landed on his head, his shoulders, his arms, his back. But then it went beyond scary—to dangerous—as the weight of them pushed him down. To an outside eye, it would have appeared as if thousands of birds had landed in the same spot of the jungle at once, but to Maybeck it meant a pitch-black flurry of wings and beaks and scratching claws. He fought them off one-handed—grabbing, poking, sweeping his arm, and knocking the birds away. But back they came.

He knew he could not sustain the weight of the birds. The pecking.

Now, crushed by the heaviness, feeling it might break him in two, Maybeck released the pillowcase to defend himself.

A tiny hand reached out . . .

A monkey hand! It snatched up the pillowcase, and the monkey took off running. As it did, the birds flew off. In a flutter of feathers, the sun reappeared, and Maybeck watched as the monkey, pillowcase in hand, hurried down the path.

Maybeck took off after it.

He looked himself over as he ran—not a scratch on him. If he were to tell anyone what had happened, they wouldn't believe him. He had no proof whatsoever. *A thousand birds attacked me!* It would sound like a lame excuse for his having lost the pillowcase and the captive bat. He had originally thought Finn's claim that the bat might be Maleficent was a bit of a stretch. But now he reconsidered. Birds didn't organize like that, he reminded himself. Monkeys were known thieves, but what was a monkey doing *loose* inside the Animal Kingdom, even if the Park was not yet officially open? He had questions that needed answering.

He ran as fast as he could.

When the monkey stole off into the jungle, Maybeck followed.

21

WILLA CROSSED DISCOVERY ISLAND, feeling as if everyone were staring at her. Could they tell she was underage? She didn't think she looked all that much younger than the other girls. The formality of the uniform helped her look older, adding a good three or four years to her fourteen. But what if they were staring because they recognized her face as that of a DHI? If caught, she could lose her family's Gold Pass, as well as her performance contract. She might no longer be one of the Kingdom Keepers. She kept her head down and wished she'd used more makeup at the costume warehouse. The ID badge Wayne had given her was clipped to her waist, helping to make her look official. With her eyes to the ground, she walked with her back straight and took determined strides, knowing the importance of body language.

She had volunteered for what was probably the most dangerous assignment that Finn and Philby had come up with: to infiltrate and search the Kilimanjaro Safari grounds. The idea was a simple one: if someone was hiding Jez in the Animal Kingdom, why not stash her someplace where people were prohibited from going? When the Park was open, the safari teemed with hundreds of wild animals. People riding on the safari were restricted to the backs of the safari trucks with a driver/guide who pointed out animals and took guests on a "mission" to save a baby elephant from make-believe poachers. But, according to Philby's research, throughout the safari grounds there were feeding stations, way points, and even some hidden gates offering backstage access. The Overtakers had once hidden Maybeck in a maintenance cage inside Space Mountain; it seemed possible, logical even, that they might hide Jez in a similarly impossible-to-access place. But if one of them got there before the animals were released . . .

"It's done in stages," Philby had explained. "Thomson's gazelles are pretty tame and harmless. Some aren't even rounded up at night, but most of the other animals are. They're fed and washed and doctored, if need be, after the Park closes to the public."

"But what about early morning?" Willa had asked.

"Before the Park opens, they return the animals in a specific order that offers the fewest problems. The trick for you is to get inside before eight AM."

Willa didn't wear a watch. She had no idea what time it was. That was an oversight. She was guessing it was between 6:30 and 7:00 AM, which gave her about an hour. But the later it was, the less time she had. She quickened her steps, off Discovery Island now, and headed toward the entrance to the Kilimanjaro Safari. A tremendous flock of black birds passed overhead— there must have been thousands of them. They streaked across the morning sky and were gone.

"If you hurry, you can catch the last one." She looked up. It was a cute guy wearing a uniform identical to her own. He stood below the sign for the Kilimanjaro Safari.

"Ah . . . yeah," Willa said. But she tensed as she felt his eyes following her. Did she look old enough to carry an ID badge?

She walked quickly through the empty waiting area, turning and winding her way down to the loading dock, where one of the trucks was waiting. There was an older woman—she had to be nearly thirty—leaning forward from the front bench, coaching the driver. Willa was the only passenger beside the instructor. It was obviously some kind of training run. The truck rumbled off down a path that wound through the jungle.

Willa called out, "I'll be hopping off at Ituri Forest."

The instructor, without so much as looking back, lifted her arm and waved.

Willa heaved a sigh of relief and held on as the driver avoided puddles and recited some memorized lines into the radio, "communicating" with other rangers who were searching for the poachers. Willa had taken the safari ride many times and enjoyed the story behind it as well as the animal-watching. But the emptiness of the place at this hour gave her the shivers. The truck rounded a bend and slowed.

"Is here all right?" the instructor called back inquisitively. Suspiciously?

The Ituri Forest, Willa realized.

"Fine!" She hopped the three feet down to the muddy ground, hoping the instructor wouldn't see that she was wearing running shoes and not the required ranger boots. She slapped the side of the truck, and it lumbered off. The minute it was gone, she regretted getting off.

Alone on the truck route, in the midst of a thick forest of bamboo and sea cane, Willa spotted a pure white ibis as still as a statue. The bird stood on one leg, perfectly balanced.

She unfolded the map Philby had given her, tried to establish her position, and punched through the forest to her left, expecting to come across a feed station within the next thirty yards. It was tough going, the forest thick with vegetation.

Had she looked behind her, she would have seen a lizard following. It was five or six feet long, with a thin tail and little claws on its feet. Not so much a lizard— more like a Chinese dragon.

22

MAYBECK LOST GROUND to the small, agile simian that moved through the jungle's tight growth in a seamless, fluid motion. He wondered if the monkey was under Maleficent's control. But if so, then why had it not been ordered to release the bat? His answer came as a slice of first light caught his eyes. Bats were nocturnal; it was sunrise. Releasing the bat was not an option.

Maybeck had to get it back. He smashed into bamboo and rubber trees, baby banyans and mangrove. He sloshed through the flooded jungle floor, quickly gaining on the monkey.

Maybeck's progress registered on the monkey's face as wide-eyed terror. It shrieked and exploded into a frenzy, briefly increasing its lead on Maybeck. But only briefly.

Maybeck broke out of the jungle and felt something hard beneath his feet. He looked down: train tracks! The Wildlife Express Train was going through its morning test run. Maybeck jumped out of the way when he heard a blast from the train's whistle. "You crazy?" the conductor shouted through the open window.

He'd been spotted. As the train passed, he saw the conductor reaching for his radio.

Not good.

The train whistle pierced the morning air, sending a flock of sandhill cranes into the blue sky. Maybeck spotted the monkey. It had been crouched in the center of the birds. He closed the distance to ten yards, then five.

The train had followed a long, sweeping curve of track but was now coming around and catching up to them. It reappeared to Maybeck's right. The monkey changed directions, going straight for the train. Maybeck skidded to a stop, caught a toe, and went down hard.

He looked up to see the monkey slip *beneath* a train car, the pillowcase in hand. Maybeck hurried to his feet and ran toward the train. The train conductor hung out of the locomotive, shouting at him. Maybeck squatted in time to see the monkey racing across a short distance of grass toward more jungle. There was no way Maybeck was about to crawl under a moving train. He waited it out impatiently. It seemed to move very slowly. Finally, Maybeck took off toward the end of the train and came around it, once again crossing the tracks.

He found himself next to the Chakranadi Chicken Shop. He came to a halting stop, looked left . . . right

. . . *there!* A flash of the white pillowcase was all he caught—just rounding a bend in the path. He took off, heading away from Flights of Wonder. Again, his size and speed overcame the monkey's efforts.

The monkey sensed its pursuer and skittered back and forth in a zigzag, chattering loudly. It crossed the path and shot straight up a dangling rope toward a concrete tower. It reached the turret, nearly thirty feet off the ground, and briefly disappeared. The next time Maybeck saw it, the monkey—still carrying the pillowcase—hurried across a set of ropes toward a crumbling Asian temple encased in bamboo scaffolding. This was on an island surrounded by a narrow moat.

Maybeck stopped at the concrete tower. The end of the rope the monkey had climbed was frayed as if it had been chewed through. He studied the layout, noticing that the rope bridges connected back to the temple, which meant that the monkeys weren't supposed to be able to get down off the towers. The moat was meant to prevent their escape from the island. But the monkeys had managed to drop a rope that had yet to be spotted. By doing so, they'd given themselves an escape route.

The monkey disappeared into the red brick temple, dragging the pillowcase behind it, and was gone.

Maybeck, understanding the importance of acting quickly, rolled up his pant legs, pulled off his shoes, and waded into the murky water. A pair of ducks startled and splashed away to the other side of the temple, squawking and quacking.

Maybeck felt the cold mud ooze between his toes. Bubbles rose to the surface all around him, giving off an unpleasant odor.

He faced a wooden door with iron bars over its small, square window. It was the only way into the temple that he could see.

He arrived there in five giant steps and, sloshing out of the water, reached for the door's handle.

23

WILLA CHECKED PHILBY'S MAP once more: he had marked the location of a feeding station—disguised as a large stump—at the edge of the savannah. Its proximity to a nighttime animal holding pen qualified it as a possible hiding place where Jez could be kept and never discovered. A clock ran off the seconds and minutes in her head—she had several such places to check before the animals were released.

She pushed though the forest, following the map, and reached the edge of the sprawling savannah: a flat plain of low grasses interspersed with trees and rocks and a few small ponds, all of it surrounded by low rolling hills. It glistened in the first golden rays of dawn.

There, quite some distance away, she saw a stump, thinking immediately that it couldn't possibly be Philby's stump because it looked so real. But the location was right, so she decided to have a look.

The problem was, there was no way to sneak up toward a stump in the middle of a field without being seen. She had to cross a hundred yards in the open. Not that there was anyone to see her, but another training truck could come by at any minute. She decided rather than run out and look suspicious, she would walk casually—just another day on the job. Hopefully, the ranger uniform would do the rest.

Then, taking in her surroundings, she happened to look back.

At first, she thought it was an alligator. Terror gripped her: alligators ate people. It happened all the time in Florida. She'd heard they could run faster than humans, and when you saw one you didn't want to run because it teased them into chasing you—and if they chased you, they considered you food. So she continued walking, though slightly faster than before. The stump—or fake stump—rose at least three feet off the ground. If she could only reach it in time . . .

But then she looked again. It wasn't an alligator after all, but a giant lizard, maybe six feet long. She'd studied Komodo dragons in school, and this looked pretty much exactly like one. Komodos didn't eat people, but they were known to bite and do serious harm. She didn't know the rule about Komodos—did you run or walk? The lizard turned sideways for a second, as if to size her up, and once again she changed her mind: it wasn't a Komodo; it looked more . . . prehistoric, with thick scales and . . . was that possible? . . .

wings, tucked in along its back. It looked more like . . .

A dragon. She'd read stories about dragons. Had seen movies. She'd always considered them mythological creatures. But now she was looking at one.

It had a disgusting, pink tongue that flicked like a snake's—but about two feet long. The tongue curled as it drew back between the rows of gray, stubby teeth.

She wanted to think of this as coincidence—the two of them had just happened to cross paths, and it was now following her. *Tracking her* was more to the point, she thought. But then something even more strange entered her thoughts: what if Jez was indeed locked up in the stump—the food locker—and the dragon was some kind of patrol for the Overtakers? After all, the safari was filled with all sorts of animals, from giraffes to zebras, but a scaly Asian dragon with wings?

The Overtakers.

It was the first thing to come to her: if Jez was being kept out here on the savannah, it seemed obvious who would guard her. And if there was a dragon mixed in with all the rest of the animals, could that possibly be a coincidence, since dragons hadn't existed for the past few million years—if ever?

So what exactly was the dragon waiting for? It just lingered back there, a dozen yards away, trolling back and forth across the grassy landscape as if sniffing around for food. If he was going to attack her, why not get to it?

Could a dragon possibly think? Could it be waiting to see if she headed for the stump? She subtly increased both the quickness and the length of her strides. She glanced back to see that the dragon had stayed right with her. It didn't seem to be moving any faster, either, and yet . . . there it was.

Now more convinced than ever that she was its intended target, she looked around and realized that she was all alone out on the savannah. She saw an ostrich in the distance—perhaps they had begun releasing animals already. A herd of Thomson's gazelles shot across the field, but some nights they were left on the grounds; it didn't mean much to see them. If, on the other hand, the animals were already being released and introduced to the savannah, then Willa hoped they might distract the dragon from its current obsession with her.

She moved increasingly closer to the stump, and now, looking back, she saw the dragon following her. If she climbed on top of the stump, she would be out of reach of the dragon. But what about the wings? Could something like that possibly fly?

She heard the sudden beating of hooves, seconds later mixing with the rumble of a truck engine. A herd of zebras had been released—again to her left—and from somewhere behind her a truck was approaching. If she was going to inspect the stump it had to be now—right now.

She ran the last few yards, and if she'd harbored any doubts as to the dragon's intentions, they were answered by its light-footed sprint to keep up with her. There was no turning back now. No changing her mind. The dragon raced toward her, its mouth open, snapping at the air.

She reached the side of the stump—though shaped like a stump, it was made of metal, with a small door in the side. She worked the snap lock off the hasp and opened the door.

The dragon charged, seemingly not touching the ground at all. It flicked its long tail back and forth, moving in a snakelike fashion, quickly closing the distance between them.

Willa dove inside and pulled the door shut behind her. It was incredibly warm inside. Enough light filtered in to allow her to see that Jez was not there. There were sacks of food and salt licks. It smelled like a pet store. A coiled hose hung from a hook.

The dragon smashed into the door, then slammed its powerful tail against the stump. Her ears rang. A rumbling in the ground grew louder. Willa looked out a crack in the access door to see the herd of zebras bearing down on her as it crossed the savannah.

The dragon took off for a distant tree and climbed it in a creepy, effortless way.

Willa sagged down to sit, trying to catch her breath.

And then she saw it: freshly scraped into the fake stump's rusty metal was a simple message that made absolutely no sense—and yet somehow she knew it had been written by Jez.

It read: *Change Rob.*

She curled up and held her breath, waiting to flee the stump once the storm of zebras had passed.

24

MAYBECK STOOD INSIDE a dark enclosure the size of a large closet. It had a concrete floor from which a low brick wall rose to waist level. From there, framed lumber intersected by long bamboo poles rose geometrically overhead, wrapped on the outside with heavy brown vinyl: fake brick. Together, it added up on the outside to what looked like an Asian temple. But inside it smelled bad—really bad—like one of those Porta-Potties at the state fair. It was surprisingly cool inside—a place for the monkeys to escape the heat. There was a white plastic tub with a metal handle sitting by the door. Alongside it was a neatly coiled green hose connected to a spigot.

The door clapped shut behind him. He turned in time to see the monkey overhead, carrying the pillowcase, climbing effortlessly, up, up, up, pulling himself between the bamboo poles and jeering down at Maybeck.

Sunlight seeped in through several square openings at the top of the temple. The temple provided shelter for the monkeys, a place to hide from storms and a cool place to sleep. The smell was the problem: the monkeys used the concrete floor as their bathroom. He understood the purpose of the hose, then, and felt tempted to give the concrete a spraying off.

If the monkey made it to the top window, the pillowcase and its contents would be gone. Maybeck considered climbing, but that was a race he was sure to lose.

The monkey crossed along the bamboo rafters, and then, to Maybeck's surprise, began to work its way back down. Maybeck's eyes slowly adjusted to the dark. And then something moved from the shadows.

Maleficent.

She stepped out to where Maybeck could see her, regal in her purple-fringed black cape, her startling green skin glowing with maliciousness.

"Hello, Terrance." A voice like grinding stones.

The monkey handed her the bag. She accepted it with an outstretched arm, never taking her eyes off Maybeck.

"Do you know what happens to *children* who play where they don't belong?"

He couldn't get a word out.

"They get . . . burned," she said. A flaming orb appeared in one hand. She cocked her arm back, ready to throw.

Maybeck dove for the hose, swiveled its nozzle, and shot a ferocious stream of water at the witch.

The monkey cried out and leaped up into the rafters.

The water stream knocked the burning ball out of Maleficent's hand but produced a cloud of steam that immediately filled the small space so thickly he couldn't see.

A dark shadow shifted inside the gray cloud of steam: Maleficent moving to cut off his path to the door. He abandoned the hose and sprang for the door. But she was much faster than he'd anticipated. He came face-to-face with the green skin and bloodshot eyes. Her breath was like a dead mouse caught in a trap as she said, "No. I don't think so."

Maybeck didn't hesitate. He kicked out, punching the door open and admitting a flood of light. Maleficent, still holding the pillowcase, moved to block his exit, just as he'd hoped.

He sprang up overhead, through the bamboo, and squeezed out the hole at the top. Hand-over-hand, he swung up the taut connecting rope—five yards . . . ten—as he pulled himself toward the tower.

Maleficent stepped out into the sunlight but jumped back—the heat of the sun's rays already too much for her.

Maybeck reached the tower and found the dangling rope and slid down, burning his hands, reached the ground, and took off running without looking back.

He understood with absolute clarity what was going on: the bat was a spy—*Maleficent's spy*—and she'd dispatched the birds and the monkey to make sure she received the bat's report.

The bat had followed Finn since Amanda's. It knew all about them. And now Maleficent knew, too.

He shuddered with the thought of that as he broke into the jungle and ran for his life.

25

THE MOMENT THE PARK gates opened to the public, Finn, Amanda, and Philby entered through the Cast Member entrance, using the IDs that Wayne had provided. Finn and Philby were determined to mix in with the crowds and reach the rendezvous in time to meet up with the others. Famous as DHIs, their faces were known throughout the Disney kingdoms, a fame that threatened—for they were forbidden from attending except on specially approved days. Getting around without being recognized was not going to be easy. They wore baseball caps to hide their faces, and they kept to themselves as much as possible.

By the time they reached the benches just inside the large gates north of the Rainforest Café, where the Animal Kingdom parade originated, a wet Maybeck and a dirty-faced Willa were waiting. Finn handed out copies of the page from Jez's diary.

Quiet at this hour, it was a good place to meet. They gathered around a bench, awaiting Charlene's grand entrance as DeVine, the ivy-covered chameleon.

Maybeck told them about being attacked by birds,

about losing the bat to a monkey, and about his encounter with Maleficent.

Willa spoke of her pursuit by a miniature dragon and her discovery in the metal stump of the cryptic message left by Jez.

"There's something to be learned from what we both went through," Willa said, continuing. "We can't trust any of the animals we see. Maleficent can control them. Whether a flock of birds, or a dragon with wings. We're no longer in the Animal Kingdom, we're in Maleficent's kingdom."

"If she went to all this trouble to be here, there's got to be a good reason." Finn heard something behind him and glanced over his shoulder into the jungle. He saw nothing. Willa and Maybeck were freaking him out.

"Maleficent's weak in the heat. She needs cold to survive. If she's hanging out here, it's someplace cold."

"But why here?" Finn asked.

"We need to keep watch on the bat enclosure," Maybeck proposed.

"I can go places none of you can," said a girl's voice from behind them. Once again Finn looked back into the jungle. Again he saw nothing.

"Up here," said the voice.

He and the others looked up to see a vine-covered

leotard, with no face and no arms. It was Charlene, in costume as DeVine, her face painted green and black. The overall effect was disarming: she'd been standing there all along, immediately behind Finn.

Philby applauded. "Outrageous!" he said.

"Whoa," said Maybeck. "You totally blend in."

"I can't believe it!" said an exhilarated Willa. "I'm looking right at you and I almost can't see you."

"I'll need to leave the area before the real DeVine comes out. But I can go almost anywhere undetected. Even Maleficent isn't going to see me in this."

"Okay, Charlene will watch the bat enclosure," Finn stated with a feigned authority. He remembered Wayne telling him that he was the group's chosen leader, though he still wasn't buying it. But to his surprise, no one argued with him.

Charlene, blending into her surroundings, waited for some Park guests to pass and then said, "Will someone please hand me the page from the diary?"

Amanda produced it, stood on the bench, and passed it up to her.

Charlene studied it. "Monkeys . . . tigers . . . a bat . . . This is enough for now," she said.

"It's possible that everything on that page is significant," Finn cautioned.

Catching Philby dozing off, he punched him in the arm. "And NO falling asleep," he reminded them.

"I'm exhausted," Willa said.

"We cannot sleep!" Finn repeated. "Wayne warned us about that. We've got to believe him."

Maybeck indicated a food cart. "Cokes all around!"

A few minutes later they were all loading up on caffeine. "Maybe Maleficent can't get Jez out of the park until after it closes," Amanda said, "or maybe the plan is to run all of you around until you tire out. If she can trap you all in the Sleeping Beauty Syndrome, she eliminates the enemy and is free to rule without challenge."

"You think she took Jez to bait us?" Willa asked.

"None of this means anything," Maybeck said, "until we find Jez. The challenge is to stay awake long enough to find Jez and crash this cloned server—if it even exists. Then maybe we hunt down Maleficent, if we're still standing. But until we find Jez, none of it matters."

"Listen!" Charlene said from high on the stilts.

The kids turned their attention toward the jungle.

"Not to me!" Charlene clarified. "To the music."

The kids perked up their ears. It was Ashley Tisdale's "Kiss the Girl," coming over the Park's speaker system.

"Yeah? So?" asked Willa. "Radio Disney plays that all the time."

"I know that," Charlene said. "But me and my family come as often as possible, and I've never heard that song in this Park before."

The kids listened some more. "You're right. It's always *Lion King* and stuff like that."

"It's Jez," Amanda stated.

"What's Jez?" Finn asked.

"'Kiss the Girl' is Jez's favorite song," Amanda said. "She abuses that song on her iPod. If it doesn't belong in this Park, then it's her. It's some kind of message."

"I think you're more tired than the rest of us," Maybeck said.

"Which is completely understandable," Willa chimed in, "given the stress . . ."

"Listen . . . listen!" Amanda demanded, raising a finger to try to shut them up. "Raven-Symoné is going to sing 'Under the Sea' next."

"Yeah, right," said Maybeck. "I suppose if your sister can dream the future, you can *hear* it."

"Philby," Amanda said, "Jez had her iPod with her. Is there some way she could use it over the sound system?"

"Hijack the sound system?" Philby said, considering the question. "Depends, I suppose. If she stripped a wire from the earbuds and tapped into—"

But he was cut off by the music changing.

Raven-Symoné was singing "Under the Sea."

All the kids went quiet.

Some visitors walked past talking about going on Expedition Everest. The parents sounded reluctant to try the ride.

But it wasn't the guests that had silenced the kids.

"Coincidence," Maybeck said in a whisper. He didn't sound at all convinced.

"It's Jez," Amanda countered, her voice noticeably brighter.

"I know for a fact that they never play that song here," Charlene said from up high. "I believe Amanda. And besides, it's softer than the regular music—not as loud. It doesn't sound right."

"Which would also explain why Finn and I overheard two maintenance guys talking about sound-system problems," Philby said.

Finn's face brightened. "That's right!"

"Then why doesn't she just send us Morse code, or something?" Maybeck complained.

"Because she can't give away what she's done," Amanda said, trying to think as Jez would think. "She doesn't want them figuring it out. So she's trying to communicate with us, without it being really obvious."

"Wait right here," Philby said, taking off at a run. The kids watched him go.

They used the downtime to review the page taken from Jez's diary.

"The animals could symbolize different things," Willa suggested.

"Like what?" a skeptical Maybeck questioned. "Listen, I see the drawing of the lightning striking a castle, and even I've got to admit it's pretty coincidental. But the rest of these? They're animals. So what? She likes animals. It doesn't mean they *mean* something."

"It doesn't mean they don't," Amanda countered. "You don't know Jez. They're clues. Clues we're supposed to follow."

Philby came running toward them.

As he did, there was suddenly no music at all: a rarity in any of the Disney Parks.

Then "Under the Sea" began playing again.

One thing all the kids knew: music never repeated in any of the Parks. Not ever.

Out of breath, Philby said, "It's playing on this side of the Park and in Asia. Discovery Island and Africa have different music going."

"That doesn't necessarily mean anything," Maybeck said. "How do we know that isn't always the case?"

Philby explained, "From what I know, the system is designed to be able to move sound around the Park. The parades require that the music follow the floats.

It's a sophisticated, computer-controlled sound system. I've never read anything about one half of the Park being sent one kind of music, and the other half another."

"That confirms it's Jez," Amanda said excitedly. "She just repeated 'Under the Sea.' We know that song doesn't belong here, and on her iPod it follows 'Kiss the Girl.' Pretty obvious she *wants* someone to hear it. Maybe us. Maybe someone to try to fix it, someone to go looking for the problem."

"Or maybe," said Willa, "the song itself is significant. Ariel. Or Ursula—"

"I hate Ursula," Charlene tossed out.

"Or it has to do with where they're keeping her," Amanda continued. "Or it fits into her dreams in some way."

"We've got to take it seriously," Willa pleaded, looking at Finn, knowing the decision would somehow be his to make.

Finn felt all eyes fall on him. He stifled a yawn. Every minute was precious. His head was clouded and heavy.

"Let's run down everything to do with *The Little Mermaid*," Finn said.

Maybeck groaned. "Isn't that wasting time? The bat is *real*. That monkey is *real*. The dragon was real. Let's follow things we can actually see."

"How do we know that?" Charlene asked from atop her stilts.

"Ariel's Grotto," Willa said. "Magic Kingdom."

"We split up," Finn said, pulling out a pencil and writing on the back of the photocopy of the diary page. "Maybeck will try to locate the animals and images sketched in the diary. The rest of us will look for anything to do with 'Under the Sea' and *The Little Mermaid*."

"I don't know if this counts," Philby said, "but when you stand in line for Nemo, over at Epcot, the ocean is painted above you. You're literally under the sea."

"I like it," Finn said. He wrote it down.

"The same thing's true at Hollywood Studios," Willa said. "On the Voyage of the Little Mermaid, you stand under the sea while waiting."

"Okay . . . Okay . . ." Maybeck said, finally going along. "I don't know if this counts, but there's this poster my little sister loves. Always points it out. It's by the Mickey's PhilharMagic line. I'm pretty sure it says something like 'A Must Sea,' spelled *S-E-A*."

"That definitely counts," Finn said, writing this down as well. "Anything else anyone can think of?"

One by one, the others either shook their heads or shrugged.

"It's a lot. And they're spread all over the place."

"It's a waste of time," Maybeck cautioned. "It's just a song."

"You have your assignment," Finn said. "Philby will stay and try to figure out the Park's sound system. Get on to VMK if you can and find Wayne." He explained how to use the Disney vacation kiosk in Camp Minnie-Mickey. "Maybe he can help." He turned to Amanda. "You will keep watch for Jez using the Animal Cam at the Conservation Station. Willa will take Ariel's Grotto and Mickey's PhilharMagic—both in Magic Kingdom. I'll take Nemo and the Voyage of the Little Mermaid. Maybeck, you stay and keep after the monkey and bat. Follow the clues in the diary, working with Charlene. Any problems?"

To his surprise, no one complained or tried to change the assignments. Maybe he actually was the leader.

"All of us have to study this page from the diary. We each have a copy. We need to write down where we've seen any of these animals, or images of these animals. This building she drew . . . this dude wearing a turban. And I'll call Rob, since his name keeps coming up."

He met eyes—tired eyes—with Maybeck, and saw Maybeck's frustration and impatience.

"I'm open to suggestions," Finn offered.

A silence hung heavily in the air.

It was broken by the music beginning again. "Under the Sea." Playing now for the third time in a row.

"Two hours," Maybeck said. "We meet back here."

"Agreed," Finn said.

The kids scattered.

26

LIKE THE OTHERS, Willa had put her Animal Kingdom Cast Member costume on over her regular clothes. She'd slipped out of the AK costume and had tucked it into a bush outside the gates of the Magic Kingdom. Using the ID Wayne had given her, she was admitted through the CAST MEMBER ONLY line.

She stopped at a pay phone and called her mother. This was critical, because she'd sneaked out in the early hours of the morning before, saying she'd gone to Mass. She did this on her own periodically—something her mother found "dear"—so she knew it wouldn't raise a suspicion. Her mother was no longer a churchgoer, not since her father's accident, so the only excuse she had to make now concerned what she was doing with her morning.

"I'm at Disney World," she told her mother, settling for the truth. For all she knew, the pay phone's caller ID had already given her away.

"But you're not allowed. They'll pull our pass if they catch you."

"It's important."

"What could be that important?"

"I'm doing it for a friend."

"Doing what?"

"Research."

"You're not tangled up with those other kids again, are you?"

"They're my friends, Mom."

"They got you into a lot of trouble last time."

"I'll be home . . . later. I'll call if it's going to be after dark."

"It is *not* going to be after dark, young lady. I want you home by five."

"I can't promise that."

"You can, and you will. I'm still your mother, and if I say five, then it's five. And remember: stay away from the Magic Kingdom. If they make us give that money back . . ."

"They won't, Mom. I'll call. I love you, Mom." She hung up. Her mother hadn't been herself since the accident. In some ways the two of them were closer; in other ways they'd kind of traded roles: Willa felt more like the parent. She wondered why certain things happened in life—happened to some people but not others. Why had she become a DHI? How very different her life would be had she never auditioned for the part. Now she was caught up in something few would believe; she didn't even believe it herself some of the time. Rescuing a girl who could dream the future? It sounded so *stupid*. And yet . . .

She kept her head down on the way to Ariel's Grotto. If she was spotted, she'd be mobbed by autograph seekers. If busted by Security, they would throw her out and take action. She hoped the little bit of makeup she had on would help disguise her. She promised herself to keep a low profile and get this over with as quickly as possible.

She charged a princess wig and Disney hat onto her credit card. A khaki-colored baseball cap, it was a little large for her head, but it held down the red wig and hid her face well. She walked briskly and turned off Main Street as soon as possible, cutting in along the Monster's, Inc. Laugh Floor and looping around toward the grotto. Not a single glance in her direction. The disguise was working.

She stopped at the tentlike structure bearing the name ARIEL'S GROTTO and studied the marquee. It held just the two words with an image of Ariel between them. Some fake flags flew.

If she remembered correctly from the night before, the Ariel parade float was adorned with colorful sculptures of Sebastian, Scuttle, Triton, and Ursula. Did Jez's musical clue have anything to do with the parade?

After a long wait in line, she stood inside the grotto, where girls lined up to meet Ariel and have their pictures taken with her. She was posed inside a giant clam shell.

"Under the Sea," Willa was thinking, searching for a possible connection to Jez's disappearance. The song played repeatedly inside the grotto. With it, she felt a tangible connection to the missing Jez.

Something in here is important to Jez. . . .

She made herself believe this, having no idea whether or not it was true.

She was now third in line, behind mothers with their daughters lined up to get their photos taken. Behind Ariel, large colorful starfish clung to the aquamarine wall, and next to her was a small wooden chest.

Nothing here seemed of interest save for the chest, the possible contents of which intrigued her. What was *in* the chest? It looked to be nothing more than a prop—something for young girls to lean against while getting their photos taken. But oh, how Willa wanted a look inside.

She stepped forward, now second in line.

A girl and her mother got their picture taken. The Cast Member playing Ariel was beautiful. She spoke politely to both the mother and daughter, then glanced ahead to Willa.

She motioned Willa forward.

"I think we have something in common," she said softly. She'd seen past the wig and hair, recognizing Willa.

"Don't tell," Willa pleaded. "Please?"

"No way!" Then louder, for others to hear. "Would you like your picture taken?"

"I forgot my camera."

"Well, then." Ariel extended her hand for Willa to shake. "Nice to meet you." She lowered her voice, "Your secret's safe with me."

"I have a favor to ask," Willa said.

"I'm really just here for handshakes and photographs."

"The treasure chest," Willa said, pointing to the wooden trunk. "What's inside?"

"No idea." Realizing others were listening, she addressed everyone. "I've never opened it."

"Could you please?"

"I've never been asked."

"If you don't mind?" Willa said.

Ariel clearly didn't know what to do. She kept her composure, but her eyes wandered as if a handler might step forward to help her. In fact, that was exactly what happened.

"May I help?" a young woman asked.

"This young lady would like me to open the treasure chest," Ariel explained.

"It's important," Willa said in a whisper.

Though the company had never publicly acknowledged the work the Kingdom Keepers had done to save the Magic Kingdom, word had spread through the community. There were few that didn't know the story by now, both inside and outside the network of Park employees. A book had been written and published as fiction, but many knew the truth.

"How important?" Ariel asked.

Willa raised the baseball cap, revealing herself. A shock of recognition overcame the girl. Willa hoped this was the right thing to do. She lowered her voice. "Did you hear about Tinker Bell last night, during the fireworks?"

Ariel's eyes widened, and she nodded.

"What is going on here?" the handler whispered hotly into Willa's ear.

"What? I don't know what you mean."

"Don't give me that! First Captain Hook comes through our line nosing around where he doesn't belong, and now you? And not fifteen minutes apart? What is it with you people?" She leaned in even closer. "Are you *inspecting* us or something?"

"Captain Hook?"

"Don't give me that."

"What did he want?"

"Captain Hook's a walkaround. He doesn't talk, in case you've forgotten. How would I know what he wanted?"

"He was just here?"

"They never used to pull surprise inspections," the handler complained. "And I don't like it."

Willa tried to process all that she was being told. The Overtakers? Here before her? Also interested in Ariel? Why?

"You want your picture taken with me?" Ariel asked. "It would be an honor." She'd opened the treasure chest for Willa: *empty*.

Willa felt her head spin. She had to beat Captain Hook—or whoever he was—to Mickey's Philhar-Magic.

"I'm fine!" she shouted over her shoulder, already hurrying away.

27

FINN ARRIVED AT HOLLYWOOD STUDIOS bone-tired, well aware that if he or any of the other Kingdom Keepers fell asleep, they might not be seen again. Ever. Worse, Jez's disappearance pressured all involved to find her quickly. He was going to be in trouble if this went on much longer. He didn't put it past his parents to go looking for him at Blizzard Beach. When they failed to find him there . . .

He hurried down Hollywood Boulevard toward Mickey's giant sorcerer hat, which towered one-hundred-and-twenty feet over the central plaza. He had his his own cap brim pulled down low over his sunglasses as he kept an eye out for any kids recognizing him—he didn't need that. He would take evasive action if necessary. He identified possible escape routes in each direction.

While checking out a Kodak shop to his left, he spotted a large black crow on the building's roof. The bird was certainly big enough to draw attention to itself, but Finn's curiosity ran deeper: it seemed to be staring at him. The bird had its head cocked so that its large black eye was trained down, not just on the street but on Finn. As Finn moved, so did the bird's head. As Finn hurried up the street, the bird flew and followed, building by building.

Finn might not have taken any notice or interest in a stupid crow, but he couldn't ignore Maybeck's tale about being attacked outside the bat enclosure by a flock of birds. He'd been bitten badly by a parrot once and could remember it as if it were yesterday.

Now, hurrying to the Voyage of the Little Mermaid, it seemed pretty obvious that the crow was following him. This, in turn, made him search the area to see if there were any other animals nearby. He spotted a group of chickadees in a tree outside the Brown Derby—but they didn't seem particularly threatening. A solo jay stood watch from a roof overlooking an ice-cream vendor. Finn's distraction with the animals caused his attention to falter.

He heard the voice too late. "Aren't you . . . *him*?" A boy of ten or eleven. His parents stood a few feet back, his mother's face bright with expectancy. Finn glanced around. How had the boy possibly recognized him? He didn't want this to get out of hand; sometimes signing a single autograph could start a big line.

"Do you like the Magic Kingdom?" Finn asked the boy, who then nodded vigorously.

"The Kingdom Keepers," the boy said. "You're Finn. You beat up Maleficent."

Finn bit back a smirk. "Not hardly. Those are just stories," he said, accepting an autograph book from the boy. "I'll sign this, but only if you promise not to tell anyone." He lowered his voice and said conspiratorially, "I'm here on a mission."

The boy's eye went wide. He shook his head, too awed to speak.

"Good." Finn led the boy over to the sidewalk, where he could sign the autograph book with his back turned to the street. In the Disney Parks, anyone signing anything attracted attention.

The boy followed. As Finn put pencil to paper, he briefly glanced up and into the reflection in the store window. Three brooms, one holding a bucket of water. He spun quickly around, dropping the autograph book. The boy bent to retrieve it.

The brooms stood facing him.

"Thank you!" the boy said, cherishing his autograph.

Finn had nearly forgotten about him. "No problem."

Then something occurred to him. "You see those brooms over there? They look real familiar, but I can't remember why. . . ."

"*Fantasia*," the boy said.

"*Fantasia*," Finn said. "I don't think I've ever seen that one."

"It's a pretty weird movie," the boy said. "The brooms show up in 'The Sorcerer's Apprentice,' I think. Mickey, the apprentice, can't control the magic—you know? It gets all out of hand. The brooms are part of that."

Uncontrollable magic, Finn thought. Yes, he knew exactly what that was about, just like uncontrollable holograms. The brooms were there *for him*. He felt certain of it all of a sudden.

Finn thanked the boy, who ran back to his mother's side.

Were the brooms part of Park Security? Were they going to bust him for being in the Park? Or were they something more sinister: *uncontrollable magic*?

The brooms swept their way across the street and drew closer.

He walked quickly away. He looked back: the brooms were definitely following.

Up ahead, he heard music from *High School Musical*. A huge crowd of onlookers formed a half moon around a street show of cheerleaders and basketball players dancing and singing.

Finn worked his way into the dense crowd, glad to

see the brooms stop at the back. But then the three split up. The one with the bucket went around the crowd in one direction; one stayed put; the other swept off in the opposite direction. He was surrounded. If they weren't Security, then they were something much worse.

The leader of the High School Musical street show called for volunteers to dance with them. A number of kids raised their hands. Finn followed one of the kids as the music started. He kept his back to the crowd and headed toward the movable stage.

The brooms all were trapped with the crowd.

Finn dodged his way through the cheerleaders and ducked behind the stage. He hurried through the plaza beneath the sorcerer's hat, running hard now. He arrived at The Great Movie Ride.

The brooms regrouped and moved through the crowd—but they didn't seem to be in any hurry.

Finn entered the ride. He was directed into one of the cars, joining a family of three on a long bench. He lowered his head to keep from being seen. But he looked up to steal a peek toward the entrance.

For some reason, the brooms hadn't followed him inside.

28

TWENTY MINUTES LATER, with no sign of the brooms, Finn joined the line for Voyage of the Little Mermaid. The ceiling was painted to look like water. His heart beat excitedly: he was "under the sea."

There was no telling what he might find. Big or small, ordinary or out of the ordinary, it could be anything.

He heard a commotion behind him—the people waiting for the doors to open were oohing and ahhing. Finn turned carefully around and spotted the three brooms. They danced and bowed and entertained as they progressively moved closer.

Finn nudged past several people. "Excuse me . . . I got cut off from my family . . . pardon me . . . I've lost my family and I think . . ." He never quite completed a sentence, thinking this made each excuse less of a lie.

People complained, but no one physically stopped him. He pushed to the very front of the line, putting a good distance between himself and the brooms. What did they want? he wondered. Would they possibly try to hurt him with all these people as witnesses?

The doors swung open. Finn hurried across a row in the middle of the large auditorium. If he kept going he'd have reached the seats closest to the exit doors, but he was afraid he might be more easily spotted there. So he took a seat near the middle.

The theater filled quickly. The brooms appeared at the end of the line. They spread out and moved along the wall to the back of the auditorium.

Before he had time to think, the lights dimmed and the theater went dark. Very dark. As an artificial rain began to fall, Finn took a chance and peeked over his shoulder. The brooms seemed to be watching the show along with the crowd. A wet mist blew from the stage, surprising the audience. A child cried out. Then there were laughs as the audience settled in for the show. The theme music rang out: "Under the Sea."

The song was the connection to Jez, and Finn searched the stage for possible clues as dozens of brightly colored sea creatures, glowing in the pitch black, began swimming across the stage to the music. Ariel arrived onstage, and the audience applauded.

Flashes of color drenched the auditorium. He stole a look to the back: only one broom.

He fought off a sense of panic. *There!* Midway down the auditorium, a broom on each side. To his relief, they still appeared focused on the show, not the audience. To play it safe, he lowered his head and pulled the brim of his cap down farther. How long until they spotted him? And then what?

The crowd laughed, but not Finn.

A cell phone rang in the audience. Several heads turned in his direction. His father's BlackBerry was ringing in his pocket. He'd forgotten all about it. He fumbled with it and shut it off, but by the time he had, it seemed as if half the theater were looking at him.

Including the two brooms on either side.

The music grew louder. The auditorium darkened once again.

Finn dropped to all fours and began crawling to his left toward the exit doors. Guests moved their legs to allow him past, creating a commotion. A storm erupted onstage. Finn reached the end of the aisle and hesitated. Light flooded the theater. People applauded.

Finn jumped up and made for the exit.

He ran straight for the broom and pushed it over.

Hitting the blinding sunlight, he took off at a full run, unwilling to look back to see if a crow was following, or a broom chasing him. It seemed to him he'd picked up nothing of value. A waste of time.

Or maybe not, he thought. Had the Overtakers been following him? Why had the brooms seemed more interested in the stage show than in finding him?

Maleficent's powers clearly extended throughout all of the Disney Parks—the existence of the brooms confirmed that much.

On his way back to Animal Kingdom, he sent a text warning to the others.

Four members checked in on DGamer: Philby, Maybeck, Charlene, and Amanada. All but Willa.

Finn tried several times to reach her, finally giving up and hoping her DS was somehow off-line.

But it didn't make sense. There was free Wi-Fi all over the Parks.

So why wasn't she answering?

29

WILLA TRIED TO USE HER ID to jump the line for Mickey's PhilharMagic, but to no use. So she joined a long line that moved in waves, as a group of three hundred guests was admitted into the auditorium.

With each surge in the line, she passed more posters—all with a funny play on words. The line moved ahead, and it wasn't long before she faced the one Maybeck had mentioned. It showed Ariel and Triton, as Maybeck had remembered. It was titled, "A Must Sea!"

A plaque on the bottom of the frame read: ARIEL BROUGHT PART OF HER WORLD INTO OUR WORLD. . . .

Willa knew this was somehow significant. She sat down to make a note of it, to copy it out exactly as it was written.

Some of the smaller kids were also waiting out the line by sitting on the floor.

Jez had brought a part of her world into *our* world, as well, Willa thought. She'd brought her dreams about the future. She had foreseen things happening in the world that had now taken place: the lightning striking the castle, for one. Finn was right. If they were to find Jez, her drawings were the answer! The poster seemed to confirm it.

Willa wrote the note and put it in her pocket. Then she leaned her head back—*just for a minute*, she told herself—and tried to think of what else the message might mean. The more she concentrated, the heavier her head became. Her eyes began to blink away the stinging fatigue.

She fell asleep.

The rest was a dream. She saw herself being helped to her feet by—of all things—two bears from the Country Bear Jamboree. The kids around her, bored with waiting, were thrilled to see the bears. As she was taken out of the line and through a Cast Member door, she felt her entire body tingle. Not a nice tingle, but like when a foot falls asleep—the same kind of tingle she'd experienced on the nights when, falling asleep, she'd crossed over as a DHI.

Where the bears were taking her she couldn't tell, but there were voices and the sound of an engine. A few minutes later came the sounds of car doors and more voices. A friendly voice welcoming people. She heard the Animal Kingdom mentioned. It wasn't long until she felt incredibly comfortable, and it was quiet again. Beautifully quiet. Wonderfully quiet.

Far, far in the distance she heard the calls of exotic animals—as if someone had Animal Planet playing on their television.

Wherever she was, it felt like she could sleep there forever.

30

PHILBY APPROACHED THE Disney Vacation kiosk in Camp Minnie-Mickey, a stone's throw from the Lion King pavilion. He clicked on Dream Vacations and typed in **yensidtlaw**. Presented with a Web page, he typed in the address: **www.dgamer.com/vmk**, as Finn had instructed. He next clicked on the logo and was asked for his username and password. A moment later, to his surprise, he arrived at VMK's Central Plaza, in control of an avatar. He navigated the avatar toward a bench at the center of the screen.

Wayne? he typed. But as Finn had warned, nothing appeared, only the question mark. He typed the name again. His speech bubble showed only his ID—**philitup**—and a question mark. Growing impatient, Philby walked his avatar around the plaza. A minute passed, feeling more like five. For a third time, he tried typing the name. *Nothing*.

As he circled back around to the benches, a speech bubble appeared above an avatar with unusually white hair. Philby couldn't remember having seen hair that color inside VMK before.

[ ]: were you looking for someone? appeared above the white head.

philitup: uncle walt's pen. finn sent me.

[ ]: follow me

As Finn had done before him, Philby followed Wayne on a long trip through the Web site to a private room Philby had never seen before. Wayne's avatar shut a door behind them.

[ ]: we can talk here. anything typed is encrypted.

philitup: okay.

[ ]: do you have a message from finn?

philitup: we need engineering blueprints for the AK. it looks like Jez may have messed with the sound system. if i can study the way it all works, maybe we can find her.

[ ]: messed with?

philitup: a song—Under the Sea—was played over the PA. not only does that song not belong in AK, but it played three times in a row, and amanda says it's the same singer jez has on her iPod, not the singer disney uses.

[ ]: i see.

philitup: finn thought you could help me get the plans. i thought about that maintenance place you showed us, but how can i get past the workers?

[ ]: you won't need to. besides, this time of day it's too risky. there's a better way. once we leave this room, we're no longer encrypted. i won't answer any questions out there, so i'll explain everything now. once we leave here, you're on your own, although i'll show you the way. i'll get you inside.

philitup: inside where?

[ ]: patience, my boy.

Wayne's avatar moved back to the door. He typed in a code that showed only as asterisks in his speech bubble. The door opened. The avatar stepped out into the hall, looked in both directions, and returned to the room, again shutting and code-locking the door.

[ ]: can never be too careful. it would appear we're all alone, which is good. VMK was not always a game. originally, the imagineers wanted to create a virtual control room for the various parks. essentially, they were lazy. they wanted a way to fix small mechanical problems, or study the schematics from remote locations—their homes, or while they were traveling. the more employees, the more sets

of plans were needed, and the paper plans were constantly changing and needing updating as systems were improved or modified. a guy named alex wright came up with the idea of putting it all online. they would encrypt access for security reasons, and each Imagineer or employee would have his or her own avatar—a mock human being with hands and feet that could not only study the schematics online but could carry out some minimal maintenance or switching procedures: open boxes, pull switches. the area they created was termed the virtual magic kingdom—vmk—and in their spare time they began to create games with each other. they built rooms and attractions in their virtual world. it was only much later it occurred to someone to allow the public inside. at that time, they sealed off what they call the mechanicals, hiding them behind encrypted firewalls. last year it became apparent the Overtakers were trying to compromise VMK. the site was closed to the public. i can get you access to the mechanicals if that's what you want?

philitup: does that include the music system?

[ ]: i would imagine. follow me. and don't write anything until I tell you to do so. it is not beyond consideration that the overtakers are monitoring

vmk. they should never be underestimated. they are devious and powerful, and it's apparent they will stop at nothing to control the kingdoms. we must be vigilant.

Philby didn't type anything. He guided his avatar toward the door and waited as instructed.

Wayne approached. Asterisks appeared in his speech bubble. The door swung open.

Philby's avatar followed the white-headed figure out into the hallway. Wayne knew his way around VMK, taking Philby to places he'd rarely visited. They entered a private room that didn't look particularly interesting. Philby realized this was a trick: the less interesting it looked, the less interested anyone would be in spending time in there. Wayne coded the door shut and then approached the far wall. Again, asterisks filled his speech bubble. A door swung open, and the landscape changed considerably. The walls and floors were silver and black. Dark blue signs with white lettering acted as trail guides: MK ⟶ AK ⟵ Epcot ↑ Hollywood ↑

They turned left, following the signs to the Animal Kingdom.

Access through the door marked AK CONTROL required yet another code from Wayne. The door opened, revealing a room with a flow chart projected on a large wall. It reminded Philby of a war room, like he'd seen in movies.

The flow chart showed: MECHANICALS, SECURITY, STRUCTURES, ATTRACTIONS, GATES/ACCESS, BACKSTAGE. Under some of these were smaller titles like ASIA, AFRICA, CAMP MM, DINO L. It looked like a giant outline or family tree, with branches connecting a main title to its smaller subtitles.

Wayne's avatar climbed into a cage on the end of a long mechanical arm. It reminded Philby of the cherry pickers road crews used to trim trees or repair phone poles. Wayne pulled the door to the cage shut, and Philby watched as he pushed levers and the cage rose to pass in front of the titles on the flow chart.

He maneuvered them to stop at MECHANICALS. Wayne reached out and pushed against the screen. Immediately, the projection on the wall changed. Now MECHANICALS was listed at the top, and there were dozens of subcategories, including—Philby noticed— PUBLIC ADDRESS SYSTEM.

Wayne reached out and tapped the title.

The lettering folded back, opening an entrance like a window in the wall. Wayne opened the cage door and led them *through* this new opening in the wall and into a massively complex room. Philby gasped. He heard his own voice and only then was reminded of where he was: standing in a small hut, in Camp Minnie-Mickey. For the past few minutes he had almost become his avatar. He'd been transported. He hadn't remembered where he was. Now, glancing behind him, he looked out through the open doorway into Camp Minnie-Mickey and reminded himself to remain alert; the Overtakers were not to be underestimated.

He then looked to the screen; Wayne was waiting for him.

[ ]: we're safe now.

Philby moved his avatar forward. He faced a large sound-mixer projected on the floor in front of him. He studied it, realizing this was a photographic image, probably of the actual soundboard somewhere in the Animal Kingdom's control room. And, like the real thing, the virtual soundboard would not only allow him to change volume or inputs throughout the Park, it also displayed cables to switching stations and the hundreds of speakers placed throughout the Animal Kingdom. With a click of a button, he could then overlay either a satellite image or a map of the Park, making it easy to identify the exact location of the various sound-system elements. Wayne was right: it offered an easy method for troubleshooting problems or identifying problem spots without being in the Park.

Slowly, he got the hang of the technology.

philitup: whoa . . .

[ ]: no one ever accused the imagineers of being stupid.

philitup: this is incredible. i can follow any wire any-where.

[ ]: and perform tests on it. i should think that was the purpose after all: long-distance testing and repair.

philitup: how much time do i have?

[ ]: no one will bother us here. take as long as you like. since i've gone into hiding, i have nothing but time.

Philby's main interest was the separation of the Park's background music, divided into the five sound areas. Each area had its own output, volume, and tone controls. He located the output wires on the back of the mixer—virtual speaker wires leading out into the Park.

philitup: what are the chances the Overtakers have jez locked up in the sound control room? she could input her iPod into this mixer pretty easily.

[ ]: i would doubt that. but i can go check if you like.

philitup: check. how?

[ ]: all the security cameras are on the screen out there. where we just were: the main screen. i can go into the security control room and view any camera in the park.

Philby had an idea. He wondered . . .

philitup: some of those cameras connect to the Conservation Station. the TVs that visitors can control.

[ ]: the AnimalCams. yes.

philitup: could i reroute *all* the security cameras to one of the AnimalCams?

[ ]: if you know what you're doing, i suspect you could.

philitup: I do all the cable TV stuff at our house. i can probably figure it out.

[ ]: let's finish up here, and i'll take you over there.

Philby spent several minutes following the speaker cables, quickly determining that from where he and the others had heard "Under the Sea" playing over the system, they'd actually been part of the Asia speaker system. He rechecked the soundboard, looking to see if he could explain Jez's iPod having played over the system. There were so many knobs and dials he didn't know exactly what he was looking at. He'd used GarageBand on his own computer, but this was far more complex.

philitup: she's either being kept in the control room or somewhere in asia.

[ ]: asia is big.

philitup: tell me about it. i'm done here. can you show me the security room?

He felt excited as Wayne led him back out to the caged lift. Wayne directed the cage to the SECURITY title, selected the menu, and then navigated to the camera control room. Soon Philby's avatar had again passed through a window in the wall and was standing in front of an enormous second wall of TV screens. There had to be hundreds of them. There was a control board here as well. It only took him a few minutes to connect a master cable from the video control board to one of the AnimalCam console inputs. This fed all the security cameras into a single AnimalCam console in the Conservation Station.

Philby wrote to Amanda on DGamer, double-checking his work. Amanda located the console and took it over. Thrilled, she wrote back how she now had control of hundreds of cameras. She could view most of the Park now: inside all the attractions, outside walkways, parking lots.

panda: this is incredible, philby. thank u.

She waited for Philby to write back. But no message was returned.

Philby never had a chance to answer her. Once

again he'd lost track of himself—so engrossed in the virtual worlds of VMK and D-Gamer that he'd forgotten to keep an eye on his surroundings.

But near the end of their discussion, he had finally looked around.

And found himself face-to-face with a very angry tiger.

31

Of COURSE, AT FIRST PHILBY couldn't believe it.

A tiger.

He'd never realized how big they were: the tiger stood as high as Philby's shoulder. Orange, black, and white stripes, like war paint. Its eyes were hypnotic; he couldn't pry his own away from them. They stared at him like he was . . . *lunch.*

The tiger blocked the door to the small hut. There was no getting past it, even if Philby's legs had worked, and at that moment he had no sensation in his legs whatsoever. He felt nothing but tremendous fear charging his system. It took him over completely. Owned him.

A tiger loose in the Animal Kingdom! Where were the sirens? Where were the animal police?

He opened his mouth to scream, but his throat proved too dry, and he croaked out a pathetic noise that didn't even sound close to the "Help!" he'd intended.

The tiger cocked his head, looking at him from an angle. Sizing him up. Preparing to attack, it crouched slowly and silently. As gracefully as a dancer, it squatted onto its haunches, its leg muscles flexing as if there were steel cables beneath the colorful hide.

Philby couldn't take it anymore. He squinted his eyes shut and braced himself for the attack.

When nothing happened, he slowly edged his left eye open slightly, stealing a look.

At that exact moment, the tiger jumped.

Philby's world went dark.

He felt nothing.

32

FINN ARRIVED TO THE RENDEZVOUS at the specified time. There was a tall guy in a Disney cap and green coveralls hanging out by the gate to backstage, and it took Finn a moment to realize it was Maybeck. With his face in the shadow of the cap, he looked about twenty years old. The two boys met up and stood to the side, near the jungle, amazed at the numbers of visitors that now jammed the Park.

Speaking under his breath, Finn explained his encounter with the brooms.

"Maybe the brooms mean the Overtakers are trying to clean things up," Maybeck said, amused by his own joke. Finn didn't dignify that with a response. "The DeVine Charlene is over by the bat enclosure," Maybeck continued. "I walked around trying to find stuff from the diary. Ended up back at the Gibbons Temple, and I gotta tell you, Whitman"—Maybeck always called Finn by his last name—"there was some serious action over there. Bunch of the rangers all making a stink. From what I overhead, some orangutans pulled a fast one. One of the apes supposedly stole a key, hid it in his upper lip, and then pulled off a jail break. Some kind of smarts, these apes. Six of them are missing. There's some serious stuff going down, no doubt about it. And far as I can tell, we're the only ones who have a clue, and not much of a clue at that."

Finn checked his watch. "Where's Philby? And Willa? Philby's never late to anything."

"Haven't seen either of them. Amanda's hanging at the Conservation Station," Maybeck said. "Philby hooked up a bunch of other cameras somehow. So now she can see basically everything going on: the attractions, the paths, and all the buildings, inside and out. But she's stuck out there. She can't leave her AnimalCam console because she doesn't want anyone to discover what Philby rigged up for her. What about you?"

"The thing about the brooms—" Finn said, starting to explain the way he'd felt. But then he cut himself off.

"Yeah?"

"Doesn't make any sense."

"As if *any* of this makes sense! Hello? Try me, Whitman."

"Okay. So pretty soon after I arrived at Hollywood Studios, I thought this crow had spotted me. Then the brooms show up. You know? But they didn't exactly come after me. They just kind of *followed* me there. At Voyage of the Little Mermaid it was almost like they were there to watch the show. The way I was."

"I don't get it," Maybeck said.

"You see?" Finn said. "When the BlackBerry rang they saw me. *Everybody* saw me. But I think the brooms were *surprised* to see me there. Or maybe they didn't care."

"I still don't get it," Maybeck admitted, though somewhat reluctantly. Maybeck prided himself on knowing things before others.

Finn blurted out what he'd been thinking ever since the encounter. "Maybe the brooms were at Voyage for the same reason I was: to look for answers. My being there both confirmed they were in the right place and threatened them."

"Threatened them how?"

"What if the crow was some kind of spy?"

"Like the bat," Maybeck said.

"Yeah! Exactly! And what if the brooms were sent to follow me? So they did. Until The Great Movie Ride. They didn't follow me into there. Why?"

"I hope you're going to answer that."

"Because by my going in there, they were no longer worried about me. And then when I got to Voyage, they weren't even looking for me. It was the show that they were interested in."

"The show," Maybeck said. "Listen, I'm not getting this. What's up?"

Finn gathered his courage. "I think the Overtakers heard 'Under the Sea,' same as we did."

"Meaning?"

"Think about it," Finn said.

He watched as the mental tumblers clicked into place and unlocked Maybeck's thought. Maybeck spoke slowly. "They're following the music clue the same way we are . . . because . . . they're . . . looking for Jez."

"She escaped," Finn declared. "They had her in the stump on the savannah. We know that much. Maybe in transferring her, maybe sometime before they ever moved her, she managed to escape. She hid someplace here in AK. And for some reason yet to be determined, she used the music as a clue."

"She's stuck in the Park," Maybeck said, "and she can't get out without our help. So she played the music to send us a clue."

"We heard it," Finn said, "but so did the Overtakers. We both started looking at anything and everything that had to do with 'Under the Sea.'"

"It makes sense," Maybeck agreed.

Finn tried the DGamer chat room again, sending a shout-out to Willa and Philby. But the screen didn't change. They weren't answering.

"So what do we do now?" he asked.

"We can't wait for them any longer. Maybe the dreams in Jez's journal are supposed to help us find her."

"We need Willa and Philby," Maybeck said. "There are a lot of drawings to make sense of."

Finn said what they both were thinking. "What if something's happened to them?"

The two boys met eyes with horrified expressions.

33

AMANDA PRESSED THE right-hand button on the camera controls, zooming in to get a closer look at Finn and Maybeck.

The AnimalCam stations—four in all—were enough like a video game that she had immediately gotten the hang of it: a small screen to her right displayed rows and columns of thumbnail images, each representing a different camera mounted somewhere in the Park. Normally, there were about a dozen vantage points offered, all of them devoted to the wildlife on display in the Park: giraffes, elephants, tigers. Philby had upgraded hers. Scrolling down the thumbnail screen, she had dozens of views available to her—maybe a hundred or more. Selecting a particular camera transferred the view to a much larger television screen mounted at eye level. She could then zoom in and out using the two buttons to the right, or maneuver the camera to look left or right, up or down, using a joystick. It provided her with a virtual tour of every aspect of the Animal Kingdom.

At the moment, she was watching Finn and

Maybeck as she was writing to Finn on D-Gamer.

> panda: have not seen either willa or philby on camera

> Finn: can u c the cast member entrances?

> panda: yes. but have not seen them. park is packed. could be here.

> Finn: i think the otakers may have heard the change in music same as us. U watch home base for Phily and Wila. also keep eye on us. watch our backs.

> panda: can do.

Finn hesitated before writing the next message. But he felt he had to tell her.

> Finn: maybeck and i think there's a chance jez escaped. it might explain some stuff that's been happening. if so, she's prob hiding in park.

For a long time the screen flickered, but no message appeared. He couldn't imagine what Amanda must have been feeling.

Finn: we could be totally wrong. maybeck and i are going 2 track down each of the diary drawings. maybe her escape was part of her dreams. ????? r u ok?

panda: scared 4 jez

Finn: my dad's crackberry does the internet. i will go onto vmk and try 2 find wayne. maybe he can help us find philby.

panda: i'll watch 4 them and i'll watch u and maybeck too . . .

The cursor hesitated. She wasn't done typing.

. . . but if she escaped, why haven't we heard from her?

Finn didn't have an answer for that.

Finn: ????? don't know.

Amanda zoomed the camera back and tried to stay with Finn and Maybeck as they headed off. It took her a minute to figure out how to follow them, one camera to the next—she lost them twice—but not long after, she pulled up their images as they moved from camera to camera. She pieced together the route they were taking to Discovery Island. At the same time, she studied the tiny thumbnail views, hoping beyond hope to catch a glimpse of her missing sister.

* * *

Finn and Maybeck walked the Jungle Trek in a hurry, though not so fast as to stick out. They kept about ten yards apart; if one of them was spotted, maybe the other wouldn't be. The Trek had an occasional park ranger at an education station—there to give hands-on demonstrations to the curious—any one of whom might be an Overtaker. Finn paid particular attention to each of these rangers as Maybeck passed, glad to see that none seemed to take any particular interest in him.

Soon, they reached the tiger-viewing yards, where they stood among the ruins of an Indian temple—the jungle and buildings so authentic that, although he'd never been there, Finn could imagine himself halfway around the world. The footpath rose here to where it was fifteen or twenty feet off the ground, the walls of the crumbling temple holding in the Park guests, offering views to either side, down into grassy knolls and fields. In the heat of the day, the tigers had taken to the shade at the edge of the wall that contained them. People crowded the temple's viewing windows to get a decent look at the wild cats. The arching windows held no glass but were divided into small squares as if they did, or once had. And while there was no pushing or shoving to win the best view, there was some seriously competitive leaning going on.

But before Finn ever reached the clot of guests at the windows, Maybeck stopped and pulled him aside.

"Check it out!"

Just Maybeck's tone of voice told Finn it was something important. Typically, Maybeck was much too cool to get excited about anything. "Son of a _____." Maybeck said a word that would have once again gotten Finn grounded for a week.

"Oh . . . man," he said, while Maybeck was busy unfolding his copy of the page from Jez's diary.

The temple's stone wall held a series of stone carvings, four feet by four feet pictographs showing different scenes. The primitive carvings were beautiful. One showed a person with his or her arms in the air, and an eagle flying overhead. Another had a fruit tree at its center, with birds in the branches and deer surrounding it. A monkey sat at the base of the tree holding a piece of the fruit. There were two others, both depicting a weird-looking guy with a mustache dancing around and doing strange things. But it was the image of the monkey that captured and held Finn's attention.

Maybeck pointed to the monkey. "That's the monkey she drew," he said. "It wasn't a live monkey, it was this one."

"Agreed."

> panda: finn, check out the diary page.

He quickly texted back to her.

> Finn: the monkey? can u c what we c?

> panda: check out the window. my angle matches the diary exactly.

"The windows," Finn told Maybeck, pointing to the knot of visitors straining for a look. He then found the incredibly similar drawing on the photocopy of the diary and pointed this out to Maybeck as well.

He and Maybeck moved toward the crowd.

"I gotta tell you," Maybeck said, "until now, I wasn't buying that Jez could dream the future."

"And now?" Finn asked.

"Yeah, well. A person's got a right to be wrong."

34

FINN AND MAYBECK steadily pushed to the front of the throng gathered at the windows overlooking the tiger yards, where a blanket of green grass was interrupted by some trees and rocks. A huge tigress slumbered in the thick shade of a bamboo stand, her back against the tall rock wall that contained her. Jez had sketched both this window and the sculpture reliefs they'd just been studying, meaning this location had played a significant role in her dreams.

But what role? Finn wondered.

"It could be she's hiding in the tiger yards," Finn said quietly to Maybeck.

"You see her out there, do you?" Maybeck asked.

"No. But—"

"That's because she isn't there."

"But it makes sense. She wouldn't exactly be able to move if she was stuck in there. Not with tigers roaming the place."

"Whitman, look around."

Finn moved to the opposite side of the walled bridge dividing the two tiger yards. He didn't have to challenge any crowds, because there weren't any. There weren't any tigers seen from this side.

"Convinced?" Maybeck said from behind him. He, too, had switched sides.

"But why would she have drawn both the window and the monkey? Can you explain that?" Finn asked anxiously. "They have to mean something."

"She drew a lot of stuff: a dinosaur, the monkey, the window, a bat, some old dude. How are we supposed to know what it all means?"

"That's just the point," Finn said. "We *are* supposed to know what it means. We're supposed to figure it out. We're supposed to help her."

"Maybe it's about the animals, not the locations," Maybeck suggested. "Something to do with monkeys, tigers, and dinosaurs. What do they have in common?"

"Nothing," Finn said, "except that they're all part of the AK."

"The server!" Maybeck said excitedly. "The second server. Didn't Wayne tell you the plan was to—"

"Make animals into DHIs!" Finn shouted a little too loudly. "You're right." He pulled out the page of Jez's diary and studied it again. "What if these animals are the ones they're turning into DHIs? Jez saw them in her dreams. They meant something to her, something important."

Maybeck wrote to Amanda on the DS.

mybest: amanda. how many tigers u c?

panda: 3

mybest: finn and me think some animals may B DHIs.

Finn joined the DGamer chat room.

Finn: otakers might use dhis 2 fake us out.

mybest: maleficent cannot be trusted. she could have made a dhi of herself 2 use as decoy or something. no way 2 know.

panda: she wants control of the parks. it makes more sense she would use the dhis 2 scare the guests, or 2 put us into sbs. she doesn't want us around. that's 4 sure.

Finn: and with jez being able to see the future, she's a real threat. what if she knows what Maleficent has planned?

panda: that would explain why maleficent wants 2 control her.

Finn: the diary drawings of animals may be 2 warn us 2 watch out for this or something.

panda: no. it's more than that. her dreams involve her. have u ever had a dream that you're not in? never! the diary is about her dreams, her life.

The screen flickered. She wasn't through typing.

panda: . . . there's a truck being unloaded behind the bat enclosure. 2 cages . . . both wrapped with tarps.

mybest: doesn't mean anything.

panda: listen to me! the truck driver has a monkey on his arm. a live monkey. the park would never allow a monkey to be running around loose. these cast members are fakes.

mybest: how big r the cages?

panda: big! big enough for a large dog or . . . a wild cat or . . .

Maybeck interrupted by typing quickly:

mybest: philby and willa!

Finn: amanda, watch every camera in that area. we're on our way!

35

FINN AND MAYBECK made their way toward the bat enclosure, just down from the tiger yard along the winding, dark trail of the Maharajah Jungle Trek. Bugs buzzed past their heads as the heat enveloped them, making their chests tight and their breath short. Birds cried out and fluttered past, winning Maybeck's unflinching attention as he recalled his earlier horrifying experience. His DS beeped and he checked for the message.

> panda: the backstage camera @ the bat enclosure just stopped working.

"That cannot be a coincidence," Maybeck whispered to Finn. "That camera was sabotaged. Something's going on back there, and we need to know what it is."

> angelface13: hey, guys. right behind u.

Finn spun around, looking for her.

Finn glanced in that direction.

Finn saw her first: a paler green shape amid the dark green of the undergrowth. She was on the stilts and ten feet into the jungle, all but invisible thanks to the twisting vine of leaves that disguised her. It was only when she made a slight motion that he was able to spot her. The boys moved closer to the jungle so they could talk to Charlene in a whisper.

"I've been keeping an eye on the enclosure as Maybeck asked," she said. "There's been a lot of activity, a lot of coming and going through those doors at the rear. The workers have paid particular attention to that big bat near the red flag on the far left. Twice they've carried him through to the back and then returned him out front. I don't know if that's the one that was in the pillowcase, but . . . it might be."

Finn and Maybeck weren't where they could see well into the enclosure. Maybeck walked steadily closer to the viewing station, leaving Finn behind. He positioned himself with a decent view of the enclosure, then turned toward Finn, and both shrugged and nodded, as if to say: *It's certainly big enough to be the same one.*

Finn said, "We need to get back there and find out what's in those cages."

"No way!" Maybeck protested.

Charlene asked, "Still no sign of Willa and Philby?"

"No," Finn answered with a heavy heart.

"I think I have an idea," Charlene said. "A way to find out what's going on back there."

Finn, surprised by Charlene's offer, turned toward the jungle to face her—though because of the way she blended in, he found it difficult to see her. Maybeck's attention remained fully focused on the enclosure. He and Charlene were opposites: Maybeck tended to react too quickly to situations and liked to work as a loner; Charlene rarely contributed in discussions, and when she did participate, enjoyed working as part of a team.

"What are you thinking?" Finn asked.

"I'm going to need a diversion," Charlene whispered. "Something big. Something everyone will watch. And by everyone, I mean every last bird and caterpillar, and especially the people and *bats*."

36

INGENIOUS, ΤINN THOUGHT as he moved through the swinging doors and into the forward viewing booth. There were three levels of viewing offered at the bat enclosure, three open-air rooms constructed of dark wood that led the Park guest closer to the risk of contact with the flying rodents. The first viewing room offered glass windows; the middle room, screens; and the final room—more of a long booth—nothing but well-spaced vertical wooden bars to keep the large bats at bay. The bars were clearly wide enough for Finn to poke his head through, yet too narrow for the extended wings of the large African bats.

Finn kept his cap pulled down snugly, hoping to avoid being recognized; that was the kind of distraction he could do without. The viewing room was staffed by a college-age girl in a ranger's uniform. Presently, she was answering the questions of two young boys who had too much energy for such a small space. Their mother seemed unwilling to contain them, which served Finn's purpose well. He slipped the case off his father's BlackBerry and stepped close to the open-air viewing windows, hoisting the phone to take a picture. He pressed up to the bars, a warm breeze striking him, and caught a fleeting and exasperated glance from the ranger, who was finding her patience taxed by the two boys.

Finn purposely fumbled with the phone and case, allowing the case to slip out of his hands and fall through the bars, down into the enclosure. He pocketed the phone.

"My case!" he shouted. He jumped up onto the sill and began to squeeze himself through the bars.

Finn was relatively slight of build. He actually got partway through the bars before the ranger's strong hand grasped him by the upper arm.

"GET OUT OF THERE!!" the girl screamed at the top of her lungs, pulling on him. "YOU CAN'T GO IN THERE!!! ARE YOU OUT OF YOUR MIND?"

The effect was exactly what Charlene had hoped for: every human eye was drawn to Finn; some of the bats were spooked by the ranger's admonishments. For a few precious seconds, the ranger pulled and Finn resisted.

"My case!" he hollered.

"GET DOWN FROM THERE!"

Finn stole one quick glance. Maybeck helped Charlene, on stilts, through the jungle door and into the enclosure. Charlene's ivy-clad costume pushed up against the rocks at the far end of the enclosure, and within seconds a miracle occurred: she disappeared. DeVine's costume fit into the environment so well that her form appeared as ivy growing up the rocks. There was no mistaking this whatsoever for a girl on stilts. The change was extraordinary.

Finn, apologizing and complaining at the same time, allowed himself to be drawn back into the viewing room, actually grateful for the ranger's efforts, since the swirling bats swooped and dove too close for comfort. The ranger scolded him briefly, then promised to have his lost case retrieved. She tried to contact someone over her headset, but clearly there was no answer. She double-checked both the headset and the radio it was plugged into, obviously annoyed by the lack of response.

She blushed, apologized, and asked Finn to stick around. "I don't know why I'm not getting anyone back there," she said.

I do, Finn thought to himself. *The people behind that door are not the people you normally work with. If they're even people at all . . .*

Once again, his eyes strayed to the far side of the enclosure, where he saw that the ivy patch on the rocks had migrated a few feet farther along, a yard or two closer to the enclosure's center doors. Charlene was moving so incredibly slowly, so expertly, that it was impossible to detect her movements. The ivy seemed to be growing and extending all on its own, blending in perfectly with the ivy already there.

37

With her back to a false rock wall, Charlene watched Finn being grabbed by the ranger in the viewing booth. The girl stopped him from jumping into the enclosure, and then the two had words. Charlene thought that Finn seemed to be looking right at her a couple of times, and she wondered how good a job she was doing at blending in.

With her face painted camouflage green, white, and brown, only the whites of her eyes threatened to give her away; so Charlene tried to keep her eyes averted. But it wasn't easy. Jangled by raw nerves, she inched her way along the wall, trying not to look at the bats. She hated bats, and the ones in the enclosure were the size of bowling pins: big, gray, winged rats, hanging upside down from clotheslines. As long as they kept their distance, she thought she could make it.

The only people who might spot her were those in the viewing station: the Park visitors and the ranger. When she did look up, it was toward the booth. She didn't know if Amanda had a camera aimed at her, and she'd lost sight of Maybeck, who was somewhere off to her right near the jungle door. She was on her own: fenced in with several dozen giant bats, in a place that smelled . . . well, funky . . . trying to slow dance her way clear around the curve of the smooth, irregular rock wall to the center doors.

She inched a stilt to her left, stepped the other along, and then froze, allowing her vines to blend in with those growing on the rocks. Then, a minute or two later, she moved again. She and the vines crept ahead, no one the wiser.

Finn left the booth, and Maybeck appeared out on the path with him. They both glanced once in her direction. She saw Finn lift his DS, signaling for her that a text was coming.

> Finn: can't c u at all, charlie. great job. we're here if u need us.

The two boys walked off.

It was the first time Finn, or anyone else for that matter, had ever called her Charlie, and she actually liked the nickname. There was something pleasing about it, something incredibly personal that made her feel especially good about it. She hoped it might stick, providing she got out of here alive.

The left stilt caught on a rock as she moved, and

the rock shot out from under it like a wet bar of soap, raising a puff of dust. This, in turn, startled the bats, already edgy from Finn's distraction. Three of the ugly things flew straight for her, coming toward her face at incredible speed, flying close enough that she could see not only the black glass, buttonlike, beady eyes, but the tiny gray hairs that surrounded their ratty faces, and the eerie translucence of their wings. Her stomach knotted, her head swooned, and a scream bubbled up from her lungs. She kept silent only by snapping her lips shut and clenching her teeth. The last of the three brushed against her hair, dislodging a carefully placed plastic vine and causing a strand to fall into her eyes—undoing her disguise. If anyone looked directly at her now, they were sure to see a length of blond hair inexplicably sticking out from the ivy—and that couldn't be good. She blew the hair out of her eyes with upturned lips and moved more quickly now, slipping her way around the curving rock wall and nearing the green doors at its center.

She was partially hidden by several trees as she neared the two doors, suddenly realizing that on stilts she was much too tall to fit through without Maybeck's help. Being near the middle of the enclosure, she was also now the center of attention. Without her knowing it, the Park guests were looking directly at her.

She wasn't going to get through those doors, and she'd come too far to turn back. She looked up: the rock wall rose high above her head, but though it was uneven and craggy, there were plenty of handholds visible. Charlene climbed the rock wall at her gym—she considered herself something of an expert.

The trick was getting her feet out of the stilts without being seen and then leaving the stilts propped against the rock so that she could return to them and effect her escape. She eased down into a squat—not an easy balancing act on stilts—and managed to release her left foot. She freed her right foot, too, and then carefully stepped out of both stilts to leave them resting against the fake rock wall. Some of the ivy strands that wrapped around the stilts continued higher and merged into those that surrounded her leotard. She managed to disconnect the tendrils one by one; far more were sewn to the leotard and remained part of her costume. These also helped disguise her as, by handhold and foothold, Charlene climbed higher up the rock face. With each small ascent she paused for what felt like a very long time, allowing her vines to combine with rock and make it more difficult to spot her. She was helped out by the trees and vegetation between her and the viewing booth. But soon she rose above the crown of the nearest tree, clinging to the odd texture of the fake rock and staying close to the line of real ivy to help camouflage her.

Then, any possible route disappeared above her. She was used to having to plot her way up a rock wall, so she paused and looked for a possible route. The only small handholds she saw moved away from the patch of real ivy. But she had no choice. As she started off in that direction, she realized she was heading directly above the double doors at the center of the enclosure. She was also exposing herself to being seen by Park guests, as she was now directly in front of the viewing booths. Because of this, she tried to move incredibly slowly. But the slow climbing taxed her strength and weakened her.

She couldn't "creep" between handholds and footholds, so she watched the viewing booths, waited for the attention of the guests to stray to one side or the other, and then made her move.

The doors swung open beneath her, and a worker stepped through.

Only then did she realize that some of the sandy texture was shredding off the wall where her running shoes touched. Painted sand rained down toward the ground, falling right on the head of the man who'd come through the doors. If he looked up, he would see her.

Counting on his entrance to have distracted both the guests and the ranger, Charlene no longer took her time. She gathered her strength, reached out, and moved with accuracy—three handholds, two footholds. She climbed quickly and deliberately, clawing her way up to the very top of the rocks, where, enclosed by the aviary's netting, she spread herself flat.

The dust sprinkled into the hair of the man below. He turned to look up. But he saw only a wall—an empty wall. He brushed the sand out of his hair and cursed the people who'd built the enclosure. The darned thing was clearly falling apart.

38

CHARLENE SCOOTED TO the far edge of the top of the wall and peered over the lip. She had a good view through the netting of the backstage area. The enclosure's wooden doors opened onto a small, courtyardlike area between the fake rock wall and a large garage with a flat roof. The steel wall facing her had been painted as a backdrop to look like rocks and vines.

She could hear a good deal of activity to her left but couldn't see what was going on. She spotted a camera mounted a few feet directly below her and aimed backstage; she assumed this was the camera that Amanda had mentioned, the one out of commission, an easy assumption, given that the wire running from it was currently unplugged.

She reached under the edge of the netting, almost touching the camera, her fingers grasping for the dangling wire. If she could only reconnect it, Amanda could take over the surveillance. It was no use—she was too far above it, and to move any lower would risk her being discovered. But Charlene was not one to be discouraged. She squirmed her upper body slightly farther off the ledge and stretched out, her fingers now only an inch or two from the wire.

She lunged and grabbed hold of it, the wire firmly in her hand.

The worker who had entered the enclosure only a minute earlier, the man whose hair she had dusted with sand, now came back through the twin doors and shut them. There was no time for Charlene to retreat. Instead, she hung over the wall ledge directly above him, her left hand holding the wire, her right keeping herself from falling.

The man stopped and put down a white bucket.

"Well done."

Charlene heard the voice—a woman's sterile voice, uncaring and even rude, if uttering two small words could be made to sound rude.

"Tie him up," the same voice said.

Immediately three big monkeys appeared from around a corner. Fast as lightning, they swarmed the worker. One tied and knotted a length of rope around the man's wrists, holding them behind his back. Another secured his ankles. Within seconds, the man was bound. The third monkey leaped at the man and knocked him over. The man fell, and the two monkeys immediately dragged him across the black-top and propped him up against a metal box, while the third tied a gag around his open mouth.

Only then did Charlene detect movement to her left, from where the voice had been heard: a flash of purple fabric and green skin.

Maleficent.

Charlene didn't actually see her, but she didn't have to. Purple and green were like Maleficent's team colors. Who else could it be?

With the monkeys' attention on the hostage, Charlene reconnected the camera and wire. The camera immediately sprang to life, tracking left. Charlene quickly retreated back to the top of the wall, flattening herself. She had a choice now: she could leave this to Amanda and the camera or . . .

She spun around and crawled in the direction of the noises. She had to see for herself. Something prompted her to glance back toward the viewing booth. From this height she could see out to several sections of the Jungle Trek path. It surprised her how much she could see— including Maybeck and Finn, who, standing to the side of the path, were shaking their heads furiously at her.

And then she understood: if she could see so much, then Park guests on the trail—like Maybeck and Finn—could see her as well. But rather than go back, she continued crawling, her curiosity ignited by the flash of green and purple, by the eerie sound of the woman's voice, and by a trio of large monkeys who had acted on orders. She crawled past a narrow wall that acted like a buttress, supporting the fake rock wall. It also screened the source of the noises, and by leaving it behind, she now saw through the netting what all the commotion was about.

Four hairy orangutans were directing smaller monkeys while Maleficent stood in the shade watching. The monkeys were unloading bags of ice from a large rectangular truck. They were stacking the bags into a heap, and the ice was melting in the sunshine and leaking out into a large puddle that disappeared beneath the truck. The whole operation looked so human—bosses and workers. And yet these weren't humans at all.

Then she saw the two cages. *Big*, as Amanda had described. They sat on the pavement, pushed up next to the steel barn. Both were wrapped in canvas tarps, but the canvas was not secured well along the bottom, allowing Charlene to see a slice of forest green fabric inside the cage: a ranger's uniform.

Willa!

She couldn't see anything inside the second cage, but she didn't need to: *Philby*. She had no doubts.

"Faster," Maleficent ordered. "We need more room. Bigger! If he's to fit, it must be bigger!"

Were they taking Philby somewhere? Smuggling him out of the Park in an ice truck? Or was she talking about some other hostage?

She tried to make sense of it all: the monkeys clearly obeying Maleficent's orders as if they understood her, the cages containing her friends, the melting pile of ice bags, the urgency in Maleficent's voice.

She knew what had to be done: she had to untie the worker and set him free. But did she dare climb down and attempt that? Wasn't it wrong not to? And if she messed up, if she got caught, would she end up like Willa and Philby? Where would that leave Maybeck and Finn, except further isolated?

Backing up slowly now, she decided this needed a team effort. She was no match for the power of Maleficent, who had once, with nothing but a wave of her hands and a mumbled incantation, created an electronic fence to surround Charlene's friends.

The climb back down the wall proved more difficult than her ascent. She had just strapped her feet back into the stilts when she heard: "Look, Mommy! What's *that?*"

The "that" was her, of course—the boy was pointing at her.

She stood absolutely still.

It felt like five minutes passed; it was more like thirty seconds.

"What? Where? The big one hanging from the rope?" the mother asked.

"Not the bats! The thingy. The creature. The vine thingy."

But no one saw her. Charlene had blended into the foliage around her. A few minutes later the unwilling boy was led away, still protesting that he could see the vine lady, and why couldn't anyone else see her?

It took Charlene fifteen minutes to work her way around the rock wall, and a second distraction—this time executed by Maybeck—to leave the enclosure.

A moment later, Finn and Maybeck joined her.

"So?" Finn asked. "Did you see anything?"

"We've got problems," Charlene answered. "Big . . . big problems."

39

FINN IMMEDIATELY UNDERSTOOD what Charlene and Maybeck did not: it wasn't Philby and Willa in the cages. Not exactly.

He took off down the jungle path, forcing Maybeck to hurry to keep up with him. Charlene had been asked to blend into the jungle and keep a strict eye on the bat enclosure. He used the DS to tell Amanda the same thing. Now that Charlene had repaired the sabotaged camera, Amanda had more opportunity to monitor events backstage.

Though winded, Maybeck kept up. "What's going on, Whitman?"

"You, of all people, should know," Finn said.

"Me? Why?"

"Space Mountain."

Maybeck said, "What about it?"

Finn stopped and pulled Maybeck to the side of the path, out of earshot of the other guests who passed in a steady stream. He spoke in a hush. "When they trapped you in perma-sleep, they put your DHI in—?"

"A maintenance *cage!*" Maybeck answered. "It

wasn't Willa and Philby Charlene saw. It was their DHIs."

"Exactly," Finn agreed. "Even someone as warped as Maleficent wouldn't put a kid in a cage that small. But a DHI is another story."

"But if the DHIs are in those cages," Maybeck said, "then why don't they just walk out?"

"Why didn't you just walk out of the maintenance cage in Space Mountain?"

"I don't know," he said. "It was like I was half asleep or something. Until you showed up, it hadn't occurred to me."

"Because we had crossed over, and you had not. With your body in perma-sleep I have a feeling your DHI is kind of in this suspended state. It doesn't know what's up. Remember, Wayne programmed the server that controlled our DHIs. Maleficent is running the second server. Who knows how their DHIs are programmed?"

"So we need to cross them back over," Maybeck said. "That's the only way to get them out of the control of the second server."

"Exactly!"

"But why would the Overtakers do this?" Maybeck wondered aloud. "Why trap them in perma-sleep in the first place?"

"There's only one guy I know who can answer that. And he's also the guy who holds the button. The remote control that can cross them back over."

"Wayne!"

"If I can get that remote from him, and we can get close to those cages, we can release the sleeping Willa and Philby—wherever they are. And I happen to think I know where they are."

Maybeck didn't dignify that with a question, but he also couldn't wipe the curiosity off his face.

"Animal Kingdom Lodge," Finn answered. "Those are the closest beds to the Park. You can reach the lodge from the savannah, and we know the Overtakers are on the savannah."

"I've got to admit: it does make sense," Maybeck said. "When exactly did you figure all this out?"

"Back there," Finn said. "When Charlene described the cages, it all fit."

"And now we're headed to find Wayne."

"Yeah. There's the terminal in Camp Minnie-Mickey. I can access VMK there," Finn said.

"I thought Philby never came back from that terminal."

"Which is why we're doing this together," Finn said. "Charlene will stay and keep an eye on the enclosure. I'll use the terminal to try to get to Wayne, and you'll stand guard. We'll use the DSs. You see anything weird, you can text me."

They started walking again.

"But what if we're wrong about the cages?" Maybeck asked.

"We're not," answered Finn.

* * *

Finn's avatar stood by the bench in the VMK's central plaza, while Finn himself occupied the small booth near the Lion King pavilion in Camp Minnie-Mickey. The air was burning hot, and he picked up the smell of popcorn, which made him realize how hungry he was. He knew that soon his parents would start to worry. They would expect him home from the water park. But he had things to do.

Knowing it would not print, he typed **WAYNE** into his dialogue box. Sure enough, it turned red in the text frame and wouldn't print.

Players' avatars entered the plaza, pausing below the billboards or circulating while waiting to meet each other. Finn's patience was wearing thin when a white-haired avatar finally appeared from his right. Wayne's avatar never stopped moving as **Follow me** appeared in the dialogue box.

He led Finn to the same room where he had taken

Philby. Wayne locked the door with a special code.

[ ]: we're safe here.

Finn: philby and willa have gone missing. we think their DHIs are being kept in cages behind the bat enclosure. i need the button.

[ ]: I spoke to philby not long ago. right here.

Finn: he never showed up. i think Maleficent is holding them to protect the second server. we can't crash the server with willa and philby stuck in Sleeping Beauty Syndrome.

[ ]: this is most disturbing.

Finn: can you get me the button—the remote control?

[ ]: yes. of course. though i'll have to use a messenger. . . . may i suggest the talking recycling bin. a few minutes from now, near the ticket gates. the remote will be taped inside the recycling bin. reach in and feel along the top.

Finn: i'll be there.

[ ]: if she's trying to protect the second server, then I fear the worst: she will either turn herself into a DHI to fool us or do harm, or she will compromise

the animal DHIs created for Animal Kingdom and use them to her advantage. this is a grave situation. in the magic kingdom she recruited Overtakers from within the attractions, most notably the pirates and the small-world dolls. in animal kingdom there are few, if any, such characters she can recruit for her army. it is our fear she has corrupted the animals themselves. five more orangutans have escaped, along with a half dozen gibbons. several snakes cannot be found. a wildebeest rammed one of the electrical fences attempting to break out. she is clearly gaining strength.

Finn: we want our friends back. Jez drew some things in her diary that have already come true. we think the diary may be—

He stopped typing as Maybeck shouted: "Mayday, dude! Mayday! Mayday!"

40

Maybeck kept watch from the side of a popcorn cart, where a multicolored umbrella was angled to throw shade onto the Cast Member behind the cart. The tilted umbrella offered Maybeck a screen from behind which he peered, spying on Finn and the Park guests milling about Camp Minnie-Mickey, as well as the surrounding jungle. Nearby, a gardener was watering some plants and hosing down the base of two tall trees, allowing the water to pool.

Because of his personal experiences, Maybeck also kept an eye on the sky, alert for any birds. But it was a lizard, not a bird, that caught and held his attention.

Small lizards inhabited most of Florida. He'd grown so accustomed to seeing them zip up trees, across sidewalks, and down the walls of buildings that he almost didn't notice them at all. His aunt Jelly, who was as close to a mother as Maybeck would ever get, called them "little dragons" and considered them close relatives to the cockroach and mouse. She wasn't beyond trying to beat them with a broom as she shooed them from the house. He'd been catching them since he was five; if you grabbed one by the tail, the tail came off. For a while he'd kept the tails—he'd had about twenty—but Jelly had found them and thrown them out, never saying a thing about it, then lying to him when he asked.

But the lizard he saw wasn't like other lizards. For one thing it was fairly big—five or six inches, instead of the typical three or four. It was also some kind of chameleon, quickly changing from the brown of the wood chips in the jungle to the grayish black of the paved path as the reptile emerged into sunlight. But more than anything, it was the way the lizard headed straight into trouble that won Maybeck's interest. Despite dozens of running shoes and sandals slapping down around it like mallets, the creature never wavered from its mission, dodging this way and that as it risked getting crushed. The lizards that Maybeck lived with spooked easily and skittered away as fast as lightning when approached. He'd never seen a lizard as bold as this one. It headed straight for . . .

. . . the Disney Vacation Web terminal.

Maybeck looked back toward the jungle from where the lizard had emerged. From there, in the shaded darkness held in place by tangled vines and leaves the size of tennis rackets, two sets of green glowing eyes stared out. He fixed his attention on them, trying to strip away the camouflage of plants and undergrowth in order to see to what those eyes belonged.

Monkeys . . . he thought at first. But the eyes were too widely set for a gibbon, and too far off the ground. *Orangutans!*

It was then that he saw the chameleon stitch its way back through the slalom course of legs and slither into the jungle, heading directly for the green flash of eyes.

As much as he resisted the idea that any of this was actually happening, he sorted it out quickly: the lizard was some kind of messenger; the monkeys were on a mission; Finn was their target.

A moment passed, and he realized he'd almost had it right.

Almost, but not quite. That's when he saw a lion slink out of the jungle. He fumbled with the DS, but it was going to take too long.

"Mayday, dude! Mayday!" he shouted.

The Park visitors saw the lion as well. A man screamed as a woman grabbed her children by the hands and started to run. The crowd scattered.

Finn turned around and froze.

Maybeck again glanced to his left—the gardener. He knew what to do.

41

FINN SPUN AROUND to see a lion strolling toward him. A big lion. A lion with a thick collar of fur, a huge head, beady eyes, and glistening white teeth. He instantly knew this was not a case of bad luck: the lion was coming for him just as the bats had come for Maybeck.

The lion lumbered toward him, now only a few yards away. The guests had scattered but now encircled an area about twenty yards across, with the beast at its center.

Heat flashed through him, and all the hairs on his arms and the back of his neck rose with his fright.

He knew what he had to do: he had to cross over. The lion couldn't hurt a DHI. But as the enormous cat began to flex, as if preparing to strike, Finn's fear was not to be conquered. The lion opened its mouth and let out a tremendous roar that seemed to come from all around. It surrounded Finn and shook the ground. It didn't sound natural. Finn threw his hands out, fending off the attack. He swooned, feeling dizzy.

And then, at once, several hands grabbed him and began to drag him away.

He heard applause and laughter.

He blinked his eyes open but was immediately blinded by the sun in the sky.

He averted his eyes and happened to catch a glimpse of one of the hands wrapped around his arm: black and calloused, with long, thin fingers. The hand was connected to a hairy arm.

Finn wrenched his head around.

He was being dragged off by a pair of orangutans. He tried to break the grip of the one on his left, and the thing bared its teeth and lunged toward his face as if to bite him. Finn jerked away, narrowly missing those teeth.

They were dragging him toward the jungle. They were kidnapping him.

And the audience thought it was all part of the show.

42

MAYBECK HEARD THAT ROAR and ran for the gardener who was watering the trees. He stole the hose out of the man's hands. Not really a man—more like a college kid. The guy didn't appreciate someone stealing his hose.

Maybeck's aunt Jelly had a mutt named Porky who considered their small backyard his domain. About once a month some stupid neighborhood dog would decide to visit their backyard without an invitation from Porky, typically resulting in a dogfight of epic proportions.

The first time Maybeck had tried to break up one of the fights, he'd nearly gotten his hand bitten off. He'd been saved by Jelly, who had broken up the fight with the garden hose. Ever since, Maybeck had used a strong burst of hose water to separate Porky and his prey.

He took the hose and sprinted toward the large apes who were dragging his friend across the pavement. He fought his way through the thick crowd, which was actually laughing and cheering.

Maybeck gave the hose one last tug, but he'd reached its limit. It would extend no farther.

He squeezed the handle and shot a burst of water at the lion. The water pressed right *through* the animal. *A DHI!*

Next, Maybeck aimed the hose at the nearest orangutan, hitting him squarely in the head. The ape was real. It let go of Finn to block the water streaming toward its face.

Again, the audience let out a cry of approval, clapping and hollering.

The ape shot a glance at Maybeck as if to challenge him, then quickly seemed to reconsider, and turned back toward Finn.

Maybeck blasted the other ape.

Finn broke loose just as the gardener jumped onto Maybeck from behind, wresting the hose from his grip.

Finn scrambled to his feet, slipped on the wet blacktop, and went down hard. Both orangutans rushed him, and Finn rolled out of the way, causing the two apes to collide. He got to his feet and took off toward Maybeck, who knocked the gardener aside, opening a small hole in the crowd, which Finn charged through.

The two took off at a full sprint, the orangutans following, their backs hunched, their teeth bared.

Finn glanced over his shoulder, but it slowed him.

"Don't look back!" Amanda said into his ear. "I've

got you. The Lion King show is running! You can lose them in there!"

"This way!" Finn shouted at Maybeck, who had heard Amanda as well.

They angled slightly toward the large, open pavilion, where a flash of bright color and loud African music confirmed the show was underway.

"They're gaining on you," Amanda warned. "Zigzag!"

Finn and Maybeck immediately cut left and right, right and left, in random patterns. Rather than run straight and intercept them, the orangutans followed their paths exactly, and the boys, having the longer strides, increased their leads.

"It's working!" Amanda cheered them on.

Together the boys burst into the show already in progress. Four sets of wooden bleachers rose from a theater-in-the-round, at the center of which were colorfully dressed acrobats performing on a giant trampoline, with trapeze artists spinning overhead.

As Finn slowed, Maybeck didn't hesitate for a second. Perhaps it was the result of forward momentum, perhaps because the Lion King stage set blocked their way; but Maybeck ran right up a ramp, hit the trampoline, and vaulted his way through the air and across to the other side. He tucked into a somersault, rolled to standing, and went running down the opposing ramp—right out of the pavilion.

Trying to avoid a collision with the ramp, Finn skidded and tucked his legs under him as if sliding into home plate. He braced himself to be crushed into the side of the stage, only to fly through the fabric skirt that surrounded it and find himself *under* the movable stage platform and the giant trampoline at its center. He crawled toward the other side, looking back to see two orangutans right behind him.

He glanced overhead. The trampoline's fabric stretched toward the concrete floor as the acrobatic show continued above him. Whenever anyone hit the trampoline, the fabric stretched so low that Finn had to lie flat; he couldn't squat without the risk of being crushed. Watching the orangutans approach, he suddenly saw his situation not as a threat but an opportunity: he could use the trampoline to his advantage.

Doubting that he and Maybeck could outrun the two apes, Finn turned and took a stand. The apes were faster and stronger than he, but Finn had the edge in intelligence. He remained directly under the pulsating trampoline, now turning to face the two apes, who immediately slowed with this challenge.

Finn egged on the apes, drawing them toward him, while keeping an eye on the pattern of the stretched trampoline fabric. There were currently four performers on the trampoline. The pattern of jumps was: the four corners; the center; the four corners.

Finn belly-crawled to the right. The nearest ape took the bait, turning to intercept him. The trampoline suddenly caved in over the ape's head, stretching toward the ground. The ape, caught between the trampoline and the concrete, was crushed by the weight of the acrobat. The ape was flattened. It cried out sharply, rolled away, and took off at a run in the opposite direction.

The trampoline came down immediately in front of the other ape, and that proved enough motivation. This one took off as well, following his buddy. Finn rolled and crawled out the other side and then sprinted for the sunlight outside the pavilion.

Maybeck had waited for him. Maybeck, who never thought of anyone but himself.

They took off running before either said a word, but as they reached full stride, Finn, the slower of the two, managed to pull even with Maybeck, though only briefly.

"Thanks," Finn called out to Maybeck. "I think we now know what happened to Philby!"

"The water shot right through the lion," Maybeck said. "It was a DHI."

"Maleficent's building an army," Finn told him. "An army of animals," he added. Maybeck flashed him a suspicious and disbelieving look. "Wayne told me," Finn said.

Finn turned and led Maybeck toward the Park entrance, still at a full run.

"Where are you going?" Maybeck huffed.

"The button," Finn said. "The remote control. We can't free Willa and Philby without the button."

43

Having witnessed the encounter with the lion, Amanda kept a close eye on Finn and Maybeck as they headed toward the Park entrance. She had a good understanding of the camera system by now, enabling her to guide the boys and check the area both in front and behind for any sign of Overtakers.

A family waited behind Amanda to use her AnimalCam. Among them was an obnoxious boy who heckled her. She wondered what would happen if she were forced to surrender her viewing station, when the person to use it next realized they had access to every security camera in the Park. Again, the boy raised his voice.

"You don't own it, you know! Give it a rest."

The outburst won the attention of a Cast Member, who then headed toward her. Amanda quickly reset the viewing menu to match what was offered by the three other AnimalCam stations, but if the next user happened to scroll down . . .

The little boy jeered at Amanda as he stepped up to the station, which worked in her favor: his mother took away his "privilege" of using the AnimalCam, allowing Amanda to retake her place.

She caught his reflection in the Plexiglas that protected the AnimalCam's television monitor.

She spun around sharply, getting a better look at the boy's arm.

The boy snapped at her, "Take a picture, it'll last longer."

"Your . . . tattoo . . ." Amanda muttered.

"What about it?" the boy asked.

"May I?" She took a tentative step closer.

The boy tried to step away and deny her, but his mother blocked him, suddenly Amanda's ally.

Amanda reached into her back pocket and withdrew the photocopied page from Jez's diary.

Amanda held the photocopy up to the light and peered through the paper to reverse the image.

It was a match, a near-perfect sketch of the tattoo: a gorilla on crutches with a yellow bandage on its right foot. On the boy's arm, "Help Care for Wildlife" was written across the top and "Disney's Animal Kingdom" at the bottom. But Jez's version offered only the image, not the words. Amanda had mistaken the figure in the sketch for a man.

"Where'd you get this?" she asked.

The mother answered, not the boy. "Here," she said, pointing toward the large windows at the far end of the area that looked in on a veterinarian suite and several laboratories where animals were housed or cared for. "They give them out if you take the private tour. The keepers."

This won an overwrought reaction from Amanda, who was thinking: *Kingdom Keepers.*

"The animal keepers," the woman clarified.

"Ohhh . . ."

"My husband is a consultant to Disney. They gave Preston and me a private tour, earlier. Really incredible, if you can arrange it."

"It was awesome," said Preston, his mood suddenly pleasant.

Boys!

"At the end of the tour, the tattoo was one of the keepsakes they gave him," the mother explained.

"Backstage," Amanda mumbled, her mind whirring as she calculated how to get herself a private tour. Jez had been back there in her dreams. She felt certain of it.

Then she reconsidered her situation: she had an Animal Kingdom Cast Member pass in her pocket.

What was to stop her from going back there?

44

INSIDE THE ANIMAL KINGDOM'S main entrance, in the large central courtyard where Park guests gathered, stood a talking recycling bin. A metal box standing about four feet high, it looked like a U.S. Postal Service box painted green. It was currently surrounded by several small boys and a pair of curious girls, amazed that when they asked it a question, the box could answer them.

Finn and Maybeck slowed and approached the recycling bin cautiously, not wanting to draw attention to themselves.

"Find a newspaper," Finn said to Maybeck.

"What?"

"Split up. We've got to find something recyclable. The trash cans make the most sense."

"You want to Dumpster-dive the trash cans for something recyclable?"

"Exactly. A newspaper. Soda can. Plastic water bottle. Doesn't matter. I need an excuse to open the flap and put my hand inside. I hadn't figured on it being so popular."

"FEEEEEED MEEEEEE," the can was saying to the giggling children. "Do you recycle at home?"

The kids were getting a kick out of the talking can, their amused parents standing back and watching.

The boys split up, and shortly thereafter, Maybeck returned with an empty water bottle.

"Perfect," Finn said, taking hold of the bottle.

Suddenly, the bin turned sharply toward Finn. The younger kids jumped back, followed by a volley of laughter.

"FEEEEED MEEEEEE," the can repeated, now aiming directly at Finn.

Finn had no doubt that Wayne had arranged this somehow.

"Eleven o'clock," Maybeck whispered at Finn.

Finn carefully looked slightly to his left and identified a casually dressed man wearing sunglasses and a pair of headphones. He carried what looked like a radio in his hands, but Finn recognized it as the remote control device that was steering the box. This man was also listening and speaking through the moving box. His sunglasses prevented Finn from knowing where he was looking, but Finn believed the man was very much aware of the task at hand.

Finn hoisted the water bottle.

The box said, "Did you know that recycled water bottles are made into Park benches, picnic tables, and car parts?"

"I did not," Finn answered.

"Are you going to feed me or not?" the box asked.

"Feed it!" one of the little kids said boldly.

"Do it!" chimed in another.

Finn knew how to play this. He approached the box warily, the water bottle extended as an offering. He reached into the bin. Then he lurched forward, as if the box were trying to swallow him. As the kids recoiled in a mixture of laughter and screams, Finn ran his hand along the roof of the box and bumped into something hard. He took hold of it and pulled. Some tape came loose, and he now had the remote in hand. He cupped it in his fist, drew his arm back out of the bin dramatically and gestured wildly, pocketing the device.

"Yum, yum!" said the recycle bin. "More! I want more!"

"I'm afraid that's all," said Finn, backing up and moving away. The bin spun toward the other children, drawing their attention and making it easier for Finn to slip away.

He glanced over at the man secretly controlling the bin and thought he saw a slight nod of acknowledgment.

His DS beeped and he checked the chat room.

angelface13: they're almost through the moving ice.

Finn: we're on our way. we did a little recycling.

45

AVING HANDED OFF THE REMOTE control device to Charlene, who stood watch outside the bat enclosure, Finn and Maybeck rode a Disney bus to the Animal Kingdom Lodge.

Charlene would, once again, use her stilts and camouflage to approach the backstage area behind the enclosure. This time, she would circle around, rather than enter the enclosure, avoiding the scrutiny of the Park visitors. Once she established herself atop the wall near the two cages and the ice truck, she would notify Finn on the DS.

The boys had to discover where the real Willa and Philby were being kept and be on hand to get them out of the hotel once they awakened. Charlene was to trigger the remote, canceling their DHI state.

They entered the Animal Kingdom Lodge lobby, and both boys gasped. Finn had never seen such a place. It felt as if he'd stepped into Africa itself: the vast floor and the columns were crafted from a dark, unusual wood; the lobby furniture was covered in brown-and-white animal skins; giant chandeliers made of spears and shields hung from the ceiling. African music played, the rhythm enchanting. The bellhops wore brown safari outfits. The lobby stretched two hundred feet or more, leading to stairs and giant windows that looked out onto an African savannah, where Finn could see two giraffes and several wildebeests.

Upon seeing all of this, Maybeck hissed a bad word.

There were people everywhere. Some occupied the sumptuous furniture; others milled about, heading this way or that. The clatter and hum of people eating and talking wafted up from a lower level to the right. A few people waited in line at the registration desk to the left. But all around, there was a feeling of excitement and mystery as families and staff came and went. Into this walked two boys, one in a Park worker's coveralls, the other in shorts and a T-shirt.

No one paid them the slightest bit of attention.

"We're invisible," Finn said softly.

"I hear you," Maybeck agreed.

Finn rarely found a place inside Disney World where he was not self-conscious about being a DHI actor, where he didn't feel the weight of eyes trained on him wondering if he was *him*, the Disney host from the Magic Kingdom. Yet here, in the wondrous lobby of this magnificent lodge, he felt transported across the oceans to another continent, one far away from Mickey and Minnie and the person he had become.

"Any ideas?" Maybeck asked.

"We can't exactly ask someone if they've seen a boy and a girl," Finn said, having already walked past a few dozen boys and girls, most in the company of their parents, but not all.

"No."

"If I could get on to VMK, Wayne might be able to look up what rooms have been checked into in the past few hours, but there would be too many to count."

"Yup."

"Not much help."

"Nope."

"So, do you have any bright ideas?" Finn asked. The two boys passed a small study, like a private library, on their left, and they continued down a long corridor of hotel rooms.

"We can't exactly go knocking on every door," Maybeck said.

"You think?" Finn stepped aside and allowed a family coming toward them to pass. "I was hoping for something more constructive."

"I've got nothing," Maybeck said.

"I noticed."

"We could divide and conquer," Maybeck suggested.

"I could take the upstairs or the other side of the hotel."

The lodge was fashioned in a giant Y, with the lobby in the stem, and the rooms stretching out into both wings of the V at the top of the stem. The V stuck out into a savannah, and the long corridors periodically offered viewing stations on either side, where all kinds of wildlife could be seen, from birds that stood four feet high to zebras and Thomson's gazelles.

"We could stay in touch by DS," Maybeck continued.

Finn stopped and grabbed Maybeck by the arm. "That's it!" he whispered harshly.

"It is?"

"The DSs," Finn said. "When a DS gets a new message, it beeps."

"So?"

"So . . . if we keep texting, and if one of us is near the door to their room when it beeps, then we'll hear it and know which room they're in."

"Sweet," said Maybeck.

"But what if they're being guarded? The guards will just turn off the DS."

"They weren't guarding you that time at Space Mountain."

"True."

"Why guard someone who's asleep and can't wake

up? Kind of a waste, don't you think?" Finn thought about how he would do it. "You'd put them on the bed, pull the drapes, put a DO NOT DISTURB sign on the door, and leave them."

"Okay! Makes sense," Maybeck said. "Then we start with rooms that have DO NOT DISTURB signs on the doors. At four o'clock in the afternoon, how many rooms can that be?"

"Not many," Finn agreed.

"Start sending messages while I find the rooms with the DO NOT DISTURB signs."

"If they're here," Maybeck said, "we're going to find them."

* * *

Finn pressed his ear to the door outside a room with a DO NOT DISTURB tag on the handle. He'd found three doors so far. With his ear to the fourth such room, he heard a faint but familiar beep and knew it was a DS.

> Finn: found it!!!

A minute later Maybeck came down the hallway toward him.

"This is their room," Finn declared. As Maybeck

leaned his ear against the door, Finn sent a text.

Maybeck smiled and pulled away from the door. "Bull's-eye!"

"You're a better liar than I am," Finn said.

"Is that supposed to be a compliment?"

"Charming. I meant to say you're more charming than I am. You're better with the ladies."

"That goes without saying," Maybeck said.

"There's a room being cleaned, back toward the elevator."

"I passed it," Maybeck confirmed.

"I think you left your family's Park Hoppers in this room, and your father's in here asleep with a headache, which explains the DO NOT DISTURB sign."

"I think you're brilliant," Maybeck said.

"Goes without saying. Can you pull it off?"

"This is me we're talking about!" Maybeck boasted.

"Same question."

"You'll need to get yourself gone," Maybeck said.

"I'll hang at the next set of windows."

"I'll text you once I'm inside," Maybeck said.

* * *

Less than five minutes later, Finn received the text message. He returned to the room and knocked softly. Maybeck opened the door.

The room held a big bed and a pair of bunks. Philby was drooling onto the pillow of the big bed. Willa slept peacefully on the lower bunk. They shook both kids, but to no avail: perma-sleep—Sleeping Beauty Syndrome.

"The one thing I remember," said Maybeck, who yawned all of a sudden, "is how much I dreamed when they had me in this state. I dreamed of being locked up. I think I was dreaming what my DHI was seeing."

Finn yawned reflexively. "Don't get me tired, or we'll end up like them."

"A nap wouldn't hurt," Maybeck said, eyeing the bunk. "We could take turns. Ten minutes."

"Do *not* go there."

"I'm tired."

"That's the point. Hang on." Finn sent Charlene a text message.

> Finn: ready when u r.

> angelface13: all set.

Both Maybeck and Finn heard the loud scratching sound at the same time. At first Finn thought it was a radio or TV in another room.

Maybeck hurried over and cracked the curtains. "Apes!" he hissed. He held up two fingers.

Two apes, Finn realized. Out on the balcony. The sliding door squeaked as one of the apes pulled on the handle from the outside.

Maybeck pointed to his own chest and then the closet. Seeing this signal, Finn hurried into the bathroom, stepped into the tub, and pulled the shower curtain closed. He heard the door swing open and the sounds of the two apes moving around the room. Were they looking for them? Had the maid told someone about letting Maybeck into the room?

A message from Charlene appeared on Finn's screen.

angelface13: i'm in position. will push remote in 3, 2, 1 . . .

The bathroom door was flung open. Finn could hear one of the two orangutans breathing hard, and the room suddenly smelled different. He reached up and turned the showerhead to face the curtains, his hand on the faucet.

Four hairy fingers appeared at the edge of the shower curtain. Finn felt as if he might pass out.

The shower curtain was jerked open.

Finn yanked the lever. Water roared into the face of an ugly orange ape. The ape slapped his own face, screamed, and jumped back.

Finn leaped from the tub, pulled a terrycloth robe from the back of the bathroom door, and tossed it over the ape. He then used the bathrobe's belt to take a strong turn around the confused ape, pulled it tight, and knotted it around the ape's legs. The orangutan fell over, kicking and thrashing and screaming, doing nothing but spinning in circles on the bathroom floor.

The second ape appeared at the doorway. Finn lunged for the other bathrobe, but it drew him closer to the ape, whose big mouth came open, teeth bared. Just as Finn feared the ape would strike, Maybeck leaped out of the bedroom closet and poked it with a hanger that he wielded as a sword.

This provoked the ape. It spun around to challenge Maybeck, giving Finn the extra seconds he needed to take hold of the robe and throw it over the orangutan. He and Maybeck made quick work of tying up this one as well. They dragged it into the bathroom and, as they shut the door, both apes were seen whirling angrily on the tile floor.

Finn shook Willa. Maybeck pulled on Philby's arm. Both groaned and squirmed uncomfortably: they were awakening! Charlene had used the remote on the DHIs in the cages, and it had worked. The cages were now empty—the DHIs gone, zeroed out by the server. Maleficent and the Overtakers with her had to be terribly confused.

And angry.

The orangutans screamed loudly from the bathroom.

Maybeck said to Philby, "I know you feel like a zombie. I've been there. But we have to hurry. We've got to get you out of here."

46

FINN AND MAYBECK escorted Philby and Willa to the train platform for the Wildlife Express Train. Amanda had announced a discovery and asked that they meet her. She'd been very secretive, and they were eager to talk with her.

Charlene was still keeping an eye on the bat enclosure. The ice truck had not been moved.

The kids stood around watching Finn as he finally made the call to Rob Bernowski, Jez's boyfriend. He had the BlackBerry on speakerphone so everyone could hear.

"Rob?"

"Yeah? Who's this?"

"My name is Finn Whitman. I'm a friend of—"

"Jez's. Yeah, I know." He didn't sound too thrilled. "She talks about you and the others all the time." *Too much of the time*, his tone of voice implied.

"Have you seen her by any chance? Heard from her?"

"No. Why?"

"Just curious," Finn said.

"What's up with that?"

"Just asking."

"Because?"

"Yeah, well . . . listen . . . I know this is going to sound stupid, but if there was one thing Jez could change about you, what would it be?"

"Is this some kind of contest or something?"

Finn hesitated. Willa was nodding violently.

"Yeah, that's it exactly," Finn said. "A contest. A school thing. How well do boyfriends and girlfriends know each other?"

"The one thing she would change?"

"Yes. That's the question."

A long hesitation on the other end of the call. "My clothes. She doesn't like my jeans, man. I wear 'em kinda low."

"Your jeans?"

"Yeah. Did I answer right?"

"I'll have to get back to you on that," Finn said. "That's all you can think of?"

"I can tell you the one thing I'd change about her," Rob volunteered, not giving Finn a chance to stop him. "I'd take her iPod away from her. She's, like, addicted to that thing. That, and all the word games she plays. She's into scrambling every word she can—making other words out of the same letters, you know?"

"Anagrams," Finn said.

"What's that?" Rob asked.

"It's what you call that: an anagram is a word that can be made from the letters of another word."

"Never heard of it." He paused. "So what about my prize? Do I win a prize?"

"Ah . . . we'll let you know. Thanks for your answers." Finn ended the call.

"Anagrams," Philby said. "You think it's worth a try?"

"Do we think *what* is worth a try?" Maybeck asked.

"Jez wrote 'change Rob' in her diary—"

"*And* inside the tree stump," Willa added.

"Some kind of code?" Finn asked.

"Give me the BlackBerry," Philby said, reaching toward Finn.

"I really don't think we should call him back," Finn said.

"I'm not calling anyone. The BlackBerry has Internet. We can settle this pretty quickly."

Finn and the others leaned over Philby's shoulder as he used the BlackBerry to Google an anagram site. Then, reaching a site, he typed in "change Rob," and hit the button to generate anagrams.

The small screen showed a long list of possible letter combinations.

"'Branch ego,'" he read from the screen. "'Corn bag he.'" They laughed. "'Herb can go.'"

"Let me see that." Willa moved in next to Philby, to where their shoulders touched. No one missed how close she got to him, least of all Maybeck, who suddenly started shifting anxiously. Willa studied the screen and spoke in a quiet voice.

"We've done this before," she reminded him. "The clues from the Stonecutter's Quill. Remember? We solved that anagram without a Web site."

"That's because we didn't have a BlackBerry. There's nothing here," Philby said.

"There are no proper names," Willa said.

"So?" Philby challenged.

Willa took the BlackBerry out of Philby's hand and held it where she could study it clearly. Then she calmly returned the BlackBerry to Philby, who passed it back to Finn.

"So I've got one," she said, capturing the full attention of the others. She meant this as a challenge. She remained incredibly close to Philby, and she was looking him directly in the eyes. "One word. A name. A *Disney* name."

"I give up," Finn said.

"I don't! Wait! Wait!" Philby barked, not wanting to lose to Willa.

"A Disney name?" Maybeck asked. "But then that's *got* to be it. What is it, Willa? Tell us what it is!"

"Give up?" she asked Philby, her voice a hoarse whisper. There was something going on between these two. And Maybeck didn't like it.

"No . . . No . . ." Philby pleaded.

"He gives up," Maybeck said. "WE ALL GIVE UP."

Willa's eyes scrunched, as if to convey her disappointment in Philby. But Philby didn't see her. His eyes were closed, his lips moving as if reading to himself.

"Chernabog!" Philby shouted out.

"And I was about to give up on *you*," Willa said, obviously impressed.

"The creature from *Fantasia*?" Finn asked.

"You ever see that movie?" Maybeck questioned. "He is one mean dude."

"And guess what?" Willa said. "Chernabog's not only the most evil of all the Disney villains, he happens to be a demon with *bat* wings!"

The kids went silent, the air suddenly shattered by the train's sharp whistle, announcing its arrival at the station.

47

"HE'S THE BADDEST OF THE BAD. The most evil villain Walt Disney ever created." Philby was in fine form, back to himself, alert from the sleep he'd gotten and able to think more clearly than either Maybeck or Finn. They waited in line for the Park train to the Conservation Station.

Charlene remained behind in the jungle just outside the bat enclosure. She blended in well there and, having found a log to stand on with her stilts, could keep an eye on the activities backstage by peering over the top of the wall. The back doors of the ice truck had been shut, Maleficent inside. As far as Charlene could tell, before entering the back of the truck neither Maleficent nor the monkeys and apes had realized the cages were empty. The tarps used to contain the captive DHIs and to block their projections from showing had also served to fool their captors.

Once the line was moving, Maybeck, Finn, Willa, and Philby separated for the ride out to the Conservation Station. They each took a place on the long benches amid the Park guests, all on different train cars. Summoned by Amanda, they were anxious to rendezvous and find out what had her so overheated.

As the train arrived at Rafiki's Planet Watch, the kids split up. Park visitors trudged up the long path toward the Conservation Station. They were a team now, protective of one another and concerned for each other's safety. These kids, who had once been strangers, were now anything but—brought together by a common enemy and the strange manifestations of a technology gone wrong. To remind them of their previous lives would have been foolish, for they could barely remember a time when falling asleep did not mean crossing over into a strange world, and where a white-haired old man had not controlled their shared fate.

Finn, who'd taken up the rear, entered the facility and joined the others in a huddle by the restrooms.

"I'm starving," said Willa.

"Later," said Philby.

"What's so important?" Finn asked Amanda, who had abandoned her viewing station. The crowd had thinned as a veterinary demonstration had begun at the central display window: a snake had eaten a golf ball and was undergoing surgery.

"We have to act while they're distracted. And I have to get back to the AnimalCam before someone realizes how many cameras that station has access to."

"Act?" Finn inquired.

"One of the sketches from the diary." She unfolded the original page of the diary and pointed out the ape on crutches. "It's a tattoo. A washable tattoo for the children. It's given to them after the private tours of the vet clinic. I think our passes will get us back there, but I didn't want to leave my station for too long. And since the veterinary clinic means *animals*, I thought it was better to get some help and maybe do this as a team."

"Agreed," said Finn, attempting to digest everything she'd just told them.

"A tattoo?" Maybeck quipped in complaint. "What about Chernabog? What about the two apes we left spinning donuts back in the lodge? Who cares about some bleeping tattoo?"

"If it's in the diary," Philby said, "then it's part of the puzzle she left us. That makes it significant. Amanda's right: we have to pursue it."

"Says the one who just got a couple hours' sleep," Maybeck complained.

"I know this may sound foolish," Amanda said, apologizing to Maybeck, "but I *feel* it's important. I really do. I wouldn't have called you out here otherwise. I know how hard you're all working to help Jez.

How much risk you're taking. I can't tell you how I appreciate it. I have no right to ask you to do anything more."

"That's true," Maybeck said.

"Shut up," said Willa.

"I'm agreeing with her."

"You're being a nimrod, and you know it," Willa protested.

"A tattoo!" Maybeck shouted, a little loudly.

"Everything in the diary has proved out," Finn reminded them. "The tiger and lion were DHIs. She drew the lightning hitting the castle days before it occurred."

"Change Rob," Willa said. She reviewed Finn's phone call to Rob for Amanda, and the discovery of the Chernabog anagram.

"And that too," Finn agreed.

"The apes," Philby added.

"And now the tattoo," Maybeck mumbled. "Okay. I get it. So what now?"

"I'm going back there," Finn said. "Into the vet clinic."

"And I'm going with you," Amanda stated, leaving no room for argument.

"I can take over the viewing station," Philby offered eagerly.

"Willa and I will stand guard," said Maybeck. "Our DSs at the ready."

"What's the code word if there's a problem?" Finn asked.

"Give it a rest, Whitman."

"Chernabog," said Philby.

All eyes fell on him.

"At least that way we'll all understand it's serious," Philby said.

48

FINN SWIPED HIS ID in the card reader. A small light changed to green. An even smaller light went off in his brain: what if the Overtakers had figured out the kids were using fake IDs and were now tracking them through the use of their cards? He shook it off.

He tried the doorknob, and the door opened. He and Amanda stepped through, leaving the sounds of activities behind them.

The hallway he found himself in reminded Finn of the veterinarian's office where his mother volunteered part-time. It also served to remind him of his mother and the fact that he hadn't yet called home. He'd messed up: soon his parents would be at Blizzard Beach looking for him. They were going to be furious. He wondered if any of the other kids were in the same predicament. One thing was certain—time was running out. The Park would remain open only another hour or so. Jez's chances of being freed were quickly diminshing.

He knew that no matter how they tried, he and Amanda still looked like kids. Tired, even exhausted, kids—but kids nonetheless. There was no getting around it. And he had no idea if unaccompanied kids his age were allowed backstage. With this in mind, he signaled to Amanda to hurry, and they moved down the hallway with an eye out for someplace to hide. Thankfully, most of the doors had glass panels, allowing them to see inside. They passed an examination room, and another, filled with medical equipment. There was one door marked PRIVATE, and another with stickers and cartoon clippings taped to it. It was this door Finn tried first. Inside was a single table and some vending machines—an employee lounge. It was empty. They ducked inside, both wide-eyed and slightly out of breath due to the excitement.

"I'm terrified," Amanda said.

"Me too," Finn admitted.

"We have no idea what we're looking for."

"No. But she must have dreamed about that tattoo. That has to mean something."

"But what?"

"The tattoos are given out to kids who take the private tours. Maybe there's something on the tour we're supposed to see?"

Amanda's blue eyes brightened. "That's got to be it! You're a genius."

Finn felt his face warm. "Hardly," he mumbled

under his breath, wondering how a guy like Maybeck could carry himself so confidently.

There was noise in the hallway, and both of them instinctively looked for a place to hide. But the employee lounge offered them nothing: a few lockers, all padlocked.

A text message appeared on both their DSs:

> angelface13: the green one just left the ice palace.

"Maleficent just left the ice truck," Finn whispered.

"Yeah . . . I saw that. But what's it mean?"

"No idea. But it can't be good." Amanda looked terrified. "Okay, here's the thing: try to look like you belong here," he advised, bracing himself for whoever was out there to come through the door.

Instead, he saw a woman dressed in green nursing scrubs leading two adults and a string of four or five kids down the hallway. A tour!

"I've got an idea," Finn said.

A moment later, he and Amanda were in the hallway trailing only a few feet behind the family. For anyone seeing them they would appear to be a group. The nurse, busy with her explanations, a memorized tour she probably did too often, seemed to pay little attention to those at the back of the pack.

The guide pointed out the purpose of several of the rooms, explaining in some detail about the care and attention lavished on the animals in the Park. This facility was so advanced it was used not only for Disney-owned animals, but for all sorts of wild animals rescued throughout the state. Finn found himself getting caught up in the tour as Amanda tugged on his shirt. They stopped, and the tour went along without them.

On the wall was a corkboard. Pinned to it were photographs of some of the recovered animals— including *a gorilla with a broken leg*. There were maps and brochures tacked to the board as well.

"The tattoo!" Amanda said.

She was right: the similarity of the subjects was unmistakable. A photo of a gorilla with a broken leg and a tattoo sketch of the same thing.

"But how does it help us?"

"I don't know," Amanda said, "but we're in the right place."

Finn studied the rest of the stuff thumbtacked to the corkboard. One of the items was a very large satellite photo of the entire Animal Kingdom. Finn spent a good deal of time—probably too much, according to his mother—on Google Earth. He loved everything about satellite photos. Using the image, it took him only seconds to establish where they were: in a complex of buildings near the top right of the photo at the end of a loop that was obviously the train line.

And then he saw them: an *M* near the bottom, and a *C* near the top.

For a moment his breath caught; it felt as if a bone were stuck in his throat. His hands were moving before he knew exactly what he was doing. He pulled the thumbtacks from the four corners of the satellite photo.

"How stupid could we be?" he muttered.

"Finn? What's going on?" Amanda asked, the concern apparent in her voice.

"Hey!" came a man's voice. "You can't do that! Put that back!"

Finn glanced to his right. The man was a long way off, at the end of the hallway.

"Finn?" Amanda said heatedly.

"They're *both* here: the *M* she wrote in her diary, and 'Under the Sea'!" Finn answered. He pointed to the satellite photo, which he had turned counterclockwise.

The man picked up his pace, heading toward them. "Hey there!" he called out.

"It wasn't 'Under the S-e-a,'" Finn spelled. "But, under *the letter C*!" Turning the photo, he traced the prominent shape at the top of Asia. It was very clearly a big bold letter *C*, formed by an arched bridge. "She's here. Jez . . . is under the *C* on the map."

"Oh . . . my . . . gosh!" Amanda squealed with excitement. "You found her!"

"It's the tiger yards," Finn said, recognizing the route of the Jungle Trek. "Maybeck and I walked right by there."

The man was nearly upon them.

Finn kept hold of the satellite photo, already folding it as he turned to Amanda and shouted harshly, "I think it's time we . . . RUN!"

49

AMANDA AND FINN turned the corner. At the far end of the hallway glowed a red EXIT sign. Finn was already in the process of texting a DGamer message.

> Finn: chernabog!

The green fairy rounded the far corner, coming between Finn and the EXIT sign. She held a black kitty in her arms.

She set the cat down, waved her hand over it, and it stretched and grew to the size of a panther. The man pursuing Amanda and Finn skidded to a stop.

"Silly, silly boy," Maleficent said, aiming her finger at him. "Won't you ever learn to mind your own business?"

"Who are you?" the man shouted from well behind Finn.

"Pest!" she called out, waving her finger at the man. The panther took off—running right past Amanda and Finn—and chased the man around the corner.

Finn pushed the fear from his thoughts and drove

away his anger. He whispered, "Examination room," and pointed subtly with his left hand, holding it behind his back. "Get the others. We'll meet up at the trek."

"I'm not going anywhere," Amanda informed him. "Not without Jez."

He couldn't allow her defiance to ruffle him. Above all, he had to clear his mind of any frustration, resentment, or ill will toward others. As he did, he felt the familiar tingling sensation in his toes and fingers, and he knew it was starting. Knew, without looking, that he was crossing over.

In the past, he had only been able to sustain his waking-DHI form for a matter of a minute or two. Somehow he knew it would have to be longer this time—that this was to be a test of his strength.

He suspected that by becoming his DHI, he risked the Sleeping Beauty Syndrome. This was uncharted territory, but he had to do something to counter Maleficent's power.

"Go!" he called out to Amanda.

"No. I'm staying."

Maleficent drew her scrawny hands toward her face, her fingers twitching, her lips bubbling with an incantation. Finn could sense a spell coming, but he would not allow himself to fear it. Even his frustration with

Amanda for not listening had to be ignored. He would be no help to her if Maleficent's spell affected him as well.

"You have a powerful master," Finn called down the hall. He watched as Maleficent's face became rubbery with surprise and wrinkled with concern.

"You know nothing of my master," came the reply.

"More than you think. Is it control over the Animal Kingdom that Chernabog wants?"

Maleficent cringed at mention of the name; it was as if Finn had spoken a sacred secret. She curled her hands into a tight ball, and Finn could feel it coming.

"Look out!" he shouted at Amanda. He turned to warn her.

Amanda was gone. Vanished. No longer by his side.

Maleficent hurled a blinding ball of energy down the hall. About the size of a softball, it spun through the air, throwing off sparks like a tiny, blazing sun, and looked as if it would burn up anything in its path.

"Duck!" said Amanda's voice.

Finn glanced up to see her *floating* horizontally near the ceiling.

"DUCK!" she repeated.

But it was too late for Finn to duck. The burning ball arrived and passed right through him. It exploded at the end of the hall, hitting a tile wall and erupting into a cloud of black smoke that rose to the ceiling. The smoke crept toward a blinking sensor mounted in the ceiling.

"But how . . . ?" he muttered.

Amanda, still floating, said, "I told you Jez and I had unusual abilities."

"You can *fly*?"

"Not exactly. I can levitate." She sank then, and returned to her feet.

Finn knew this discussion would have to wait until later.

Maleficent twisted her ugly fingers. A cage of blue-white lines surrounded Finn and Amanda.

Finn wasn't scared of the laser cage. His DHI stepped right through it, coming closer to Maleficent. Amanda floated off her feet and swam through the air, slipping through a gap between the electric bars. She sank back to the floor.

"Or is it the other way around?" Finn called out to Maleficent. "Is it that the Animal Kingdom controls him, and you're going to 'save' Chernabog? To free him! His powers are limited here. Is that it?"

Maleficent took a step back, away from Finn. It was the first time he'd ever sensed an ounce of retreat in her. He savored the moment.

By gloating, he briefly lost his DHI.

"My master's powers are anything but limited," she said. "Just you wait!"

She threw an arrow of flame at Finn. His cherishing Maleficent's retreat had cost him more than half his DHI. He was now half kid, half light. And as he turned his back against the oncoming arrow, he unknowingly offered her his mortal half.

Seeing this, Amanda leaped in front of him.

The arrow struck her in the chest and was totally absorbed. Her arms and legs glowed as she sank to the floor.

Maleficent grinned an evil grin.

"Looks like your girlfriend shouldn't play with fire," Maleficent said.

Amanda lay unconscious on the floor at Finn's feet, a burn mark on her shirt. His fear removed him from his DHI state and exposed him to Maleficent's powers.

But something else overcame him—a wild, pent-up anger that he could no longer control. He charged the witch.

A wide-eyed Maleficent seemed to sense her situation. As her lips muttered another incantation, she was too late.

Finn hit her with a body block, his momentum slamming her against the wall and pinning her there. He brought his hands to her throat.

Her skin was ice cold.

He said, "Release her this instant. You bring her back . . . or so help me . . ." He tightened his grip. Her cold skin was like nothing he'd ever felt.

Maleficent's sickly green skin turned yellow. He was choking the life from her. She had no voice. No incantations.

"RELEASE AMANDA!!" Finn shouted, holding the wild panther at bay with his voice. He tightened his grip. Maleficent's eyes bulged. She waved her hand.

Amanda coughed and sat up, coming back to consciousness.

"Are you all right?" Finn asked.

Amanda coughed hard but nodded.

Finn squeezed even tighter. "Tell Chernabog it's over," he said. "He will never regain his power. The Overtakers are through."

He threw her to the floor, turned, and ran, grabbing Amanda by the hand just as the smoke reached the smoke alarm.

"You saved my life," Amanda said, clinging to his arm. "Maleficent was *scared* of you!"

"I was . . . mad," Finn said.

"I didn't know you cared," Amanda teased him, just as they opened an emergency door and sprinted outside.

"Who says I do?" he said to her, his voice breaking.

"Boys . . ." she muttered.

50

THE KINGDOM KEEPERS and Amanda stood watching the AnimalCam, with Philby at the controls. All but Charlene, who kept vigil at the bat enclosure, her DS in hand. Philby, being Philby, had quickly located two cameras that served the tiger yards and a third that looked back toward the arched bridge that separated the two enclosures. It was this bridge that caused the *C* on the satellite photo.

"They keep tigers on either side of the bridge," he explained. "Both sides have water and some trees for shade. From the bridge you have a good view of either yard."

"But if she's under the *C*, she's under the bridge," Finn said.

"I don't know that that's possible," Philby said, switching camera views.

"Zoom back!" Willa said in an excited voice.

Philby did as she asked.

Amanda stepped forward, her finger pointing to the screen. "The window! That's from the diary."

"Yes," Finn said. "You showed us that before, when Maybeck and I were over there."

"She dreamed about this place," Amanda said. "No question about it."

Willa pushed her way to a closer view of the screen.

Maybeck said, "Are we just going to watch TV all day? Let's *do* something."

Willa pointed. "Zoom in on this."

"On what?" Philby said.

"Just do it," Willa persisted.

Philby used the AnimalCam's joystick to aim the camera where she pointed: a section where the wall met the dirt.

"Zoom in," she directed.

It wasn't dirt, as it turned out. Slowly a geometric shape became apparent: a wooden hatch with grass growing around its edges.

"That couldn't be what I think it is," Maybeck said.

"It's a trapdoor!" Amanda declared.

"A trapdoor in a tiger yard," Maybeck said. "Yeah, that makes sense."

"She's in there," Amanda said. She looked to Finn for support. "Don't ask me how I know, but she's in there."

"Philby?" Finn asked. "What's a trapdoor doing there?"

"You're going to think I'm crazy."

"Try me," Finn said.

"Let's say you're the person running the tigers. How are you going to get any tigers into this lower yard?" He switched camera views. It showed a slowly rising hill of grass.

"How 'bout trying the gate?" Maybeck asked.

"There is no gate. Not in the lower yard, only in the upper yard. We know from what Wayne told us that all the animals are accounted for each evening. They're kept in barns and pens backstage. I'm thinking they probably move a couple tigers into this upper yard in the morning—then they open the hatch. It leads to a short tunnel that connects to the lower yard. Tigers are cats, so they're smart. They learn fast." He zoomed the camera to where a second hatch could be seen, this time in the lower yard. "Once the first tigers are in the lower yard, they close the hatches and put two more tigers into the upper yard. Tigers are territorial, so this system keeps them apart."

"Brilliant," said Willa.

"I don't mean to play devil's advocate," said Maybeck, who thrived on playing devil's advocate, "but if they let them in in the morning, then don't they let them *out* in the evening? So if Jez is down there, which personally I don't believe, doesn't that mean . . . ?" He didn't finish his thought.

"That if she's still down there at closing, then the tiger gets her for dinner," Philby said.

Willa gasped.

"How could she have gotten down there in the first place?" Maybeck questioned.

"She could have crossed the savannah," Willa proposed, "after escaping the tree trunk. Jumped a wall, or entered an open gate, only to find herself facing tigers. Maybe the hatch was already open; maybe she opened it herself. We won't know until we find her."

"One thing," Philby said, "supporting this theory . . . if I were rigging the sound for the Park, the wires would follow the path. It might make sense to have a junction box down in the tunnel connecting the yards. Workers would have a place to check the wires that's out of the view of the guests and safely away from the tigers."

"No matter what," Finn said, "I think we talked ourselves into checking out that tunnel."

"A tunnel we don't even know exists," Maybeck reminded them.

"But there's something else to think about," Finn said. "The *M* on the satellite photo is a match with the *M* in the diary."

"So she could just as easily be hiding someplace on the *M*," Maybeck said, pleased to have some evidence to support his view.

Amanda shook her head. "No, I don't think so. She played that song over and over. She has to be *under the C*."

"Then what's the *M* about?" Maybeck asked.

"Well, for one thing," Willa said, "it's your initial."

Maybeck looked as if he might stick his tongue out at her, but he resisted.

"In the diary there's a blob of ink on the lower right stem of the *M*," Philby pointed out. "That could be a mistake, or it could mean something. And I might add that everything in the diary so far has meant something."

"Agreed?" Finn said.

"So look where it is," Philby said.

"Dinoland." Philby looked around at the others. "Do any of you ever come to this Park?" he inquired sarcastically. "Dinoland is ridiculously boring except for one attraction."

"That research thing—Dr. Grant Seeker," Willa said.

"Dinosaur. Remember anything special about it?"

"Only that it was really cool," Willa answered.

"Not cool—well, yes, it's cool—but it's also *cold*. And it's computer controlled. Majorly computer controlled. There have to be some serious computers running that ride."

"The second server," Finn whispered, "could be hidden among them."

"As good a place as any."

"Listen to you!" Maybeck sniped. "We don't know any of this for sure!"

"No . . ." Philby said. "But there might be a way we could find out. If I can get back on VMK, and Wayne gets me into the control center, I may be able to track network bandwidth usage."

"Speak English," Maybeck snapped.

"Think about it: if we go after Jez, how is Maleficent going to come after us?"

"With birds," Maybeck said.

"And monkeys," Willa added.

"And lions," said Finn.

"And DHIs of all of the above," Philby said. "The more DHIs she uses, the more bandwidth usage on the network. What I'm saying is this: we *want* her to come after us with everything she's got, because when she does, I can probably locate the second server. And if I do, then maybe I can cut it off the network. That would take all the DHIs of animals out of the equation."

"So we split up," Finn said. "Maybeck, Willa, and Philby will team up to take out the second server, to destroy it if possible. Charlene, Amanda, and I will get inside the tiger yard and get into that hatch."

"Oh, yeah, like that's going to happen," snipped Maybeck.

"Philby said the tunnel makes sense for maintenance. If that's the case, do you think the maintenance workers go through the tiger yards every time there's a problem? I don't think so. There's going to be another entrance—a hatch, a manhole, something—probably hidden in the jungle. Something that Jez can't get to, or isn't strong enough to move. Philby can check it out when he gets into VMK. There must be a way to open the hatches in order to move the tigers. Philby can look for that, and we'll be in position, ready to move."

"There are still a few sketches in the diary that we haven't run into," Amanda reminded everyone. "We shouldn't forget about them. There's the hairy gorilla and the owl on the branch. There's the elephant and the hunchback guy who looks sort of Indian."

"Everyone will stay alert for those," Finn said.

"Alert?" Maybeck said. "I'm half asleep on my feet."

"No sleeping!" Philby warned. "Willa and I messed up things by getting caught. We're both sorry and appreciate everything you did for us. But the Park is closing soon: six o'clock. And that means the animals will all be moved backstage, including the tigers. If there is a tunnel between the tiger yards, and Jez is down there . . ." He didn't have to finish the sentence.

But apparently Maybeck felt obliged to. "Then she becomes kitty chow."

51

CHARLENE INSISTED THAT she could slip over the wall of the upper tiger yard with no one the wiser.

"I don't think so," said Finn. He, Amanda, and Charlene were assembled along the edge of the Jungle Trek, very near the tiger yards.

"I can stay close to the wall, like I did at the bat enclosure," Charlene said. "No one'll see me, and that includes the tigers."

"Tigers are fast," Amanda reminded her. "Very fast. And they can jump, let's not forget."

Charlene nodded. "But also lazy. I'll be on the opposite wall. If the tiger moves or shows any interest, you can warn me. I can vault the wall in a nanosecond. It's not as if it's going to get me."

"No, probably not," Finn said. "But it's also not worth the risk. At the very worst, we wait until they try to move the tigers. If we're right, they'll open the hatches at that point. Jez will get out of there. Our jobs will be to distract the tigers so Jez doesn't get attacked."

"Tiger bait?" Amanda asked, horrified. "Your plan is to use us as tiger bait?"

"My plan is to rescue Jez. At the very worst, we wait out the Park's closing."

"Let's look for a maintenance entrance," Amanda encouraged. "If it actually exists, it can't be far from the bridge."

"Agreed. And Charlene promises not to jump the wall," Finn said, looking up at her. "I would suggest you scout the perimeter looking for other hatches, gates, or anything else we should know about."

"I can do that. But I can also—"

"Don't even think about it," Finn said, interrupting her.

Amanda and Finn set off down the path toward the tiger bridge. At Finn's suggestion, they kept a few yards apart in case they came under attack from the Overtakers. They sharpened their senses, alert to what was overhead and all around them for anything out of the ordinary—especially monkeys and orangutans.

They scouted both tiger yards from an old Indian temple made of stone and plaster, which was at the top of the tiger bridge. Amanda stared out the window that matched what Jez had sketched in the diary. An enormous tiger was stretched out in the shade about twenty feet below and across the yard. She couldn't see the trapdoor from where she stood but could place it just to her left in her mind's eye. She switched sides and kept looking around.

Finn patrolled the center of the bridge, also switching sides and looking into both tiger yards. He'd hoped to see a manhole cover in the path—some indication of maintenance access—but there was none.

"I think I have something," Amanda said from behind him. She faced some plants and a beautiful section of the wall, where four large stone panels had been carved, each depicting a unique scene. Finn recalled these from having seen them earlier, and he said so.

"I don't think we should be seen staring, so I'm going to turn my back, but check out the second panel," Amanda said, spinning around.

"The owl!" Finn said. "And the elephant with the headdress."

"Both of which she sketched in her diary," Amanda reminded.

"It's a secret panel," Finn said. "The access to the tunnel."

"We don't know that," Amanda protested.

"Screen me," Finn said. "I'm going back there and looking for some kind of switch to open it. The way it's on the corner, it's perfect for maintenance, because you're hidden to start with. No one's going to see me, but just to make sure . . ."

"I've got you covered," Amanda said.

Finn slipped into the vegetation and stepped into

shadow. The ground here was disturbed, and he noticed several large shoeprints in the mud, convincing him all the more that they were right about this.

He ran his hand along the edge of one of the large stone panels, hoping to find some kind of trigger. *Nothing.* He tapped on it lightly. It sounded hollow. "This has got to be it," he hissed. "But I can't find anything to open it."

"Try the owl," Amanda called over her shoulder.

Of course! he thought. He stretched to reach the owl, opened his hand, and pushed. The tile with the owl moved. The panel clicked and popped open an inch. Finn threaded his fingers behind it and pulled. It was incredibly heavy.

"I've got it!" he announced.

But behind the panel he saw a metal gate. And the gate was padlocked. This helped explain why, if Jez had found this entrance, she'd been unable to get out.

He didn't hesitate for a moment. Understanding the risk he took, Finn flushed all thought from his mind. He was neither anxious nor excited. Neither angry nor tired nor hungry. He felt the now familiar tingling in his arms and legs and witnessed a slight glow on the back of the stone panel that hung open: he had crossed over. He stepped through the wrought-iron gate, his glow illuminating a dank, stone stairway that spiraled down to his left. He turned around, his DHI already fading as fear crept into him. Fear of the dark. Fear of the unknown. He was himself again. He reached through the gate and grabbed a heavy iron handle on the inside of the panel. He pulled with all his strength, and the massive stone door clicked shut.

He'd acted a little too hastily: it was pitch dark.

He couldn't see a thing.

52

FINN FELT HIS WAY DOWN the damp stones as the stairs beneath him fell away in a spiral to his left. It smelled at once of dust and mold, like his grandparents' basement. He counted the stairs as he went: *ten, eleven, twelve* . . . before they leveled off. He walked on the flat now, straight ahead, his left hand skimming a rock wall, the occasional cobweb tangling in his fingers and making him jump. Finn didn't like spiders.

The sound of his running shoes scraping the concrete changed; he could feel he was in a more open area. His vision, which had shown him nothing but sparkles and curlicues, improved to where he could make out a haze both to his left and right. It hung in the air like a gray mist. And now, slowly forming, a lump, an interruption in the mist. An imperfection in the horseshoe-shaped glow that continued to define itself.

"Jez?" he called out softly.

The lump moved. He thought it might have turned in his direction.

He called her name again, this time a little more loudly.

"If you're a dream, go away!" Jez's voice!

"It's Finn," he said, taking steps toward her, his hand still guiding him along the wall.

"Why can't I wake up?" she muttered.

Finn felt good. His heart swelled in his chest. It was not simply the pride of success, of beating the odds and finally finding her. It went beyond that, to something more. He felt an importance in being here. A significance. He was saving Jez. He was doing something that really mattered, not just studying or wasting time on his computer. It gave meaning to all the effort they had gone to, all the risks they had taken.

And then the tunnel filled with a colorful glow, like a light warming up. And it *was* a light warming up. *His* light. *His* DHI. It filled his end of the tunnel, and what had been a lump of darkness transformed into Jezebel. She stood up from her slumped position looking almost angelic and came toward him slowly, as if she were floating. He couldn't sustain his DHI, and it vanished. He pulled out the BlackBerry, using its glowing screen as a flashlight.

He thought of her as having jet black hair and bone white, almost translucent, skin. Intriguing eyes. That had been how she'd looked when he'd first met her on the Sports Complex soccer field, what seemed like years earlier. In fact, it had only been a matter of months. But Jez had made a radical transformation when Maleficent's spell had been lifted. Her hair was now a shocking blond—almost white. Her thin lips shined luminously red.

She came into his arms, like a young child hugging a parent, and then let go.

In the BlackBerry's weird light, they both looked vaguely blue.

"I didn't think . . ." she stammered. "I hoped and even prayed, though I'm not very good at praying . . . I wired up the iPod but couldn't be sure . . ."

"Amanda found a page in your diary," he explained. "We followed your sketches."

"I don't even remember what I drew."

"Dreams," Finn said. "Amanda said it was what you dreamed."

"Nightmares is more like it. I've had them here as well—down here in the dark."

She explained the ordeal she'd been through. It was much as the Kingdom Keepers had come to suspect: her detention on the savannah; her escape, which turned on a mistake made by one of the monkeys; her flight across the savannah and over a wall that turned out to be the tiger yard. The early morning release of the big cats and her finding herself following one down a wooden hatch and into the tunnel while being stalked by another left behind in the upper yard.

"The hatches both closed at the same time, and I was trapped. At first I realized how lucky I was, because the Overtakers would never think to look in such a place, but then as time went on, it occurred to me that *no one* would look down here. That I was not just hidden, I was trapped. And that's when I realized that a dream I'd had—of a landscape, but from above, like from a plane—made all the more sense. I was in the tunnel, under the *C* in the photo."

"It was a satellite photo," Finn said, explaining. "One of your sketches led us to it."

"And that's when I realized the song on my iPod might help you find me. I used my earbud wire to connect to a box." She turned the glowing iPod, revealing a series of three junction boxes mounted to the stone wall and a number of wires leading from them. "I couldn't be sure it would work, but I thought it probably should. And maybe you'd hear it. *If* you were even here in the Park. And so I decided to save the battery and only play the song every few hours." She pointed at the glowing face of the device. "It still has some power, though not much, I'm afraid."

"We need to get out of here. Amanda and Charlene are up there waiting for us. Philby is on VMK with Wayne—"

"But VMK is closed!"

"Wayne fixed that. The two of them are monitoring network traffic and also trying to see if they can control the hatches in the tiger yards." Finn had nearly forgotten about the DS. He checked that it was turned on.

No signal. He tried the BlackBerry: no bars, no signal.

"To get down here," Finn said, "I had to cross over to get through a maintenance gate. You can't turn yourself into a DHI the way I can. You can't cross over to get back out." He paused, trying to think clearly. "We're kind of stuck down here."

"You can still get out."

"That's not going to happen. I'm not leaving without you."

"You don't happen to have a hamburger and fries in your back pocket, do you?"

"I'm going to try the DS again, closer to the hatches."

"I'll take that as a no."

She disconnected the iPod and carried it in front of her as a very dim flashlight. Finn did the same with the BlackBerry. The tunnel's floor was concrete, its walls, stone. The tunnel was longer than Finn expected. Nearing the far end—the end leading into the upper tiger yard—the tunnel floor began to rise, forming a ramp. The space became lower and tighter, ending in a box of concrete three feet square, a space Finn could just tuck himself into.

"It's exactly the same on the other end," Jez said.

Finn already knew their situation had improved: the static in his ear had lessened. "Have you tried opening it?"

"Yes. Of course. It doesn't open."

"What if two of us pushed?"

"It's not that it's heavy. It's latched shut. Tigers are much stronger than either of us. I'm sure it's constructed to stop a curious tiger from opening it." She paused a moment. "Why do you keep checking your watch? It's only a few minutes later than when you first looked."

Finn said nothing. But he checked his watch again. She was right, it was 5:18. He'd last checked at 5:15.

"What is it?" she asked.

"The Park closes at six."

"So Amanda and the others will have to leave. That's not the most awful thing."

"It isn't just that," he said. "They move the animals—all the animals—out of the Park at closing."

"Including the tigers." Jez made it a statement.

"I'm afraid so."

"And if we're down here when they move them . . ." Her voice trailed off.

Finn caught himself nodding.

The DS beeped, indicating a connection.

> philitup: Finn? Finn?

> Finn: i've got jez!!! she's ok!

Messages started to compete, but Philby cut everyone off with an announcement.

> philitup: found the virtual switch. i think i can open the hatches. want me 2 try?

Finn looked up at Jez. "What do you think?"

"Do we have a choice? I'd rather get eaten running for my life than trapped in a tunnel."

"Yeah, I know what you mean."

> angelface13: ten apes just entered the tiger yards. looks like someone knows what we know.

Finn explained to Jez, "A guy saw us take the satellite photo. It's possible that the Overtakers heard about it and figured out you were down here the same way we did."

"There are monkeys out there?" Jez asked, unable to keep the tension out of her voice.

"Mean monkeys," Finn confirmed. "Though the orangutans are the worst."

"Well, that's certainly reassuring. And we're going out there?"

"I'm not sure we have any choice."

53

MAYBECK AND WILLA stood guard at the Dream Vacation kiosk in Camp Minnie-Mickey. With their backs to Philby, who occupied the computer terminal, they kept their eyes on the crowd as well as on the jungle, acutely aware that the last attack had come quickly and without warning.

Philby had his hands full. While he was negotiating an intricate set of networking cables, represented on-screen by a rainbow of wires that spidered out from various network hubs to the myriad attractions, security cameras, and cash registers throughout Animal Kingdom, Wayne had worked his way through the virtual schematics to find a switch he believed responsible for the tiger-yard hatches. Philby had double-checked Wayne's work and, agreeing with him, had called Finn over the DS.

> philitup: changed a timer. in 5 minutes the tunnel hatches will open.

"Five minutes," Finn said, sounding anxious.

With Charlene's announcement that the monkeys had arrived in the tiger yards, Philby noticed that the volume of network traffic increased exponentially. Data flowed along the colorful cables, not in data streams, but in data *rivers*. Philby worked the cursor to move his avatar along the virtual catwalks that carried the network cables like colorful hoses. Screen by screen he followed the increase in color that signaled a rise in data flow. Blue indicated outbound data—from various servers placed throughout the Park—while red signified data returning, check sums used to tell the server the data had reached its intended destination. Like data over the Internet, it moved in pulses, or parcels, which when combined added up to a whole message or image. With the jump in data traffic, the blue lines pulsed sky blue, and the red lines turned fire-engine red. The pulses got faster and the bursts brighter, until all at once a good number of lines turned into a shimmering purple—a combination of the red and blue, the data moving in such quantity and at such speeds that the two colors became a third.

These were the lines that interested Philby, for as life-size graphic images, holograms consisted of phenomenal amounts of data. His avatar hurried, staying with the same purple data line through a half dozen screens, making sure he never confused one purple line for another. (By simply rolling the cursor over the purple line a corresponding number appeared—like an ID tag. He followed number 518912.) The data was passed from one network hub to another, the largest and most complicated being a hub marked Discovery Island Hub.

From here, the purple lines traveled southeast across a bridge. Just before the bridge, a network line led to a structure marked Flame Tree Barbecue. Philby's avatar reached the far side of the bridge and turned to follow the purple cables as Wayne's white-haired avatar popped up from below the bridge. Wayne's avatar held two silver swords cradled in his arms.

[ ]: here. one is for you. i fear we may meet resistance. and remember: although only a virtual world, if your avatar is killed or captured, it's Game Over. i won't be able to reconstruct you and reinsert you into VMK for at least an hour or two, and I fear by then it will be too late. if you're to accomplish your mission you must stay in the game.

philitup: a sword?

[ ]: it's all i could find on short notice.

philitup: how many of them?

[ ]: no idea. maybe none. but the closer we get to destroying them, the bigger the fight they will put up. they know you were in vmk earlier. I assume they've adjusted their defenses accordingly.

Philby took hold of the small sword—it looked like a silver toothpick—and swung it back and forth. It took him a moment to get the hang of it. Then Wayne stepped in front of him and the two sparred, Wayne handling the weapon with surprising aplomb. In fact, the more aggressive Philby got with the sword, the more effortless Wayne's motions. They continued to duel, Wayne's avatar dancing circles around Philby. Then Philby held his sword to his chest and typed a message.

philitup: you've done this before.

[ ]: a little, perhaps.

philitup: more than a little.

[ ]: there was a time . . . a *long* time ago . . . when the overtakers challenged the kingdom. this is why uncle walt left the stonecutter's quill in the first place. I was a member of the team sent to repel the overtakers.

The Stonecutter's Quill had been central to the Kingdom Keepers' first attempt to defeat the Overtakers. Philby found it interesting, important even, to hear the history. He told himself to remember everything so he could tell the others.

philitup: sent?

[ ]: disney world was just being built at the time. the real power of the kingdom lay in disneyland, as it does to this day.

philitup: what kind of power?

[ ]: it needn't concern you now.

philitup: but it does.

[ ]: patience, my young friend. if the battle ever returns home, believe me, the kingdom keepers will be part of it.

philitup: you were a swordsman?

[ ]: we learned many defenses, the sword but one of them. surprising how easily it comes back. you're doing well enough. just remember: it is double-edged. it cuts just as easily on the backswing. conserve your energy and always swing in *both* directions.

philitup: I'll try.

[ ]: it's all that can be asked. now let's be off . . .

Together they continued along the catwalks, up and down staircases, always following the pulsing purple cables. A group of cables ran to the right. Philby stopped to examine them: none was purple. Others continued straight ahead.

[ ]: we're in dinoland. those are restaurants to our right. the rides are to our left: fossil fun games, primeval whirl, and triceratop spin.

Six cables continued straight ahead—four of them pulsing a rich purple. What had left the Discovery Island hub as hundreds of data cables had been reduced to just a few, the majority of which were purple, indicating a large amount of data transfer. The cables were nearing the source of that data—*the second server*.

Philby was scared. For Finn, the key was to defeat the second server, to eliminate the DHIs Maleficent was using to increase her army. Who knew how many of the monkeys, birds, or tigers were real? The only way to absolutely know was to shut down the second server—for good—and that task now fell to him and an old man with toothpick swords. If they were going to encounter resistance, it was going to be soon.

He didn't need to ask Wayne where those cables

led. There was only a single attraction at the bottom of DinoLand USA.

Philby, the boy, not the avatar, briefly released the VMK controls. He turned around, found Maybeck's face in the crowd, and called out, "The Dino Institute. You and Willa . . . as fast as you can!"

Then he turned back to the screen to see that he was too late: Wayne was under attack.

54

*T*WO MINUTES . . .

Finn counted down the seconds on his watch. He heard his mouth speak before he meant to say anything.

"The first time I saw you I was scared of you," he told Jez. The two were huddled close together just below the hatch in the upper tiger yard.

"Me?"

"Your long hair. The way you looked at me."

"I was under Maleficent's spell," she reminded him.

And I was under yours, he thought. "Yeah," he said. "The thing is, as it turned out, there was nothing to be afraid of."

"Are you trying to tell me something?" she asked. Their faces were about a foot apart. Only a tiny bit of light seeped in from around the edges of the hatch, emitting a dull glow. He saw the shape of her head, nothing more.

"Fear is a weird thing. It can totally take over, or you can push it away and suddenly it's gone. That's how I'm able to be a DHI—I remove all thought, all fear, and suddenly I cross over."

"It's going to be scary out there," Jez said, suddenly understanding what it was Finn was trying to say.

"Yeah, I think so."

"Why can't boys ever say what they actually want to say? If you were Amanda, you'd have just said, 'Heads up, girl! It's going to be freaky out there.'"

"Heads up, girl," Finn said.

"Ha-ha," she mocked him.

"I will try to leave the hatch as my DHI. If Charlene's inside the tiger yard, she will be near a wall. Have you ever been to a rodeo?"

"Are you serious?"

"In a rodeo, the clown's job is to distract the bull. To draw the bull's attention away from the bull rider to give the rider enough time to get over the fence, out of danger. Think of Charlene and me as the clowns. You're the rider."

"They're coming after me," Jez said.

"They'll come after all of us," Finn said, "but they can only hurt you. They don't know that, so that's to our advantage."

"It's not much."

"No. But it's all we've got. If Charlene has jumped the wall, then she'll know the way out. You *must* follow Charlene. No matter what happens to me, no matter what you see, ignore it. Stay with Charlene."

"I don't like the sound of this."

"I'm just saying."

One minute . . .

"Finn, if you're trying to impress me . . . I already have a boyfriend . . ."

"Rob," Finn said. He saw her head cock to the side in curiosity. "'Change Rob'—it was in your diary. Amanda told us Rob was your boyfriend. It took us forever to realize why you'd written that."

"And why had I written that?"

"It's an anagram for Chernabog," Finn said.

"Like the guy in *Fantasia*?"

"The same. We think he's Maleficent's boss, or king, or whatever you'd call it."

"Superior," she said.

"Whatever. He's the one in control."

"I think . . . oh my gosh."

"What?"

"I think I had a daydream," she said. "While I was down here in the dark. *King of the Mountain*, I called him. Big and ugly, and really hairy. He was trying to kill me. Me and Amanda. He had this club in his hand. No! It wasn't a club. It was—" She gasped. For the first time in the dull light he could see her face clearly: her eyes were squinted closed.

"What?"

"It wasn't a club in his hand," she repeated. "It was . . . you, Finn. He had you by the legs and was swinging you like a club."

Finn knew the strength of Jez's dreams. He found it hard to breathe, his chest tight, his throat dry.

Fear!

He had to push it away. He had to find a sense of calm. He needed to cross over to his DHI.

Because at that moment, the hatch above their heads began to squeak and groan. Light flooded in and blinded them.

The hatch was coming open.

55

PHILBY RAISED HIS AVATAR'S SWORD and blocked the swipe of silver steel that aimed for his head. Wayne was fighting two at once, his sword nothing but a blur of shining light.

The things coming at them—there were four altogether—were hunchbacked trolls with exaggerated noses, long hair, and strong arms. Never mind that they were avatars, they were horrendous-looking creatures, incredibly quick with their swords and determined to eliminate Wayne and Philby from VMK.

Philby blocked a second swipe and then a third. He backed up and moved to his right, noticing that the troll pivoted on its left foot as it turned to stay with Philby. Philby raised his sword as if to strike a blow to the head. The troll crossed its sword to block, but Philby released the sword, allowing it to fall and, as it did, he bent forward and was there to catch it before it hit the ground. He swung at the troll's left leg. It sliced in two at the knee. The troll stepped forward and fell over onto its face. It tried to stand but was useless without a left leg.

Philby stepped around it in time to engage the

sword of the third troll to attack Wayne, who was already busy defending himself against two of the attackers. Philby caught this troll's sword as it swung back over its head. The contact spun the troll around and it came at Philby with a series of swift slices to the air, narrowly missing the chest of Philby's avatar, which was in steady retreat. The troll reared back and lowered its sword with power and speed. Philby sidestepped, tripped, and his avatar went down.

The sword smacked into one of the purple networking cables, cutting it in two. The purple color immediately switched to gray, and Philby realized that since this was an internal maintenance site, anything done to the mechanism was for real and affected the real world. Wherever that data feed had been headed, it was now null and void. He considered cutting all the cables. Wouldn't that have the desired effect? Wouldn't it stop all the data—and more than likely all the DHIs? He thought it would, but at the same time, without that vivid color, he wouldn't be able to follow the cables to their source—the second server. And that was the ultimate prize.

A troll left the fight with Wayne. It squatted and jumped a phenomenal distance, landing right in front of Philby. It raised its sword to do Philby in. It was now two against one. Philby spun in a full circle, his sword outstretched. It was similar to a martial arts move, and it caught the two others by surprise. He hit the first in the arm, severing it. The second took the tip of his sword across its chest. Philby spun again, this time taking a step forward.

The one-armed troll merely switched hands, now holding the sword with its right. It lowered it at Philby, who danced to the left just as the blade came down like a guillotine. It chopped off the end of Philby's right foot.

Philby moved and saw his avatar sway, about to fall. He jerked left and maintained his balance: he could still stand, but his steps had to be shorter.

Wayne had dispatched the remaining troll. He came at the two on Philby from behind, and soon there was a flash of swords as Philby battled the one-armed troll and Wayne took the wounded one. Philby moved to his right, seeing that Wayne was moving that way as well. And now Philby saw Wayne's scheme. The two trolls were battling in close quarters, too near one another. They each pivoted on one leg as they turned— a faulty design—and Wayne was working to tie their legs together, to cross their legs.

It worked beautifully. One more move to his right, and Philby watched as the two trolls tumbled over. Before Philby could even lift his sword, Wayne had removed these two from the game as well. Wayne hurried to the one spinning on the floor and stopped it with a sword thrust.

[ ]: if we don't hurry, they'll generate another fifty of these and send them our way. can you find the server?

philitup: I'm sure I can.

[ ]: then do it. and tell your friends up top we may need their help. my guess is these trolls aren't going to let us anywhere near that server.

56

Their eyes adjusting as they climbed up the small ramp and out of the open hatch, Finn and Jez beheld an intimidating sight. The upper tiger yard was a large enclosure, an open expanse of sloping green grass surrounded by fifteen-foot-high walls. The enclosure's boundaries were broken by bamboo trees, wild grasses, and jungle shrubs. In the shade to their left, and just coming to her feet, was an enormous tigress, six feet from shoulders to tail with a huge head, and paws the size of oven mitts. She glanced back at them with her amber eyes and let out a thunderous growl—they were intruders and she didn't appreciate being awakened from her nap.

Directly ahead of them, coming over the crest of the small rise, were two more tigers—barreling toward Finn and Jez at full speed and, to the right of the yard, a half dozen monkeys and four large orangutans were also charging. The number of wild animals, as well as their combined ferocity, every twitch of muscle aimed directly at Finn and Jez, froze the kids. They stood absolutely still, which was a good thing.

Then Finn spotted the ivy creeping along the right wall—just behind the gang of monkeys. *Charlene.*

"Finn?" a terrified Jez said, her voice breaking.

"No fear," Finn whispered. He had tried to cross over on his way out of the hatch, but his excitement had prevented it. He didn't want Jez to know this, so he spoke with authority.

"Move to your right," he said. "Stay close to the wall."

"But the monkeys!" she said.

"I know."

A hollow growl reverberated from behind them: another tiger, this one coming through the tunnel from the lower yard.

Finn picked up a stick and stepped forward, putting himself between the charging monkeys and Jez. The two center tigers continued their advance, while the one in the shade to the left had spun fully around to face the hatch. If he didn't do something quickly, he and Jez were going to be animal crackers—a late afternoon snack.

"Go!" he said.

Jez took off along the wall at a run.

Finn attacked the line of advancing monkeys and apes, swinging the stick like a baseball bat. The monkeys skidded to a stop, forming a semicircle around him. He saw a flash in the eyes of one of the orang-utans: the ape had spotted Jez fleeing along the wall. He chose this ape to go after, chanting under his breath: *Nothing can hurt me.*

He charged the orangutan, swung the stick, and forced the ape to dance backward, out of the way of contact. In doing so, the orangutan left a small gap between him and the ape to his side. It was just big enough for Finn to squeeze through. He ran forward and shot the gap. The ape turned.

This offered Jez the opportunity to run even harder, quickly moving along the wall toward the slowly advancing Charlene, who, posing as DeVine, was high atop her stilts.

The large cat to the left stepped out of the shadows, her strides calculated and controlled: she was hunting. If not Finn, any one of the monkeys would make a worthwhile snack.

The monkeys saw the cat as well, their hackles raised in alarm.

Finn was facing the wall of monkeys as the second cat climbed up and out of the tunnel. He glanced over his shoulder: the other two cats would arrive at any moment.

He'd done a fine job of pulling attention away from Jez, but his own situation was far more tentative. If he didn't think of something quickly, his lone stick was not going to be enough to defend himself.

He held the stick high overhead and cried out loudly in a war cry.

"Go ahead, try it!" he shouted, watching Jez continue her progress. But the monkeys grew daring, tightening the circle around Finn.

Preparing to strike.

PHILBY'S AND WAYNE'S AVATARS ran along a catwalk of steel mesh, following the few remaining cables like train tracks toward an unconfirmed destination. But everything pointed toward the Dino Institute. Finally, the first wall of the institute appeared, and then the identification on the schematics.

The trick for Philby was to juggle back and forth between the DS and the computer terminal. It wasn't easy.

> philitup: it's definitely dino-institute.

> mybest: we're almost there.

He studied the wires ahead of him. The purple wires turned right just inside the doors of the institute.

The virtual blueprint spread out before him and Wayne. As they neared the entrance, the plan shifted from two to three dimensions. He and Wayne moved inside the guest entrance. Philby stayed alert for any other ways to get in.

Wayne's avatar stopped at the edge of the doorway.

Philby typed a message to Wayne.

philitup: what's wrong?

[ ]: i sense a trap.

philitup: why?

[ ]: we should have met more resistance. i am familiar with their tactics. this is unlike them.

philitup: maybe they've changed.

[ ]: not likely. the overtakers never rest. they are cunning and clever and they possess many spells. i would suggest we look for another access point.

philitup: there's no time. besides, the cables are right here.

[ ]: have you considered the cables themselves may be part of a trap?

Philby had not given it any thought. The data flow had convinced him he was following the right cables. If it was a trap, then Maybeck and Willa were also walking right into it.

[ ]: please . . . another door. it's safer for *all* of us.

Philby hesitated, incredibly tempted to follow the cables. But Wayne had gotten him this far. He had to trust him. He backed his avatar out of the entrance, took his hands off the controls, and texted a message to Maybeck's DS

> philitup: if u can get backstage @ dino institute, u r looking 4 a rack of servers. there will b thick blue or gray ethernet cables clipped into the back of each server. there may be a hub—a box with flashing lights.

As his avatar stepped out of the structure, the schematics returned to two dimensions. He studied the full schematics. The biggest backstage areas were to the right.

> philitup: workshops are @ end of ride. must destroy server.

He waited to make sure Maybeck had received the messages.

> mybest: got it . . i hope.

58

THE APES AND MONKEYS ENCIRCLED FINN, closing around him like a net. How simple to cross over briefly into his DHI and just walk right through that hairy line, but it was not to be: he was terrified. He wasn't going to cross over on his own.

He spun, looking for the weak link in the circle. He considered charging some of the smaller monkeys, breaking the line there and running for it. But they all were ferociously fast on their feet and, at the moment, baring their teeth in a display of aggression and anger.

He caught sight of Jez as she reached Charlene. Excitedly, the two girls worked it out to where Charlene was leaning her back against the wall, and the nimble Jez now climbed up the stilts—using them as a ladder—toward Charlene's waiting hand. Finn looked away as the fingers of the two met, confident that Charlene would get Jez up and over to the other side.

"Over here!" a high-pitched voice called out.

Finn heard guests shout: "Check it out!" "Look at this!" "There are kids in with the tigers!"

Where had she come from? Finn wondered. It was

Amanda. She was *inside* the tiger yard, the huge, prowling cat to her left, the circle of monkeys directly in front of her.

Disney Security would be on them in minutes. They had to get Jez—and themselves—out before they were either eaten by the tigers or caught by Security.

The other two cats arrived at the same time. They, too, began to circle, along with the tiger that escaped the hatch—a wider circle than the monkeys, one that included Amanda.

The escaped tiger still confused Finn: *how had it gotten into the tunnel in the first place? Was the lower yard hatch open? If so, who had opened it?*

Only the prowling tigress that had emerged from the shadows remained on her own, majestically moving with long, confident strides, restlessly back and forth. She seemed to be agitated, studying the commotion in her yard, calculating a strike.

Several of the monkeys spun around, distracted by Amanda, and broke their chain. Finn took advantage of the distraction and shot for the opening.

The two charging tigers turned at the last minute, now aiming for Amanda.

Finn took two steps toward her, intending to defend her, but then witnessed her leaving the ground. She levitated, floating higher and higher. The monkeys, carried by their own momentum, ran right through the space she had occupied. The two charging tigers leaped into the air, reaching their claws toward her. One caught the leg of her jeans, but there was no sound of tearing fabric. No scream.

The leaping tiger flew through the air and landed with a roll.

The slinking tigress sat back on her haunches and sprang for the charging tiger. It looked as if the tigress were trying to defend Amanda. The two tigers growled at the tigress and the three cats began to circle each other.

Ignored, Amanda lowered herself to the grass.

"The wall!" Finn called out to Amanda as he raised his stick toward the remaining two monkeys.

Amanda sprinted toward Charlene.

Finn turned his back in their direction, battling most of the monkeys, who darted about him trying to sink their teeth into his legs. He knocked them back with his stick, but apparently they barely felt it.

Looking over the heads of the monkeys, Finn saw the tigress swiping her huge claws at the other two grand cats. It looked as if the cats made contact, but none of them reeled with pain—they held their ground.

Charlene let out a squeal as Amanda climbed up

her stilts; her hand had become caught between a stilt and the wall.

With that squeal, all three cats turned. One minute fighting each other; the next, acting like curious cats. They clearly saw the monkeys, then Finn, and finally the girl in the distance clambering up a wall.

They charged.

Finn had his hands full with the monkeys. He had not an ounce of strength nor a second of time to deal with three enormous cats barreling down toward him.

This is it, he thought. It was too late to turn and run. Too late to escape.

The cats were lightning fast. They seemed to pull the earth, and Finn with it, dragging him toward them. Without looking, the monkeys knew. They darted to their left, removing themselves from the tigers' line of sight.

Finn readied his pathetic stick; it was all the defense he had. He was going to be eaten alive.

The two smaller tigers leaped into the air when just five yards away, perfectly calculating the distance. They would land on Finn, crushing him, then snap his neck with their powerful jaws and start the feast.

Finn braced for the end.

59

PHILBY'S AND WAYNE'S AVATARS HAD, only five minutes earlier, moved around the right wall of the Dino Institute, as it appeared on the virtual schematics.

philitup: if you helped create the place, how about a little hint of how to reach that room?

Near the south wall of the institute, the purple cables terminated. The blueprint showed a series of walls around them, but no door. So was the server in a closet? A workspace? The ceiling? The hiding place in the floor?

[ ]: computers came way after my time. I have no idea where that is.

philitup: none? are you sure? they don't need much space, but it has to be a cool room, and they require a lot of cabling, so they would be over a tunnel or sewer, or—

[ ]: storm sewers.

Wayne's avatar lifted its arm to point.

[ ]: I remember a meeting, years ago, where routing data lines over the storm sewer pipes was

discussed. storm sewers carry the rainwater out of the park. the sewer lines are in maintenance conduits throughout the park.

philitup: but this is a server they want to hide, that they don't want anyone to find.

[ ]: the employee bathroom in the Dino Institute is way too cold. and every bathroom has drains, right? some drains feed the storm sewers.

Philby grabbed hold of the DS. It was worth a try.

> philitup: dhi server is in an employee bathroom close 2 the south wall.

> mybest: on our way.

> philitup: wayne and i will try 2 cut the cables. u try 2 find server.

Philby looked back at the VMK screen and, as he did, the screen popped and sparkled. It occurred to him that someone could be monitoring them. The Overtakers could know that he and Wayne were online. Could they trace their locations? If so, both he and Wayne were at great risk.

philitup: hurry up! we have to cut the cables.

Wayne's avatar rushed to keep up with Philby. It forced Wayne to keep his hands on the mouse and off the keyboard: he couldn't type a message as long as Philby kept him moving.

They traveled around the corner of the institute and back to the catwalk that carried the data cables. Philby struck the purple cables with his sword. Once . . . twice . . . three times. All the cables were cut. They immediately turned gray—the data stream was dead.

Why wasn't Wayne helping? Philby turned his avatar to look.

Wayne's avatar wasn't moving.

philitup: come on! hurry!

The white-haired avatar just stood there not doing anything.

Philby wished he could scream at Wayne, instead of just typing. Why wasn't the old guy following him?

Then the impossible happened: Wayne's avatar dissolved.

60

MAYBECK AND WILLA occupied the backseat of one of the exploration vehicles inside the Dino Institute. The front seat stood empty, and given the size of the crowd lined up for the ride, this should have told them something; but they'd been too preoccupied with Philby's instructions to pay much attention to anything beyond looking for doors offering employees backstage access.

The ride was dark and very cold, with stunningly real dinosaurs appearing at every turn. Asteroids fell to Earth in a shower of fiber optics. The vehicle rounded a long turn. The prehistoric creatures looked up and turned toward the truck.

"How are we going to do this?" Willa asked Maybeck in a whisper. "We can't jump from the car without setting off the alarms."

"We'll find a way backstage," Maybeck promised. "The trick is to know where we're going." He indicated the part of the ride to their right. "This section is all interior to the track. Philby said a workshop or bathroom. Those rooms are going to be in spaces between the ride and the exterior walls—or currently to our left."

"Are you sure about that?" she asked.

"I'm not sure about anything," he conceded.

The next scene showed a tyrannosaurus eating a lizard.

"It's creepy the way their eyes move," Willa hissed. "It feels like they're looking right at—"

But her words were cut off as the dinosaur's giant tail swiped over the engine of the open-topped vehicle. Maybeck reached out and pulled Willa down onto him a fraction of a second before the massive tail nearly beheaded her. The tail broke some equipment off the vehicle, and it tumbled to the track.

Maybeck dared to sneak a look and pushed Willa back up.

"Was that . . . supposed to happen?" she gasped.

Maybeck pulled at a lap belt at his waist; then he tried Willa's. The belts wouldn't release—they were locked shut. The kids couldn't jump out of the vehicle even if they'd wanted to.

"I don't think so. No," Maybeck answered. "I think that was intended for us. Heads up!"

He glanced back. No vehicles in sight in either direction.

The ride was designed so that no car ever saw another. There was no use calling out for help.

"You remember Small World?" he asked her.

"I was on Winnie the Pooh with Charlene," Willa answered. "We nearly drowned, don't forget."

"I haven't forgotten. My point is: I think this is like that."

"I think you're right."

If they could have jumped from the car, the sensors would have stopped the ride, but the locked seat belts prevented their escape.

Suddenly, a pterodactyl shot down at them from out of the pitch-black ceiling. It was dark and angular, with a wingspan of over six feet. With its sharp talons extended, it descended too quickly for Maybeck to react, catching him by the wrist as he shielded his face from the attack. At the moment the talon grabbed hold of him, his seat belt released, the timing too perfect to be coincidental. The bird locked on to his forearm and dragged him up and out of the vehicle.

Willa screamed, spun, and grabbed him by the boots. Maybeck was now stretched between the overhead bird and Willa, still locked in her seat. Neither was willing to let go. He groaned in agony—it felt like every joint was separating simultaneously.

He twisted his forearm to the left then quickly to the right, breaking the bird's grip on him. The pterdoactyl's long beak bent back to peck at Maybeck, but too late. Maybeck reached out and snapped the bird's leg at the knee. The creature cried out, flapped its wings, and was absorbed into the darkness of the ceiling.

Was it alive?

Willa pulled him down into the backseat, but he avoided the seat belt.

The pterodcactyl's broken leg in hand, Maybeck studied it. An electrical wire extended from the broken knee.

"You're bleeding," she said.

He studied the three holes in his skin. "It doesn't hurt much. I'm fine."

"It *got* you."

"Dang right it did." Only Maybeck didn't say 'dang.'

"This ride is *trying* to hurt us!"

"You think?" he snapped sarcastically. "You're not surprised by that, are you? There are sensors on every ride. Probably cameras, too. Throw in a little artificial intelligence, and how hard can it be to program a server to defend itself?"

"You think the *server* is doing this?"

"I think it knows we mean business. It has every right to be scared. I'm going to fry its innards if—*no, when!*—we find it."

"But how—?" Willa began. She cut herself off as

Maybeck stood up in the seat, grabbed a light, and turned it to show them something of the track in front of them.

Back behind the jungle plants, he illuminated a black door and a disguised device protruding from beside it.

"Ten-to-one that's a card reader," Maybeck said. "That's our way in."

"But I'm stuck," Willa reminded him, indicating the locked seat belt. She pulled and squirmed, but there wasn't any way she was going to slip out of its grip.

Maybeck glanced around sharply. The car had already moved them past the black door. They were rounding a turn toward the end of the ride. They would be caught and—at a minimum—thrown out of the Park. If the Overtakers got hold of them, then things were about to get a lot worse.

"There has to be an emergency release," Maybeck said, trying to think like Philby. *What would Philby do?*

"If a car stops," she said. "Like a fire or something . . ."

"The belts would release!" Maybeck nearly shouted, agreeing with her.

"We're going to have to move fast," he said. A rhinoceroslike dinosaur stepped out of the scene up ahead and lowered its head. It was going to head-butt them.

Maybeck jumped from the vehicle.

Nothing happened.

He'd expected flashing lights and sirens and for the vehicle to stop. But the car continued forward, aimed directly at the armor-clad beast with its head lowered.

Maybeck tore loose a branch from a tree. He hurried to the front of the research vehicle and swung the branch repeatedly at the vehicle's bumper and grille.

"Terry!" Willa shouted, calling Maybeck by his first name.

"There has to be . . ." Maybeck muttered to himself as he continued to bash the vehicle while he backed up toward the waiting dinosaur. His pants belt snagged on something on the front grille. If the beast charged now, it would crush him against the car.

Again, he smacked the front of the car.

It stopped.

He'd knocked out a front sensor.

Struggling to free his hooked belt, he turned and glanced over his shoulder. The dinosaur broke loose from his scene—*the thing was definitely alive!*—and charged.

With the stopping of the vehicle, an alarm now sounded throughout the building.

Willa's seat belt released, freeing her.

She leaped from the backseat. "The black door!"

Maybeck called out calmly. Again he wrestled with his belt. Now he fiddled to unstrap it: he was stuck.

The dinosaur snorted and charged down the track at him. Only at the last second did Maybeck spot a small pool of oil along the track—one of the vehicles ahead of him was leaking oil. As he noticed it, he elected to stay perfectly still.

"MAYBECK!" Willa cried out.

His belt still caught, Maybeck turned around and faced the charging animal.

His belt buckle came loose and slipped out of the loops on his pants.

He dropped to the floor.

The dinosaur slipped in the oil and crashed into the front of the vehicle, demolishing the rover into a twisted V of bent metal.

Maybeck was lying directly between the dinosaur's legs.

He scrambled to his feet.

Willa held the black door open.

Maybeck ran like he'd never run. The dinosaur turned and followed, not slowed by the crushing impact with the vehicle.

Maybeck literally dove through the black door. Willa swung it shut. The wall shook as the dinosaur impacted the metal door and concrete fire wall. Willa took Maybeck by the hand and pulled him to his feet.

"You could have been killed."

"I saw that his legs were like stumps. As long as I stayed *between* them . . ."

"That was too big a risk to take."

"It's not like I had forever to think about it," he replied.

He looked around. They were in a long, curving hallway. There were no markings on the gray walls. Overhead, hundreds of wires were carried in a kind of metal ladder that hung from the ceiling; it ran in both directions and out of sight. Among the wires were dozens of blue ones.

"We follow the wires," Maybeck said.

"But in which direction?"

"This way," Maybeck said.

"But how do you know?" Willa asked.

"I don't," he said. "Some things we've just got to take on faith."

"Faith? This is you speaking? What have you done with the real Maybeck?"

"Give it a rest."

They were hurrying now, the alarm still sounding. Perhaps employees all rushed to assigned stations in emergencies—or to unload guests. Whatever the case, the hallway was empty.

Maybeck moved not with his eye down the hall, but in the tangle of wires overhead. Willa did much the same.

"There!" she said, pointing out a massive group of blue wires running from the wire carrier through a hole above a door to their right.

Maybeck swung open the door.

Workbenches ran along the far wall, covered with spare parts, soldering guns, tools, and hydraulics. In the middle of the space to their left was a metal rack, floor-to-ceiling shelving holding dozens of computer servers, network hubs, and surge suppressors.

"We've got it!" Willa proclaimed.

"No!" Maybeck countered. "It can't be this easy. Philby said we should look for a closet or a bathroom."

"But these are computer servers. It could easily be—"

"No, it couldn't be here. This ride uses all these computers. The nerds that work on them would notice a server that didn't belong. Philby's got to be right."

"Then where?"

"The wires," Maybeck said, hurrying around the back side of the rack of computers. There had to be several hundred wires—both blue and black—the blue wires interconnecting the servers and the hubs. The black wires ran to power supplies. Some of the groups of wires were well-organized and held together by plastic ties; others had been added hastily and were in a tangled clump of spaghetti.

Maybeck looked this all over and said, "We're not going to find it here."

"How can you tell that?" Willa asked.

"Because the same guys that work the computers know the wires. They could spot wires that didn't belong."

"In this mess? I don't think so." Willa stepped forward and dragged her fingernail along one wire, then another.

"What are you doing?"

"Every girl knows that makeup can hide anything," she said. "The way you fool the nerds is you paint the blue wires black. Then they don't notice—" She cut herself off as her thumbnail flaked away some black paint, revealing the blue wire below. *"Voilà!"*

"If I hadn't seen it with my own eyes," Maybeck said.

Footsteps . . . coming fast down the hall.

"The door!" Maybeck whispered.

Willa raced to the door and quietly spun the lock.

The people in the hall ran past. She looked at Maybeck and rolled her eyes: that had been too close.

As she rejoined Maybeck, he followed the painted

network line to where it had been run along the underside of the bottom shelf. Together they traced it and three others to the interior wall, and along this wall and another set of shelves to where a small hole had been drilled through some plasterboard. A door stood immediately to Maybeck's right where a wall jutted out. He tried the doorknob.

Locked.

Willa pointed to a small sign that identified the door: JANITOR.

"That's perfect!" Maybeck said. "It's certain to have a drain—which is how Philby says they run the wires around the Park."

"I need something the size of a credit card," Willa said.

Maybeck looked at her curiously.

"I have brothers who are constantly trying to lock me out of the bathroom. They think it's funny."

She found a metal plate on a workbench. She slid it into the crack next to the doorjamb, and the dark room popped open.

"Sometimes I hate being an only child," Maybeck quipped.

The room was a pile of junk—a neglected storeroom. It took him a minute, but Maybeck located the server mounted beneath a photo-developing bench—

a blue-and-silver Dell that looked a lot like a piece of a home stereo.

If they were right, this small box controlled all the holograms of the animals they'd battled, and it possessed the power to erase them all.

"What now?" she asked.

"We don't just pull the plug. I know that much."

"A magnet," she said. "We need a magnet!"

Together, the two returned to the workshop and began searching for anything magnetic. Willa found a couple of small magnets, but they both agreed they wouldn't be powerful enough to do any real damage. They needed to rearrange all the magnetic information on the hard disk. It was going to take something . . .

"There!" Maybeck said too loudly.

At that very moment, another line of footfalls had been coming down the hallway. The noise stopped just outside the door. A fist banged on the door.

"Block it!" he hissed, instructing Willa.

For what he'd spotted was currently up near the ceiling. It was a very large device with two metal plates connected by wires; it hung from the end of a hydraulic arm and was clearly meant to raise and lower heavy pieces of the dinosaurs that were under construction or repair.

Willa rolled a tool chest in front of the door and then locked the wheels.

Maybeck threw a switch and worked the hydraulic arm, attaching the magnet to the end of it. He found the power switch and tried it: a wrench and three screwdrivers jumped off a workbench and stuck to the magnet. He'd gotten it too close to the workbench, but he'd proven his point.

He flipped off the switch, and the tools dropped to the floor in a cacophony of banging metal.

Now the people on the other side of the door tried all the harder.

Maybeck wrestled with a giant cotter pin that held the magnet to the arm. He got the magnet free, extended the wire connecting it, and was able to stretch it to all the way inside the dark room. The thing was massive. He knew it had to be right on top of the server to corrupt the hard drive. It took most of his strength to lift the magnet and all his strength to hold it under the counter and against the hidden server.

"Throw the switch!" he called out.

"I'm a little busy here," Willa said, having dragged a leg of a tyrannosaurus to block the door.

"I . . . can't . . . hold . . . it," Maybeck gasped. "Throw the freaking switch." Only he didn't say "freaking."

Willa abandoned the door and ran to the controls. She threw the switch.

The magnet leaped out of Maybeck's hands and

glued itself to the server. A small, green LED on the front—meant to indicate hard-drive activity—turned to amber, then flashed red. Next, all the lights on the server failed completely, and there was an electrical smell in the air.

The second server was dead.

Maybeck and Willa hugged, only to realize what they were doing. Then Willa pushed him away and said, "Don't disgust me!"

Maybeck brushed off his clothes and quickly changed the subject. "I probably should have checked with Philby before doing that. I hope it doesn't mess things up."

The workroom door banged open an inch, the tool carrier sliding on the concrete floor.

Two inches.

Then five.

"What now?" she asked, her voice tight.

Maybeck glanced overhead: it was a drop ceiling, maybe a foot or two lower than the one out in the hallway.

"How are you with small spaces?" he asked.

61

THE TWO TIGERS VANISHED IN MIDAIR. As did four of the six monkeys and two of the orangutans.

The big tigress from the shadows remained and so did the massive tiger that had come through the hatch. Finn counted two monkeys and two orangutans.

DHIs, Finn realized. Two of the tigers and several of the monkeys and apes had been holograms. No wonder his blows with the stick hadn't done much.

Amanda's climb had distracted the charging animals just long enough for Finn and Jez to get past them. Meanwhile, Philby's team was about to defeat the second server.

Now it was time to get out of there.

Finn took off running. A caged-in jungle Jeep appeared from over the rise, a flashing light atop its roof.

The orangutans moved to intercept Finn. Jez ran toward Charlene and the wall.

Incredibly fast, and easily as big as he was, the apes came at Finn with wild eyes and drooling snorts of intention. The first of the two bounded toward Finn, made one gigantic leap, and would have torn his head off with its outstretched hand had the tigress not sprung. The cat scared the orangutan. The ape rolled into a ball, came to standing, and saw the cat bearing down on it once again. Forced to choose between pursuing Finn or confronting the cat, the orange ape turned to escape. Now, faced with a Jeep coming at it headlong, the orangutan sprang for the bamboo grove and disappeared, the huge cat following hotly on its tail.

The second ape saw its partner flee and beat a hasty retreat. Thankfully for Finn, that retreat took it into the path of the Jeep, which veered sharply to avoid a collision. The Jeep skidded to a stop near the open hatch, away from Charlene, who remained poised, her stilts pressed at an angle against the wall. Jez was nowhere to be seen. She'd made it over the wall.

"How about a lift?" Finn shouted.

Charlene bent low and offered her cupped hands as a boost.

Finn climbed up, lay flat, and offered Charlene his hand. She took it, stood, and, as rangers hurried from the Jeep, shook her legs violently, managing to kick loose first one, and then both of the stilts. Some of the ivy that connected her costume with the stilts tore loose. She left the rangers with a pair of stilts in their hands as she and Finn both lowered themselves down off the wall.

Dozens of guests had gathered to observe the excitement. Some applauded as the Kingdom Keepers dropped to the path, but they didn't stick around to take a bow.

Charlene said, "This way!" and led the others directly across the formal gardens and into the jungle on a route she now knew well.

But just before they entered the dense jungle, Jez pulled to a stop, transfixed by something to her right.

All the kids stopped and looked in that direction. They saw a snowcapped peak of a towering mountain.

"That mountain was in my dream," she told Finn. "The dream I told you about."

"*King of the Mountain*," Finn said. "Where you and Amanda were under attack."

"Yes." Jez reached out and took Amanda by the hand. She said nothing, but the look that was exchanged between the two "sisters" would have quieted even the most cynical person.

"That's Expedition Everest," Charlene said.

"Then, like it or not, that's where we're headed," Jez said. "Never once, not once, has one of my dreams lied to me."

62

Having reconnected on the DS's, all the Kingdom Keepers, along with Jez and Amanda, reunited in a small patch of jungle. Behind them towered Expedition Everest, and screams were heard periodically as the roller coaster thrilled its riders. After a quick celebration of Jez's return, Finn brought up the daydream she had had while trapped in the tunnel.

"But so what?" Maybeck asked. "We had two things we had to do: get Jez back and kill the second server. We've done both. I'm so tired I can barely stand. Let's get out of here while we still can."

"You all can go. It's all right," Amanda said matter-of-factly. "We will never be able to repay you for all you've done."

"But your dream," Charlene said. "The giant attacking you. Finn in his hands."

"All the more reason," Maybeck said, "we should just boogie and forget about all that."

He looked to the others for agreement but saw only vacant faces.

"Come on, people!" Maybeck chastised. "Quit

while you're ahead. Ever heard of that?"

"Leave no stone unturned," Finn said, "might be more appropriate. Wayne has gone missing."

"Philby cut the data lines. Who knows how that affected the data flow in the Park? Besides, it wasn't Wayne. It was his VMK avatar! Are you kidding me? We're going to stay and try to find a missing avatar? Are you *serious*? Half the Park is out looking for us."

"Maleficent serves Chernabog. We know that Chernabog defeated Mickey at the Fantasmics. Wayne told us that a long time ago. That means he has major powers. He's the one Disney demon that we know virtually nothing about—"

"And let's leave it that way!"

"But Jez dreamed something awful. And Maleficent could have hidden in any of the Parks. Why here? Why now? What's being planned? With Wayne missing, it's up to us to find out."

"You're hallucinating," Maybeck said.

Philby stepped forward. "Without Wayne we'd have failed. I promise you that. Maleficent's got him. Don't ask me to explain that, but I just know it. And if that's true, it's my fault—it's all of our faults. Can you honestly just go home and go to bed knowing that?"

Maybeck hung his head and shook it back and

forth. "No." He sounded so despondent.

"No," Philby agreed. "I didn't think so."

Charlene unfolded the photocopied page of Jez's diary. She pointed to the sketch of what looked like a gorilla. "What if this isn't a gorilla at all? What if it's the yeti?"

Jez spoke up. "You just told us that Chernabog was missing from his float, remember? Maybe Maleficent thought that that was the real Chernabog, only to discover it a fake. The bat . . . the monkeys . . . something could have told her the real Chernabog was locked up here in AK."

"Or maybe this whole thing," Finn said, "was cooked up by Maleficent to use us to lead her to Wayne. Has anyone considered that possibility?"

He drew stunned expressions.

"What if we did *exactly* what she wanted us to do?" Finn asked in a softer voice. "We couldn't have gotten Jez without Wayne's help. He knew they were looking for him. So Maleficent cooks up this plan to basically use Jez as bait. We think she's after Jez to keep Jez's dreams from forecasting what Maleficent is up to—and that could be right. But it doesn't mean there wasn't a bigger plan."

A light breeze broke the silence between them as, once again, it carried the cries from Expedition Everest.

"One thing we know," Willa said, "is that Everest is cold. At least, it represents the cold." She indicated the gorilla on Jez's diary page. "What if this is the yeti, like Charlene said?" The other kids stared at her with puzzled expressions. "What if, like Maleficent, the yeti can't handle the heat? So Maleficent's job is not only to get him out of the Park, but keep him cold. Keep them both cold."

"The ice truck!" Charlene said.

"Exactly!" agreed Willa.

"But to what purpose?" complained Maybeck.

"How do we know? A refrigerated truck can take him anywhere he wants to go."

"But where?" asked Finn.

"So Expedition Everest was a way for Wayne and the others to control Chernabog?" Charlene asked. "The Imagineers basically locked him up in a deep freeze?"

"It could be," agreed Willa. "They locked up Maleficent in the dungeons, let's not forget."

Philby spoke confidently. "I say we get inside Expedition Everest and check out the yeti. That could be where the answers lie. Jez drew it in her diary. It has to mean something!"

"It means that's where the danger lies," muttered Jez.

Finn said quietly, "Chernabog is using Maleficent—maybe to get him off of Everest or even out of the Park. Maleficent used us to reveal and capture Wayne. If they eliminate Wayne, then they take away years of knowledge about all the Parks, all the history of this place. If they're trying to gain control of the Parks, Wayne has to go. He's proved that."

"He has the knowledge and leadership," said Willa, "to stop them."

Leadership, Finn thought. Wayne had given him a lecture on how to be a good leader. *Had Wayne known what was coming?*

"Wayne is not the only one they need to get rid of," Maybeck reminded them. "I'd say we've become a pretty big pain in the—"

"But!" Finn said, interrupting, "there's obviously stuff we haven't figured out. Maybe a lot of stuff. It's pretty obvious we don't have it all. We can't make any conclusions without going in there, without knowing more. I'm going in there. And I have a hunch Amanda and Jez are, too, because Jez dreamed about it."

The two sisters nodded.

"This is stupid," Maybeck whined. "It could be a trap."

"Which is why you and Willa and Charlene will remain outside of Everest," Finn directed. "If we get nailed, you'll have to come save us." He knew if there was one thing Maybeck loved, it was being the hero.

Maybeck snorted. "Okay," he said, relenting.

"Philby will come with me because he's so good with tech stuff, and if there's one thing we know about Expedition Everest, it's that it's high-tech."

"I haven't studied it much," Philby cautioned.

"We'll take our chances," Finn said.

"The Park closes in, like, five minutes," said Charlene.

"That may work even better for us," Finn declared.

"What about the fact that Jez's daydream has Ape Man swinging you around like a drumstick?" Maybeck crossed his arms, believing he'd finally found a hole in Finn's plan.

"But what he doesn't know," Philby said, "is that we already know that, and that's gotta be to our advantage."

"Not if you're the one being swung around," said Maybeck, clearly challenging Finn.

"I'll take my chances," said Finn, staring back at Maybeck's twitching smile and wondering why he'd volunteered.

63

THE LINE FOR EXPEDITION EVEREST had been shut down fifteen minutes prior to the Park closing to make sure the roller coaster was free of passengers by the appointed time. The line twisted through a startling reproduction of a Nepalese village, complete with prayer flags and Asian memorabilia.

Finn, Philby, Amanda, and Jez stuck together. They passed into the backstage area through a "Park Rangers Only" gate and simply walked into the enormous structure that housed the exotic roller coaster.

Finn had expected to need his ID and perhaps some quick talking to get them all inside, but with the closing of the ride to the public, someone had left the backstage door open, and the kids simply walked in.

"It's three structures in one," Philby explained in a hush. "The massive superstructure that supports the exterior building, the roller coaster, and the yeti."

"I thought you hadn't studied it," whispered Jez.

"I haven't studied it thoroughly," Philby replied, "but that doesn't mean I haven't read up on it a little."

"We may need the roller coaster for our escape,"

Finn said to Philby. "Why don't you stay and try to handle that?"

"Done," said Philby. He could be a handful when he showed off.

"See you up there," Finn said.

The metal stairs reminded him of a fire escape. The three of them climbed and climbed. Then they climbed some more. Far below they suddenly heard men's voices. The lights went out. Then a reverberating *thunk* as a door was slammed shut with a finality that Finn felt up his spine.

With the lights out, the building's vast interior was held in an unnatural haze caused by the few emergency lights strategically placed throughout.

No one said anything at first, but a tremor of fear passed between them.

Finn couldn't lose the image of his being swung around by his feet. Step by step he felt himself drawn to that fate.

Amanda started talking, possibly to break the mood established by the lights going out. "What is it that something—someone—like Chernabog wants?"

"Power," Jez answered.

"Exactly," Amanda agreed. "He's been locked up in here ever since they built the ride, and now he wants freedom and power, probably in that order."

"And you're saying he'd have gotten both if I hadn't dreamed what I dreamed," Jez said.

"He still may get both," Amanda cautioned. "And what's the one thing anyone seeking power is afraid of?"

"What is this?" Finn complained, "a social sciences class?"

"Answer the question," Amanda pushed.

"His enemies," Finn answered.

"Yes! His enemies," Amanda agreed. "In particular, any enemy who is potentially more powerful than he is. So who are his biggest enemies? You—the Kingdom Keepers—or Wayne, or Jez, or whom?"

"All of the above," a winded Finn replied. The stairs seemed to go on forever. The trio passed along the roller coaster's high-tech tracks and the arctic scenery that only made the chill of the air all the more convincing. "Or none of the above," Finn said, his mind racing.

"You're messing with us?" Amanda said accusingly.

Finn answered, "Chernabog is rarely seen in any of the Disney stuff. *Fantasia* and Fanstasmics are it, I think."

"And all the postcards and stuff that show the Disney villains," Amanda corrected.

"That, too. But in the Fantasmics—he's beaten by the sorcerer, Mickey," said Finn. "And in *Fantasia*, by the sun."

"Interesting," said Amanda. She didn't sound winded

at all. Finn wondered if she was levitating herself up the endless stairs.

Jez asked, "Are you saying he has to defeat Mickey before he can be assured of maintaining any power he gains?"

"Defeating Mickey," Finn said, "defeats us all. Without Mickey, there *is* no Magic Kingdom, no Animal Kingdom, no Disney at all."

"But then why kidnap Jez? Why involve the five of you? What do you guys have to do with Mickey?" Amanda asked.

"Nothing," Finn answered. "That's what's puzzling. But think about it: the sooner he eliminates Mickey, the sooner there's no one to stop him from overtaking the Park."

mybest: ice truck just arrived!!!

Finn told the two sisters the news. "The ice truck pulled up around back."

"Then this is it," Jez said, her voice trembling. "Whatever Maleficent has been planning, it's happening right now."

They rounded a corner and then quickly jumped to one side to hide.

What they'd witnessed was emblazoned in their

362

minds. Far above them towered the frightening figure of the yeti. It stood thirty feet tall or more, leaning out over the track—the embodiment of evil: monstrous and otherworldly.

At the yeti's feet stood a tall figure in a black robe. They were too far away to see the purple fringe on the cape or the green skin, but no one in the group doubted it was she. Hidden by an outcropping of rock, they continued higher until the steady chanting of her voice could be heard. She was conjuring a spell. As the staircase curved, following the rocks, they were forced to drop to their stomachs and belly-crawl up the metal stairs. Then Finn raised a hand signaling the others to stop.

He didn't know exactly why they'd come here—only that they couldn't turn away from Jez's daydream. Perhaps they were here to witness whatever Maleficent planned, perhaps to stop it. He believed their attendance here critical to Wayne's rescue, yet he knew they were no match for the yeti. Not if Maleficant awakened the thing.

And then it became perfectly clear to him: they had to stop her from awakening the yeti in the first place. Chernabog must not come to power. This was the secret to preserving the peace in the Animal Kingdom. This was why Jez had dreamed it in the first place.

More than anything, Finn's concern for Wayne remained at the forefront of his thoughts. He had to find out what had happened to him, where he'd gone. And to that end, he must not be afraid.

This became his focus: *he must not be afraid.* He felt a tingling sensation wash over him.

It was true: he did not see the green skin or the fringe on Maleficent's robe, and he was betting she couldn't make out the sudden slight shimmer to his skin, either.

He rose to his feet and called out boldly, "Do you really think you'll get away with it?" His electronically-edged voice echoed in the cavernous building.

Amanda and Jez slunk back and down, once again hiding in the lee of the rock outcropping.

Far below—miles it seemed—a loud *pop* was heard, followed by sudden humming. The round rail to the left of the stairs carried a slight tremor.

The roller coaster had been switched on.

64

IT ALL HAPPENED SO QUICKLY: his words echoing around the building; the steady increase in electronic and mechanical sounds as the roller coaster started up; Maleficent's arms shooting up from her sides and lifting her robe like magnificent wings.

The twitching of the yeti's fingers, like the paws of a sleeping dog.

Too late! She had already awakened the giant.

His massive head moved side-to-side, and a loud *crack* thundered through the snowcapped mountains.

The hum and whir of the roller coaster grew steadily closer.

"Silly, silly, boy!" Maleficent spun around and shot a ball of fire at Finn. The size of a soccer ball, it exploded at his feet, flaming out.

And whereas once Finn would have been terrified by such things, would have stood transfixed by the power she displayed, something had come over him. She was nothing but an illusionist, a magician using her substantial skills to scare him. He was no longer convinced she even possessed the ability to kill him—

or, if she did, then why hadn't she done so?

"If you were going to kill me," he shouted, "then you would have done that the first time we met. But you can't, can you? Walt Disney would never allow a creation of his imagination to take a life."

The tingling grew stronger; he felt it in a way, a degree, he'd never experienced. This confrontation was making his DHI stronger.

"But I am not of his imagination," Maleficent said. "I am of the old stories—tales that existed for hundreds of years in places all around the world. Tales of things that actually happened." She shot another ball at him. Again, he did not move from his spot. Again, the flames fell short.

The giant yeti was awake now, towering over them all, eyes blinking. Finn did not recoil. He could not picture Wayne and the other Imagineers building creatures designed to harm them.

The roller coaster sped closer.

"I will kill you," Maleficent said, "when you are no longer of use to me." She bent backward and looked up at the hairy creature above her. "When Lord Chernabog has no further use for you." She let out a laugh—a bloodcurdling cackle—that for the first time challenged Finn's DHI status. His feet and hands grew cold, and it took all his will to overcome this poison and return to his full DHI.

The beast had the reaction time of a snake. One

moment Finn was standing on the stairs. The next, the yeti had him by the legs and was swinging him overhead.

His legs . . . not the legs of his DHI.

Amanda and Jez jumped out from their hiding places and Jez shouted, "Let him go!"

"Ah!" Maleficent cried out. "If it isn't the Fairlies."

Amanda craned forward, her neck thrust out. Maleficent knew way too much.

Finn knew the secret to his own survival was to push away his fear, but being swung at thirty miles an hour over the head of a forty-foot-tall giant proved a difficult challenge.

Maleficent suddenly floated—levitated—off the platform, clearly, nothing she'd planned for herself, for she flailed her legs and arms, dog paddling like a kid struggling to swim for the first time.

"You put me down, child!" she roared.

She hurled a ball of flame at Amanda, who leaned slightly left, allowing the asteroid to pass. It exploded into the Himalayas.

"PUT HIM DOWN!" cried out Amanda, "OR I WILL DROP YOU AS YOU WISH!"

Maleficent moved like a puppet twenty feet to the left. Now there was nothing but a sixty-foot fall to concrete beneath her.

Finn felt the tingling return, and, as it did, the yeti's

hand closed shut through his body—nothing but light. Finn clamored up the beast's arm toward its massive head. The yeti swiped at him, but again his hand passed through Finn's DHI, unable to touch him.

He caught a glimpse of Maleficent as she began to transform into a crow. But as she did, Amanda released her and the green-skinned creature fell fifteen feet straight down before stopping in midair.

"You try that again," Amanda warned, and I'll drop you before you have the chance.

Maleficent looked down and seemed to consider her odds. Then she looked back at Amanda.

"You harm me, you little tart, and your friend will never see his precious Wayne again!"

With the mention of Wayne, Finn slipped. He fell off the yeti's shoulder, and the sensation immediately removed his DHI. He slid down the side of the creature, grasping at the matted gray hair and somehow controlling his fall. As he reached the yeti's leg, it moved. Then the other. The giant's feet broke free of the platform where it had stood for several years. The entire building shook.

A series of screams was followed by the roller coaster shooting up at them through the darkness. Philby, Maybeck, and Willa zoomed past—backward—and out of sight.

Maybeck waved at Maleficent.

The witch proclaimed: "You will bring me the Stonecutter's Quill, or you will never see the white-haired man again."

At that moment, the yeti began to change. The hair was sucked inside its arms, turning the gray skin smooth; the legs and arms shrank, and the neck grew thinner, while the head also lost its hair and sprouted horns. The giant creature had been reduced to a figure much greater than Maleficent, but no longer a thirty-foot-high beast. Horns sprouted, while black webbing formed under the thing's arms like . . . bat wings.

Chernabog.

Finn heard the roller coaster slowing in the distance. It would be returning—and when it did, he, Amanda, and Jez needed to be on it.

The pen, Finn realized. The Stonecutter's Quill was the pen Walt had used to imagine the first plans of the Parks. It had demonstrated great powers the one and only time Finn had seen it used. Powers, he assumed, that could be put to evil use as easily as they had been to good.

A wall of tension formed between Amanda and Maleficent. The witch produced another ball of fire, but this time Amanda levitated it as well. It hovered next to the witch, burning hotly and illuminating her green face.

"You will regret this, little one," Maleficent muttered, clearly afraid of her own fire. "You are playing with things you know nothing about."

She grew the head of a vulture. Wings began to sprout.

Amanda released her. Again, Maleficent fell abruptly, before slowly being carried aloft. Evidence of the vulture was gone; the green-skinned fairy hovering over the precipitous fall.

The strain on Amanda was evident. She had quickly grown pale, her body now shaking.

Finn saw that Maleficent was merely playing for time. She knew Amanda couldn't keep this up forever.

"Release Wayne!" Finn called out, "or she'll drop you."

"The Quill," Maleficent said, "or you'll never see him alive again." She looked over at Finn, who held to Chernabog rather than drop to the platform where the creature might squash him like a bug.

Amanda's strength gave out, and she collapsed into Jez's arms.

"You harm any one of us and you will never see that pen!" Finn shouted. He let go, jumped, slid down the mountain slope, and aimed straight for the two girls, hoping his timing was right, for he could see the roller coaster from the corner of his eye. Chernabog stepped forward, raising his arms in defiance. But he was too late.

Finn's wild slide down the mountainside connected with both girls at the exact moment the roller coaster arrived. He stretched out his arms and caught both Amanda and Jez, his momentum carrying all three of them headfirst into the passing roller coaster. They tumbled into a middle car.

But the safety bars on the ride were already set, having been locked at the start; and, as the cars gained substantial speed, Finn held on to the weakened Amanda as Jez reached out to cling to the car, and with Maybeck, Philby, Charlene, and Willa calling out from the back, the Kingdom Keepers plummeted down into the dark.

65

HERNABOG MOVED WITH surprising agility for something that was a beastly demon with a pair of batlike wings the size of boat sails.

To the surprise of all, Chernabog made no attempt to stop the Kingdom Keepers. He flew toward the bottom of the ride. For once in his life Finn willed a roller coaster to go even faster.

He did not want to lose them.

Finn had ridden on Expedition Everest before. Within a matter of seconds they would be thrown into a spiral that would crush them against each other if they couldn't hold on tightly.

Holding on with one hand each, he and Jez wrapped their free arms around the other's shoulders and, with Amanda pinned between them, leaned forward, braced for the spinout.

Expedition Everest roared into its climactic spiral, the G-force driving Finn and Jez to their right, their hands slipping along the restraining bars. The force nearly threw them from the car, but together Finn and Jez managed to keep Amanda pinned in, and soon the roller coaster began to slow to a stop.

As it came to rest, the restraining bars released, and Maybeck and the others hurried to join Finn, Amanda, and Jez.

Finn left Amanda in the care of her sister and led the others through the building and out an enormous garage door that was standing wide open.

They ran out into the street where they caught a final glimpse of the back of the ice truck as it sped away.

"What now?" a gasping Philby said, clutching his sides.

"They got away," Finn said.

"But we can't just let them go!" Maybeck said.

"We got Jez back," Finn said, "and we crippled the second server." He looked at each one of his friends. "I think it's safe to say that Jez and Amanda are now officially Kingdom Keepers."

The others nodded.

"We have work to do," Willa mumbled.

"Let's get some sleep," Finn said. His suggestion met with no resistance.

66

THE STORY MADE THE morning news: a refrigerator truck, being driven poorly, had been pulled over by the local police. The officer swore that he'd been knocked over when he'd gone to open the back of the truck, and that two creatures had been seen hurrying away. He refused to describe them. He said only that they had traveled in the general direction of Disney's Hollywood Studios theme park, and that from everything he'd seen, that was where they belonged.

For nearly two weeks, Finn—who'd been grounded for a month—sneaked onto VMK the way Wayne had told him. He hoped to find Wayne by typing the name into a text screen. When the white-haired avatar failed to appear, Finn organized the other kids, most of whom were also currently grounded.

So it was that exactly a month after the event at Expedition Everest, Finn went to sleep fully dressed, holding a small black remote button in his right hand.

As he fell asleep that night, he intentionally dreamed of the Magic Kingdom, and he awakened there on a Park bench, his body glowing under the moonlight.

He was at the hub near the entrance, at the end of Main Street, USA.

Soon, the other Kingdom Keepers joined him. Only Charlene was still in her nightgown, having forgotten to change into street clothes before going to sleep. Or maybe this was how she wanted to dress.

The five headed up and into the small apartment above the firehouse in the Magic Kingdom. It was exactly twelve midnight.

This was Wayne's apartment. Most had visited it before. There was incredibly sour milk in the refrigerator and food that now wore a coat of green fuzz— Wayne had not been here in a very long time.

They searched for over an hour for the Stonecutter's Quill, but to no avail. If Wayne had hidden it, he'd hidden it well.

"What now?" Charlene asked.

"Is there any choice?" Finn asked.

"But without the pen," Philby said, "what leverage do we have? We can't win his release without that pen."

"We'll think of something," Finn said.

"Or maybe Jez will dream it," said Charlene, "and give us more clues to follow."

"The point is, we did save Jez, and we pretty

much saved the Animal Kingdom from being overrun by DHIs. We can't be giving DHIs a bad name, after all."

They laughed. Five shimmering kids, glowing as they enjoyed a rare moment of levity.

"Maleficent used us to bring Wayne out of hiding," Finn said. "We failed him. And although we don't know enough about Chernabog, we've seen his power. And I have a hunch that the bat with green wings was him all along, although I'm not sure how to explain that."

"We know that even Maleficent cannot transform herself for very long," Philby said. "Especially in this heat. She and her animal army may have been planning to take over AK. They had the ice truck as their back-up, in case they failed. It was only when we crashed the server that she resorted to moving Chernabog. What's strange is that if they hadn't captured Jez, if she hadn't been in that tunnel to have that daydream, we might never have known what Maleficent was planning, might never have been there when she was freeing Chernabog."

"I think it was intended—us being there. I think if we'd failed to defeat the server then the animals would have caught us all and taken us to her. I don't know what would have happened, but I think she had plans for us. Amanda saved us all by levitating her. Without that . . ."

"I always thought staying up that late would be fun," said Charlene. "But it—"

"Stank." Although Maybeck used another word.

"We've got work to do," Finn said. "And we need to act quickly. Who knows what secrets Wayne might have in that old head of his? Secrets no one should know."

"Tell us what to do," Willa said.

All eyes fell on Finn. They waited for him to say something.

He smiled, a warmth filling him and making his DHI glow even brighter.

Wayne would have been proud.

"We'll meet after school. We've got to find Wayne."

He raised his right hand. In it was the black remote with the small button at its center.

"Ready?" he said.

The others nodded.

He pushed the button.

ACKNOWLEDGMENTS

The Kingdom Keepers novels depend on a team, in part because the research conducted inside the Parks, and also *about* the Parks, is both complex and time-consuming, and ultimately essential to the story.

First, I want to thank my co-writer (from other novels), Dave Barry, who, during a car ride to Orlando's airport made suggestions to the outline that formed and framed the book, forever changing it. He jokes how I'm the "plot guy" in our partnership, but for once he *is* "making this up." He set the clock in the book ticking and gave me one of the most important twists. Thanks.

The real dedication of the book should probably be to Alex Wright, a Disney Imagineer, a man with tireless patience, who has endured (and I am *not* making this up!) *hundreds* of e-mails where I picked his brain for details. Alex also hosted several behind-the-scene tours for me in Animal Kingdom and introduced me to:

Dr. Joseph Soltis—Wildlife Tracking Center
Dr. Don Neiffer—Veterinary Hospital
Debbie Weber—Animal Nutrition Center
Matt Hohne—Animal Barns
Jason Surrell—Disney Imagineer (and AK tour host/insider)

I'd also like to thank my niece, Blair M. Daverman, for filling in some blanks about the sport of lacrosse.

My wife, Marcelle, along with Laurel and David Walters, as always, copyedited the various drafts. And Tanner Walters, who in sixth grade reads more than I do, gave me an early read and caught a bunch of problems. So did my daughter Paige. And thanks to daughter Storey for reading KK1 and telling me what she liked!

Special gratitude to Nandy Litzinger, my office manager; Wendy Lefkon, Disney editor; Amy Berkower, agent; Matthew Snyder, film agent; and Jennifer Levine, Disney publicist.

It obviously takes a village.

—*Ridley Pearson*
January 2008
St. Louis, Missouri